Grim's Door

Eric Schoch

Grim's Door by Eric Schoch
Copyright © 2021. All rights reserved.

Published by Pen It! Publications, LLC
812-371-4128 www.penitpublications.com

ISBN: 978-1-954868-99-1
Edited by Jen Selinsky
Cover Design by Donna Cook

thewyrdwolf.com
@wyrd_wolf

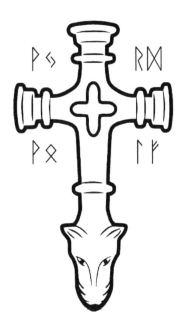

WYRD WOLF

This story is dedicated to Beatrix. Our little princess Bee.
Wir sehen uns in Valhalla

- Eric Schoch

The Architect

A Foreword by the Author

When I use the term The Architect, I am not referring to myself, nor am I referring to the people who helped format this novel. I am, instead, speaking of something or someone far more unknown. I use the word 'unknown' not to baffle you, nor to add some pretentious mystique to my words. I use it because I have no other way of describing the being of which I am about to explain. Or, try to explain.

Would it be breaking too much of a writer's wall for me to start at the beginning?

In the beginning, of my life, anyway, I have always been struck with the double-edged curse-gift-hybrid of imagination. It allowed me to escape the early childhood traumas of watching a parent dissolve before your eyes into a hospital bed. Instead, I was able to wander away into a land of my choosing, where wolves would run alongside the car window and dragons would battle in the sky above me. What it did leave me with, alongside this superpower of mental invisibility, was a crippling case of OCD.

By the way, this will all make sense, it is not merely a chapter of me complaining.

With OCD, as many others will have found who carry this lifelong burden, it brings one into a voyage of self-discovery. Asking questions about life, the universe and purpose. Why do I have to touch that lightbulb sixteen times when Jack can just leave the room and feel fine? Why has God decided I have to work ten times as hard as other people just to stop from screaming in the middle of every sentence? Just...why? Which, then, naturally brought me onto the addressee of my formal complaints, God. As a young man, in my teens and early twenties, I studied religion, at college and university level. This was at first going to be physics until I realised I could fathom the darkest reaches of space, but had a difficult time with long division. So, what other study could I undertake that tried to comprehend the very nature of reality and life? Ah...religion. Specifically, philosophy more than theology. Having gone through the school system of the UK within a traditional Catholic setting, I attended both college and university at Catholic institutions, therefore it cannot be too strongly judged as to why I became a staunch Catholic. Pro-life, pro-mass, Pro-Marriage, pro-guilt, the whole lot. Then, what came next? Obviously...the priesthood. My life was planned.

So why, some might ask, did I never make it to the priesthood and don the vestment and robes of the Godly man? I could not tell you precisely why, and if I were approached today by the pope himself and asked to cast aside all earthly belongings and join him in a crusade, I probably would. As far I can comprehend, myself, it is because Catholicism was lacking something. I loved the mass and the medieval setting, the history, and the community. What I just could not get my head around was the afterlife. Catholic afterlife, though no doubt several times more interesting than Protestant heaven, just sounded...boring. Eternal happiness. Bliss. What did that entail? Perpetual Netflix and Ben & Jerry's until the universe collapsed on itself? What about, well, women (for me, men for others)? Are you married in heaven? Can you sleep with whoever you wanted? If so, why was that frowned upon so much in mortal life? Is there an endless bar filled with every intoxicant known to man? Is that good or bad? Or, as I saw it, do we just sit beside a perfect stream all day and night gazing up at the glory of the heavens? Because after a while, would that not just because a little tedious?

Questions. Questions. I apologise.

This then led me to focus my studies on 'other' religions. Some major, such as your Buddhism, some minor, such as animistic native communities of the Pacific Islands. When I was perhaps in my final year, I saw a map of the world. On said map, someone had placed a perfect circle around a small portion of the world. It covered most of Egypt, North Africa, Lebanon, Palestine, Israel, and other countries verging around the eastern coast of the Mediterranean. The quote that accompanied this circular conglomeration of countries was (not verbatim) as follows, 'Do you think all of God's truth came from this small area?' which was, of course, referring to the Holy Bible. And it was a small area, in comparison to the world. It made sense and it did not. I felt myself to be a deeply religious man and tried in depth to understand God as best I could. Was I being so naïve that I could think every word of the Holy Bible was true and no other truths existed across the thousands of world religions?

What do you think?

Not long after this shaking of faith, did I discover *American Gods*, by Neil Gaiman. One of my now favourite books and if you have not read it, I suggest you put this book down right now and go read that. Obviously come back and read this! Then, tell your friends to read it, too. Anyway,

American Gods, in a bad summary, is a story of how every god, every deity ever known exists, some as tulpas, and every god has their own truth. And I completely got on board with the idea. We bring along our own gods and they all exist together. I was completely on board with it, for about a month. No, maybe less, I'm a quick reader. The theology, or philosophy, was lacking something I felt was an innate truth deep inside my soul; There may be many gods, but there is only one God.

That capital letter is perhaps the most important capital letter in the universe.

So, who was this God? This ultimate. Aristotle described his idea of this being as the 'Unmoved Mover'. A being or energy that had to be the original cause of creation. Not until many years, 2173 years later as a rough guide, when the first law of thermodynamics was laid out in writing. This law states that energy cannot be created or destroyed, it can only be transformed. Then, how in the world, pardon the pun, could the Big Bang Theory even exist? Yes, take that atheists. It is implausible to place one's faith in science and to put forth a belief that goes entirely against its primary principles and laws? No. there was something there. Something big. Something omnipotent.

I could not put my finger on just what.

It was during the last year of University that I was invited into a certain fringe organisation. One that has existed for many hundreds, possibly thousands of years. I shall not name or even allude to the mysteries of the brotherhood, but shall only let it be known that this is where I finally understood the nature of reality – in no short accomplishment. Or should I say – this is where I finally came to the realisation that I knew nothing of the universe.

Enter The Architect.

For this is what He is. God. The Unmoved Mover. The Prime. The Alpha and the Omega. The one God amongst many gods. The Designer, Creator and principle of humanity, the cosmos and time itself. The Architect. This is when my love of worldly religions could come out in full swing. I studied Hinduism and its concept of Brahman and though they have many smaller gods, they believe in the end we all return to this one great creator being. Then, I fell in red-discovered my ancestors' faith of Asatru and the old-world Nordic and Saxon beliefs. The Hall of the Slain. Yggdrasil, the Tree of Life (which if you study in itself describes not only the solar system and our connecting worlds, but permeates as an understanding across almost all human religions). Odin. Thor. Freyja. Frigg. Baldur. And of course, Loki, the trickster god. And I could believe in these gods. I could believe in them just as much as I wanted. I could even study Druidism and Wicca, (update - of which I now have) and still hold true to that one core belief, that at the centre of it all lies The Architect. I mean, come on, you show me someone who would rather go to Christian heaven for a day, or Valhalla and ill point back at the most boring individual on earth.

The book.

This is not the first book I have written, nor is it the first on which I have begun to breach the subject of The Architect. You can probably find my other collections of short stories somewhere online, or in the bargain bin of a local bookstore. Nevertheless, this book, *Grim's Door*, was the first in which I decided to commit my philosophical beliefs my knowledge and imagination, all poured out in written word and laid bare for the world to see. I do hope you enjoy the story you are about to read, or perhaps have read and returned to. I hope that you feel the essence I was trying to capture and how I feel the universe fits itself together. After all, there may not be many happy endings, but would it not be fantastic if all of our favourite things existed? And not only existed, but could co-exist. My mother was mostly the inspiration for this manuscript. Her favourite book(s) are *The Chronicles of Narnia*. (mine and my fathers were *The Lord of the Rings*, as you can probably see bleeding out through the pages). My mother still, to this day, enters a wardrobe in every antique shop she visits and closes her eyes before opening them, just on the chance that one day she might feel that luring breeze from the world beyond pulling her into a world of fantasy, adventure and magic. So, here it is, *Grim's Door*, and I hope and pray that you can find that magic, too.

- Eric Schoch

Places, People and
Names of Importance

The Architect – Sometimes known as Lord, or God. In early Christianity, there existed a sect of believers called the Gnostics referred to as the Platonic Demiurge. A God above gods. what Aristotle first described as his Prime Mover. The Creator of all things. In modern day, a certain fraternal brotherhood derived from the remnants of the Knights Templar refer to this divinity as the Great Architect of the Universe.

There may be many gods, but there is only one God.

The Adversary – The opposing face of the coin. Call this being what you will; Devil, Anti-Christ, Deceiver. An evil exists that permeates our world, and it has a source and a name.

Old Grim – Grimnir, Gallows-Walker, Blindr, Alfodr, Old One-Eye, Skilfing, Wotan, Woden and, of course, Odin. There are more names than I can list and still more I do not know. Allfather of the Norse pantheon of gods.

Aishling – Little Ash-Tree.

Loki – Lokke. The Hidden-One. Hveðrungr. Demon. Trickster-god. Father of Hel (Hella), Fenris-Wolf (Fenrir),

Jormungandr, Sleipnir and many others less monstrous. Part of the pantheon of Norse Gods.

Aesir – The pantheon of Norse gods.

Valhalla – Valhöll. The Hall of the Dead, where warriors go after death in battle.

Fólkvangr – Where many of the victorious dead may be taken.

Valkyries – the winged warrior women who carry the dead to Valhalla.

Helheim – Land of the dead who die outside of battle. Home to the Corpse-Hall, Corpse-Ripper and legions of undead and demonic entities. Akin to the Latin Hell or the Inferno. Ruled by Hel (Hella).

Midgard – Earth. Middle-Earth. Home.

Altheim – The Old World.

Table of Contents

Prologue
Grim's Fair

ק

Now are sung the High-one's songs, in the High-one's hall, to the sons
of men all-useful, but useless to the Jötunns' sons.
Hail to him who has sung them!
Hail to him who knows them! May he profit who has learnt them!
Hail to those who have listened to them!

- Hávamál

Of course, the carnival was in town.

It came every year and every year the same repellent
mess was left afterwards. Heaps of soiled clothes collected
from the rags thrown away by the carny folk. Tins, jars, and
glass bottles had to be swept away from streets and parks lest
the rats be coerced from their sewers as if the Pied Piper
himself had drawn them forth. Still, the carnival gave the
residents of Myersville a break from their lives, if only for two
weeks out of the year. Betty just hated that it had to set up
right across the street from her. There was another much
larger area of land, just on the other side of town where she
could leave the sights, sounds and smells behind. She sighed

again, as the last of the colourful wagons rolled on down the street. There was already a sweet scent in the air, as though someone had brushed cotton candy beneath her nose and held it there until her mouth began to water.

The Halsteds had a small kitty set aside for rainy days. Most of the cash they had spare was not even their own. Their house and almost all the new possessions inside had been paid for with what her mother called, Uncle's Retirement Plan. He had never retired. You cannot retire at twenty-three. Instead, as Betty got older, she understood what it meant.

At the age of five, she had watched her family break down at the news of Uncle's death. The sergeant who had come to the door, holding the folded American flag and bundle of letters, had explained that Uncle Joe had earned several Medals of Honour during his time in France: most notably for saving the lives of thirteen British soldiers from enemy fire in Ardennes during the Great War. She, like her mother was loathed to hear how Uncle Joe, that once bright-eyed and giggling youth, succumbed to his fragmentation wounds almost a whole week after being found face-up in the tears and the mud and the blood.

A slow and painful death for a hero, she thought, remembering how much Uncle Joe loved nothing more than the smell of cotton candy on a long summer night in Myersville.

Almost a decade after Uncle Joe's passing, the family still kept a tradition. They would toast to his good health at midnight, June 12th, the day he had earned his medals. Pop a couple of beers for the doughboy. So few had returned that year. So many had remained across that beautiful blue Atlantic. Betty had been almost too young to remember the day they came back. But she could still see the scars to this very day.

Unseen scars. Shaking hands. Hollow eyes. Faded smiles. How could a fourteen-year-old sheriff's daughter know what horrors these hollow soldiers had brought back from their war. Because it was *their war*. It belonged now, only to them. In their nightmares. In the haunted reflection in their bedside mirror. During those nights, they woke screaming, sweating, and clutching loved ones as though some brilliant fiery ball might drop from the sky to take them away forever. Of course, there was no burst of artillery fire. Not here, in Oklahoma. Still, each night the war drums beat, and the visions returned. Betty could, at the very least, see that. In their eyes.

Brushing away the thought, Betty was about to turn back towards her house, when she saw a curious wagon round the corner of Main. She had never seen this one before, it must have been new. Although judging by the chipped paintwork and wobbling axis of what appeared to be a LaFrance Fire Truck, perhaps not. Betty had loved cars, they fascinated her from the first time she had seen Dr. Goodfellow's Model-T Roadster flying down Broad and Sixth. This old truck, now passing her by, looked as if it should have been in a museum, which was a thought that troubled her in a way she could not describe. A thing both grim and old. As much as she wanted to go inside for Ma's cooking, it was all she could do to keep watching the ancient vehicle trundle its way into the park, smoke firing out of both ends. Its Donner party-looking wagon following and not quite turning as it should, bearing the sign,

Old Grim's House of Doors

"Betty, get in now, it's gone cold," Her mother beckoned from the window. She heard the pane slam shut and sensed a foul mood in the Halsted House.

The next morning came carrying with it a gentle, clean breeze. It was a relief from the typical June weather of Oklahoma. Dust, sun, and more dust. On the wind came the carnival. This morning, however, it was not sugar, spice, and everything nice. It was instead chocked full of cigar smoke, burning rubber, and old hose. Betty came home from a day watching her father piece together paperwork at the Sheriff's Office, to find that Janey and Elmer were already waiting with eager anticipation to head off to the carnival. They had a bulging purse between them that their mother had given. The Cuttlings were the richest family in town, and a part of Betty wondered if that was why their families had been so close for so long. A long line of successful businessmen tied to a long line of law enforcement. Such partnerships seemed to go hand-in-hand and as one family rose, so did the other. It was how they had escaped the worst of the financial impact of the war. They had never once bought bonds. Not once. It was a word she had heard in school. Along with 'debt', 'repayment' and 'subsidies'. Not words she ever heard at home.

'Hey, Mr. Frank, can Betty come out yet?' Elmer smiled at her father with a mouth of tiny teeth. The doctor was unsure why his adult teeth had come in so small and far apart, the medical condition had not been discovered yet and it left Elmer with the appearance of a kid far younger than fourteen. Not helped by his croaking voice which could change to the highest and lowest pitches in a single sentence.

Betty's father held up his hand, then cocked his head towards the front door with a shrug, to suggest that it was probably a better idea that they wait to see what the woman of the house decided. As it turned out, her mother was just fine about it, which surprised both Betty and Frank and even the Cuttling Twins. The Cuttling's were not identical twins. Far from it. One had long, mousy brown hair, and the other had a bowl-cut of almost bright blonde. One had a long, drawn face, and the other had pudgy soft cheeks that made her appear overweight from the neck up. Her father often made the joke that one belonged to the milkman, while the other belonged to the postman and the third they had to lock away in the attic because it was somehow even weirder looking than the twins. Betty did not understand all of the joke, but she laughed whenever he said it, mostly because her mother would shoot him a look of annoyance every time he did; especially in public.

Crisp air became crisper, as the afternoon became evening. A curious time of day in which the sun descended into a lasting orange glow over the hills, leaving the primeval brain to wonder, if only for a moment, if it will ever rise again. The carnival had awoken. Betty had spent almost a whole dollar already on candy and sodas. Her mother would have been furious if she had known just how much they were now charging for a ride on the Ferris wheel. Still, there was nothing greater than sitting above the houses and streets and seeing everything in town for a handful of coins. On the third go around, the goateed man on the control lever had to ask the Cuttling's to leave, after their pushing and shoving had caused the ride to squeal with the sound of a dozen slaughtered pigs. They took the tutting and the shaking heads of the neighbours with laughter and ran off to see what else the carnival had in store.

There was the freak show, of course, which was perhaps the main attraction every year. It amazed people with such fascination, horror, and disgust that they almost threw their money onto the stage to see more frights of human nature. There was the Lion-Boy; an aging man now, from Czechoslovakia, who had enough hair on his face and head to cover Betty's entire body. Then, there were the Ying Sisters; three of them, with only a single body between them. Betty felt sorry for the most sideways sister. Her head had sunk further each year so that her mouth had become sallow and drawn to the right as her upper body failed to stay as upright as her sisters. Of course, everyone in town was amazed by the acrobatics of the dwarves; Mog and Mull, who flung one another around with such appearing carelessness that every time it happened a gasp of anticipated horror swept up from the crowd. Betty was certain that more than a dozen onlookers were secretly praying that this would be the year they watched one of the tiny humans slip and break their neck. What a tale to tell at the diner the next morning, 'Did you see the little guy fall?', 'Aww, I can't believe I missed the midge break his neck.'

Betty wondered why she came to the carnival sometimes. It gave her joy and excitement, but also filled her heart with a soft pang of guilt. Why? She had not done anything wrong, surely?

'We're paying so them folks can eat something what's not been stewing for five days,' had been her father's rationale, whenever he had seen that distant, glazed-eye look she often got, as if this young girl growing up in such a small slice of Americana had an old and worldly soul lying within. It was the same at the zoo. They had only been the once, when Betty was far younger. She had cried softly the entire time. Maybe it was the bear with less hair than her father had, stooped low to the ground on gnarled claws. Or maybe it was the way the monkeys looked at her, staring out from behind those iron bars with all the hopeless desperation for freedom as a death row inmate.

Turning around, Betty found she was suddenly alone in an ocean of flashing lights and bumping shadows. Beneath her feet the once, almost-green, grass had become shallow, bent and etched with a haze of dry earth. *Where have the twins gone?* She decided to take a stroll and would no doubt bump into them gallivanting around the candy shop again. Those two had a sweet tooth only God could cure. Westerly, the sun had sunk to its lowest point now, without leaving the world in complete darkness. Streetlights popped up around town, one by one, but had no chance of drowning out the dazzling lights around her; supressed in beauty only by the emerging, distant glint of the heavens.

A young boy dropped an ice cream beside her and began to wail uncontrollably, as his mother failed to see the event and carried on, eventually dragging the poor boy by his chubby arm. Each softening whimper send an ominous chill fluttering over her skin like spiders' legs. When she looked away, *it* had appeared to her like a vision from a dream. Something she had recognised only in the deepest memories of her mind's mausoleum, yet had never actually seen in reality. It was different now.

All things changed under the light of the moon, but this time, she felt as if the owner had truly outdone himself. A new attraction to the carnival. A fresh façade dropped from the heavens into the dustbowl of Oklahoma. In Betty's head, through her eyes, it was made of old wood from a pirate ship, bolted together with rusty medieval nails and had spent so long travelling the world and inhaling the sights it had seen that it was now alive itself. Sure. And why not? Why could a building not grow a soul, the way a tree grows flowers, if has experienced more than most of these simple folks would never dare to dream exists?

The building was much larger than she had imagined. Stretched out across the edge of the carnival it would have dwarfed any other attraction nearby, and yet it seemed to hold its breath, waiting for its first customers. Old wood and iron filled with glittering lights, twisted and turned into the allusion that this was someplace Betty wanted to be, and not what it was, just an old shack barely holding its own against the weight of the modern world. Each slab of ancient wood had been plastered in black paint and within that paint were etched a variety of curious symbols that seemed to Betty as if missing, taken from someplace far beyond and left here, where they should not exist.

The whole area surrounding the building Betty was now focussed on, seemed clear and devoid of life, as though someone had seen fit to erect an attraction just for her. There was little interest from the rest of the carnival attendees who seemed focused in clapping rounds of thunder, on the fire-show and the exotic dancing girls on stage. Betty stepped gingerly towards the huge sign that read. *Old Grim's House of Doors.*

The words were lit up with a sort of faint red glow, which she failed to place to a source, as if each word of the sign was somehow a light in itself. It was made even more unnerving by the fact that the last letter flickered every few seconds, trying to perhaps disappear, back into the strange realm from which this odd façade had sprung from.

Betty was pulled back into the carnival, with the sound of one of the Cuttling's voices calling to her.

'Betty. Would you come over please and talk to him?' Janey was pouting, a dozen yards ahead of her, walking slowly towards where she stood beside the pool of melted ice cream. How long had she been entranced by the old wooden shack?

'W-what's wrong, Janey? What's he doing now?' a sense of familiar anxiety and annoyance over Elmer washed away the strange otherworldly dread that had tickled her mind.

Janey stood, hands on hips, with a look that said more than she ever had to explain to her friend. The look simply said, 'Come on, just see.'

****

'I don't wanna have my fortune told by some kooky old broad,' Elmer's voice shifted to a high whine, making him sound more childlike than ever, especially with that thin whistle behind his elongated vowels. 'I just came to visit the weird-looking house. Job done, Jack. That's all. Betty will you tell him, please. Old fart won't let us in without speaking to some ancient crone who wants to tell our futures.'

Betty eyes looked up at a man at least a half foot taller than her father, and Frank Halsted was not a short man by any stretch of the word. The keeper to this unknown realm of attraction looked foreign. Though most of the carny folk here were at the very most second-generation Americans. He had a thick, platted beard, forked into two long tails that poked down to his chest. They each held old, bronze beads intertwined in them, giving the one-eyed man a somewhat medieval appearance. Yes, he was one-eyed. His left eye was covered in a grey patch, that hung there without need for straps or ties. Over the patch was a curious symbol; several poorly etched white lines, aligned in a circle, much like a clock. A deep, three-inch scar grooved its way above and below the cloth.

Must be a veteran, Betty mused. *I wonder if he ever met Uncle Joe?*

When he spoke, the man had the parched, rattling voice of a man twice his age, 'Those are the rules, young sir. Not one soul is allowed to enter the House of Doors without first making sure he is not going to come foul of any accidents while inside. We would not want a young American leaving our *reserhem* in the back of a *likvagn*.'

He was foreign for sure. His 'wubbleyous' sounded like v's and his c's had the faint sibilance of a hissing viper. An accent she had never come across before.

'Look, Jack. Just let me peek inside and if I like what I see, I'll do your stupid fortune. How's that for a deal?'

The man, who might have been 'Old Grim' himself shook his head defiantly and crossed his arms in a childish manner, 'There will be no deals. Fortune first, or do not come back.'

Janey nudged her brother in the ribs, hard enough to make his face contort.

'Fine,' Elmer whined, 'fine. Let's get it over with. I already know I'm going to die an old rich bastard like my grandpa.'

It still shocked Betty to hear Elmer or Janey curse. If her mother ever caught her using such language, she would not see the light of day for a fortnight.

'*Tack*,' the carny unfolded his arms and let one outstretch, leading the way into a small tent beside the entrance to the House of Doors. Betty's stayed focussed on the tall, one-eyed fellow. Something in the way he moved, slow and unblinking, unnerved her more than the creepy old shack itself.

If any of the three were brave enough to be outspoken about the sudden dread that seemed to eke out from the tent, it would have been Elmer, and still he was trapped in that paradox of childish fear. How social anxiety can prevail over perhaps even the darkest of devils. Not one of them, especially *he* would be the first to admit that the shivers on their skin were unrelated to the gentle June breeze.

A warm glow surrounded the interior of the tent. It smelled of ancient times, foggy woodland, and roaring fires deep in the lands where tress still spoke, and the critters of the undergrowth still listened. For the third time that day, Betty felt as if her nose could travel not only across vast distances, but also whisk her back in time, to envelop her in every story that this tiny, rugged tarp had heard. Behind her, she was again knocked out of time by one of Elmer's patented tongue clicks. It was as loud as her father's hunting rifle being cocked.

'Creepy guy.' Elmer grimaced, peering around the tent.

There was a camping sheet unfolded across the floor, but still carrying the long, wide creases from when it had been hauled all those miles in the back of that awful, painted wagon. There was little on the outside walls, but a length of netting separating what must have been the owner's private area, where they could change, reflect, and most likely count their takings for the night. The owner herself was not as Betty had imagined. Mostly, the average age of these travelling folk hit at around mid-forties. And, if you were to ask someone to draw what they imagined a fortune teller to look like, they would more likely than not, sketch a woman as old as time. She would have at least one wart, perhaps one large one just on the cusp of her nose. Her hair would be long and ragged and her dress a mismatched tapestry of gypsy rags. This is likely due to the circulation of Gothic novels, comic books and those odd Penny Dreadfuls that the Cuttlings' mother seemed to own, though they were English and why she had such imprints was beyond anyone's comprehension, let alone *Mr.* Cuttling.

Yet, here and now, the woman sitting by the octangular table, wearing her bright green, flowery skirt and shirt without buttons or sleeves, was young. Very young. Early twenties, perhaps, if Betty made a guess. But to a fourteen-year old's mind, anyone over eighteen could range between there and thirty-eight. With bright yellow hair, hanging down from what looked to be jet back roots, the woman's face was plastered in a curious pale-shade of makeup. Betty assumed, like the rest of these United States, that European behaviour was a little more *elocuted*, if that was the right word. A little more advanced in society and culture than they. Still, it was not only her nose that was telling her she was out of her depth here. Out of her time. Smiling, the young woman offered the three of them a seat each, at three of the edges of the octagonal table, which was covered in a plain, black cloth and had only the woman's bejewelled hands, and two items on it: a small brown bag and a wooden box, presumably a card holder.

'Have you ever had your fortune told before, lass?' the woman asked Janey directly, in a thick Irish accent. A dialect different to the ones she heard in the Cuttlings' factory. Broader. Deeper. Older.

Janey shook her head, 'No, ma'am.'

The woman nodded. Every move she made was slow and gentle, as if she were caressing the air with each, even subtle, movement.

'My name is,' and before she continued, shot Betty a curious, lingering glance with the brightest blue eyes, 'Aishling. I was born myself from the great Tree itself…'

As Aishling spoke, Elmer scoffed, and Janey had to kick him under the table and whisper, 'It's part of the trick, jerk.'

'… born many lifetimes ago in a land far from here, where the wood grows thick and the fog of dreamlands grows thicker.' Aishling continued without heed for Elmer's coarse attitude to her performance.

'Ireland?' Betty asked, already entranced by the tale and inching closer so that her chin was in line with the edge of the table now, gazing wonderstruck at the foreigner.

Aishling nodded, 'Aye. Many moons ago. I haven't seen the old land in a long time. I travel the world with Old Grim, spinning yarns of foretelling and foreboding to all those who care to lend an old hag an ear.'

Laughing inside, Betty thought, *But you aren't old. You're beautiful. The most beautiful woman I've ever seen.*

'How much is this gunna cost us, lady?' Elmer cut through the atmosphere with the bluntest knife at his disposal; his own poor wit and carelessness.

Aishling slowly turned her stare back to the boy, 'It'll cost ye five drops,' then added, 'at first. Who knows how much the Norns will ask of ye?'

'What the fuck? What's a drop? How much is that in dollars, lady? I got a buck fifty to spend, and I ain't throwing it all down on some silly game of "guess who dies first".'

'Five drops, lad,' Aishling flicked her eyes back at Betty, gave a wink faster than a flash of lightning and returned to Elmer, 'of blood. Five little drops, and I shall not only tell ye the hour of your death, but I can also tell ye how you kill your first wife.'

Janey gasped and nearly fell back on her chair, bringing her hands up to catch the air escaping from her gaping maw.

'I'm only joking, lass,' Aishling touched her upper lip with the tip of her tongue, and a sly grin folded in the corner of her mouth. 'He doesn't marry, this one. Dies alone and poor.'

'Hah,' Elmer guffawed. He was beginning to like this woman. Her dark sense of humour appealed to him, and her dry wit had ensured that Elmer would stay and do almost everything she asked. Betty could see it in the way he folded his arms across his chest. Not in defiance, but in a statutory, intrigued state.

'Shall we begin?' Aishling asked. 'Who will be the first to ask their fate of the Norns?'

Betty did not know what a *Norn* was, but could only conjure up an image of everything she had known about the mystical and the fantastical. She saw three old women, hunched over a smouldering fire, in a land of fog and snow. Maybe it was those Penny Dreadful covers she had seen at a glance. Or maybe it was the Boulder Falls production of that Shakespearean play she had seen last year which clung to the fore of her mind? Whatever or whoever these Norns were, Betty felt a strange air enter the tent and unfold around them like a thin blanket of quiet, silencing the noise of the world outside.

Janey, sitting opposite Aishling, raised her hand. The fortune teller tilted her head and with a wave of her hand, the box of cards opened without her touch. Of course, Elmer inched his head around the edge of the table to see what sort of mechanical trickery was at play, but the girls were awestruck once more. They saw Aishling for what she was, or at least what they perceived her to be. Aishling placed five cards, face down on the table, in the shape of a solar-cross. She moved her right hand clockwise over the spread and took in a deep, rasping breath of air. It was then that her voice changed.

'Ah,' Aishling muttered and with an accent similar to Old Grim's now, closed her eyes. 'Janet Mary Cuttling.'

Janey gasped again, but the sound did not interrupt the fortune teller, if it was still her that resided in the body of Aishling.

'I see a Fool. Here. In a present and living soul.' Aishling folded over the central card, and smiled, lifting her chin as if smelling something sweet in the tent. 'How much optimism resides in such a young body.'

The proceeding cards revealed by her hand, showed first a Papal looking man, above which the word *The Hierophant* was written. Then came *The Sun* at the top, followed by the *Three of Swords* at the bottom. She left the most left card unturned.

'A man. A handsome man, full of life and vigour. You will give your heart, soul, and life to this wondrous creature. There will be three beautiful children,' Aishling's smile grew sour and cold, 'but they shall not be yours. Though your beauty is admired by so many and your success clings to your form like a gown, your face cannot hide the true nature of your soul. A needle filled with desire will prick your veins and draw everything from you. Love. Happiness. Beauty. Your yearning for greater heights of pleasure will see your star fall from heaven, cast into a pit of your own abusive lust. There is no Crone to be found on your shore. The Maiden prospers, and the Mother remains barren and lonely.'

With a quick snap of her head, back towards them, Aishling opened her eyes wide, blinked them successively and peered around the room, as if searching for someone she expected to be there and who had somehow left without her knowing.

'Wow.' Elmer said, snorting a happy chuckle. 'Sis, I always knew you were never gunna be a real Cuttling.'

Janey kicked out her feet from the table and turned her back on Aishling without saying a word, storming out of the tent. She stood there for a moment then sank her head into her hands and sobbed silently.

'She'll be fine, lass.' Aishling, now Aishling again, accent and all, looked over at Betty reassuringly, 'Just give her a moment. As for you, lad, hold out your hand, palm *up*.'

Still grinning innately, Elmer thrust out his left hand, willingly. The fortune teller lifted an object from the table Betty must have missed. A small, thin sewing needle. She turned the cards over again, face down. With a deft manoeuvre, she grasped hold of Elmer's wrist so tightly that he was unsure if he could have broken free if he had tied his hardest. His fingers began to retreat and curl, but he thought it best to just see the charade through. Who knows, he might get some good yucks out of this gypsy yet. Aishling pricked Elmer's index finger with the needle and flicked his hand over. As the blood began to form and collect into a droplet, she guided his palm over the cards, allowing five drops to drip: one onto each of the blue-coloured rectangles. Her fingers flung open and fell back to her lap. Elmer drew his finger to his lip and sucked on the tip like a small child, furrowing his brow as his did. His face said the words lingering in his mind, *This better be worth it, bitch.* Aishling winked at him, as though she heard every word. Then, she turned over every card without resorting to her accented doppelganger form.

'I could have guessed,' she raised one eyebrow. The cards had changed.

Isn't that *a trick?* Betty was unaware that her jaw had fallen, as without changing the cards, they had overturned with new faces. Every one of them. *Real magic.*

Again, Elmer's face remained locked in a state of unimpressed boredom. The cards now left staring up from the black cloth, for all to see, showed a reading that Betty was sure she did not have to be an expert to show some meagre level of understanding. And it was not good. A man hunched over in a field, with ten long blades piercing his back: The Ten of Swords. A tall building filled to the brim with fire and smoke: The Tower. A beggar wandering the cold, snow-filled streets, in front of a stained-glass window depicting five stars with five points each: The Five of Pentacles. The last two were the worst, surely? Death and The Devil.

'Well, lad,' Aishling smiled a curious smile at Elmer, as if she were more than pleased with the outcome, finally finishing with, 'yer fucked.'

It was when Betty eventually managed to draw her eyes away from the grotesque ensemble of painted figures on the deck that she was able to see something she had never seen before. Elmer was fixated on the cards. Betty felt the air change and the thin blanket of calm begin to pulse with each passing second. Elmer's face had turned whiter than mother's sheets and his mouth had pursed up into a grim spectacle of despair as he failed to blink at the cards. What was more unnerving was the watery pool forming in the corner of his eye, that Betty had not seen since they were too young to fully remember when. Not speaking, not even to give a dry witty remark to the woman, or even to insult her, Elmer stood, still pale, and stumbled unblinking from the tent. *What has he seen?* Betty watched as Janey, waiting outside, tried to place her arms around him, but her brother kept walking, unevenly, out into the carnival, head down, eyes streaming with tears. Betty realised what the situation was now. She flicked back, agitated, staring back into the bright blue eyes of Aishling. She was next.

'Relax, dear,' the fortune teller stretched one, warm hand over the table and took Betty's in hers, nodding. 'I promise ye, nothing in your future could hold a candle to the demons in that boy's mind.'

'But,' she continued, 'I'd be more than understanding of ye, if ye wished to walk out that door right now.'

It was posed as a question, but Betty felt it might have also served as a warning. Still, it was so difficult to imagine leaving. Walking away from those powerful pools of blue and that beautiful, haunting smile. After a moment's quiet consideration, Betty shook her head, and Aishling took back her hand and softly grasped the small, brown bag. There was a slow, trickling sound, as two dozen or more thumb-print sized objects fell onto the black cloth. They were stones. Unidentical, hand-carved grey rocks like little pebbles she imagined she could find out in the cold wastes of Aishling's homeland. Maybe she came from a country where beaches and sand were as abundant as dust and grain where she lived. Maybe she came from a land where people swam through lakes, bathed in snow, and wandered barefoot across green fields. Maybe that's where Aishling got her stones. She awoke one morning with a fresh breeze drawing her outside. She donned a cloak and walked into the misty blue fields, carrying her collection in her hand.

Whoa, Betty snapped back towards the table. The fortune teller had seen her eyes glaze over in lost admiration.

'Aye. Took ye to a place far from here, did they? Curious little things. Me sister once made some from small twigs, but they never carried the same magic as mine.' Aishling rubbed a finger and thumb over the stone. Her eyes flickered rapidly behind their closed lids. 'Run your hand over the pile and pick up as many as call to ye in the moment.'

Her young, pale fingers inched out over the pile and hovered for the briefest second, before being immediately drawn to the centre of the pile, right at the bottom.

'What are they?' Betty reached forward and picked up the most unusually shaped one. The mineral felt cold and wet to the touch.

'Runes,' Aishling answered. 'Each carving and letter can represent both a single and multiple voices. Would ye care to see what they sing?'

They sing? Betty furrowed her brow, turning her stone over and over with inspectional and quizzical confusion, 'there's nothing on mine.'

'You have a strong bloodline here,' Aishling said, ignoring her question, fumbling the edges of the runes, squaring their arrangement into a neat line across the table. 'Very strong. Ancient. Almost as ancient as mine. I must admit, I suspected something as ye approached my dwelling, but I had to be sure. Old Grim has waited some time ye see. Ages and ages of time. I'll not lie to ye. This a very special communion we're having together. A gift so promising has not been offered in all my years of service to the Tree.'

Again, and again, Betty heard words she did not understand and sentences that seemed to begin with comprehension, only to trail away into dismal, unsatisfactory confusion. She wanted nothing more than to know just what the fortune teller was talking about. What those fancy words described meant and how she, a fourteen-year-old Presbyterian from Oklahoma slotted into the jigsaw of this tale.

Aishling took her left hand and delved the slender, jewel encrusted fingers down between her cleavage to produce a bronze, slightly rusted key. Aside from the general wear and tear, the key felt old. It felt older as it was offered to Betty and she felt its weight dip her hand slightly.

Curious how something so small could carry such weight, she wondered, running her fingers across the lock-opener and feeling a series of minuscule indentations that might have been words she could read, should she have a magnifying glass in her pocket. Yet her mind also told her that even if she could make out the inscription, it would be in a language she, nor probably a handful of people in America could decipher.

'What does it open?' she asked, not bluntly, but with a sense of longing in her voice.

Aishling smiled her usual, wry grin, looking as pleased as Betty, 'a very unique and very special door.'

Outside the House of Doors, Betty realised she was alone. Not because Aishling or Old Grim had left, they still watched her eagerly as she walked, but because her friends had gone. Just gone, without a word. She could hardly blame them, seeing the way Aishling had presented them with such dismal fortunes. They could have at least said goodbye. She would find them later, she supposed. It seemed that right now, nothing was more important than seeing this door the gypsy had spoken of. Seeing it for herself and opening it. Maybe it would be full of treasures? Gold coins in a pirate's chest? Or jewels, just like Aishling had? It had to be special, for her to have to go through all this trouble just to even get inside the House of Doors.

'That's it, little one. Go on. You might see things and hear things that appear quite scary to a young girl, but they cannot harm ye.' Aishling walked just a footstep behind her now. 'Nothing to fret over, lass. Ye'll be able to find your way around with the key. It knows a thing or two. Let it guide ye around the maze. I'll be right outside should ye get too flustered.'

Betty looked back and saw the fortune teller smiling, ushering her onwards with both hands. Just behind her, Old Grim half-closed his one eye, as though something about the little girl was untrustworthy. That whatever she might find, she might not be worthy of.

The House of Doors was dark and numbing. Everything past the gate was too crisp to be enjoyable. Too dingy to understand. Betty found herself lost, all at once. The gate had gone. The darkness overwhelmed the House and she felt trapped within its bleak walls.

'Aishling?' She muttered, seeing a hint of her own breath form from her mouth, rising up into the rafters of the House.

'I'm here, little one. Keep going.'

Her foot reached out into the darkness and held for the briefest moment, before pulling her body through its shadowy veil. Step by step, the veil opened up to her and eventually began to provide a series of glimpses into its heart. At first, Betty was unsure that what she was seeing was real, as she had no reference in her mind to place the object. It might have been a tree, but for all its many shapes, the towering object seemed to thrive with life and move its gnarled branches to and fro, as though growing with each passing heartbeat of hers, which became quicker and heavier. On the lowest branch of the lowest limb of the tentacled, writhing sapling, a man stood. Betty could not see a face with which to identify the figure. Her soul did not fill with dread to hear the shadow speak, but rather with sorrow.

'A twelfth I know, if high on a tree I see a hanged man swing,' as the voice sang out; the man placed one foot over the edge of the branch and allowed his body to sink towards the black soil beneath.

With a shriek of horror, Betty turned away, cowering. Aishling had not heard her. Or had heard her and had not cared for the shrill, splitting cry. Through her fingers, Betty returned to the tree and saw that it had left. Though the hanged man remained. He danced there; the jig of death on his own gallows. Letters began to emerge around her. Great lightning blues and visceral greens. The letter, no not letters… what had Aishling called them? *Runes*. They glistened like starlight. The only light to be seen. Betty reached out one palm and felt her hand glide through the ethereal literacy. It appeared to be an S. Almost like an S. A ᚾ.

A flash. A spark of life filled her mind. Visions of men marching the streets, their hands covered in blood, their guns belching fire. Two runes covered their faces, shielding the world from the terror behind their eyes. Two runes. ᚾ. Betty could not cover her eyes, for the visions came from inside, however hard she looked away and hid. An army scorching the earth with bombs and smoke and death. Above the blistering ground, a broken cross hung in the sky. Betty finally shuddered enough to pull free her hand. The world was dark again. She was alone. Even the hanged man had vanished. Still, the runes remained.

'Not all magic is used for good, little one.' But it was the voice of Old Grim she had heard now, not Aishling, whose sweet accent she now longed for. 'Every man makes his choice, and every man must pay his brother's price. I ween that I hung on the windy tree, hung there for nights full nine.'

When Betty took a step backwards and found herself at a distance to the glimmering runes, it was then she understood. They were not runes. Not *only* runes. They were doors. Two dozen doors of different shapes and sizes. Different creations and designs. One which looked to be marked with an M. No, a Ɯ. When her hand braced the handle, the letter became an Ɛ. The door churned with wooden life. The eye of her mind stretched far across the world and saw horses. Dead and dying. Hundreds of them. They lay in pastures void of life and green grass, now all bare and grey. Great armadas of flies scoured the littered corpses. A pale eye caught hers, and she wept. How strange it is to weep without eyes and without form. It is only when she screamed once more her body was given back to her. In a great and terrible voice, the Hanged-Man announced, 'Despised was he by strangers when he was washed ashore, and shunned was he as if he were plague-smitten and foul.'

'I want to leave. Now.' She cried and turned this way and that, searching for the gate through which she entered this abysmal domain. Flitting across an endless chasm of darkness, a world filled with doors and empty of exits.

Outside, she heard their voices, Old Grim and Aishling, and though they try to whisper she can hear every word clap like thunder.

'This is not supposed to happen.' Grim barked, and he may have been trying to turn something in his hand.

Aishling sounds furious, 'get her out, Grimnir. Get her out, *now*.'

'Bah.'

Did he strike her? Betty's fear exploded into panic.

Aishling sobs. Soft, controlled tears.

'She must find the Silver Door.' Grim rattled the handles of Betty's enclosure over and over, forcing shadowy sparks to zip past her, this way and that.

They cannot hear her scream, though she can hear them calling.

'Find the Door, *barn.*' Grim bellows. 'Use the key. Use it now. Go.'

Betty wiped her face with the back of her hand and fumbles for the key. It was gone. She had just held it. Just placed it in her purse for a second. Just one second. She dropped to her knees and scurried across the ethereal, obsidian floor. Nothing. Nothing. Nothing. The floor was clean and marbled. Cool and blemish free. Anything that touches her hand must be…the key. She did not touch it but saw it. Just an arm's length away. Betty swiped forward and…missed?

'When you have it, just call for the Door. The *Silver* Door. It will take you home, *barn.*' Old Grim blared his command from every direction, hand still rasping against the gate like a drum.

The key floated above the ground for a second. Only a second and then quick as a flash spit forward. Betty heard the familiar mechanical *click* and *thunk* of a lock being opened somewhere ahead of her. Three flashes of brilliant, incomprehensible light appeared. The light was dark and white at the same time. Just looking upon it made Betty's primal mind recoil in fear of the unknown. as if she were the first beast to create fire and now stared in terror at what she had done. The three lights glowed until their light consumed the world and then, just like that, they faded into a dim, hollow strips of crimson. Edges of a door.

'I can hear it.' Old Grim's voice reappeared, this time filled with gratitude. 'That's it, barn, open the *Silver* Door.' Then he tried to whisper, 'she might save us all yet.'

Betty gulped down a lump of fear and gave him a confused reply, 'but it's not *Silver.* It's *Black.*'

Unaware or unable, Betty could not hear the shrieking voices outside. They screamed until their throats gave out, and the screamed again. They called to her to 'run', 'to stay away', 'stay away from the *Black Door.*'

How can she, when it is so beautiful? A shining, Stygian door. Its very essence hummed, calling to her to come closer. Come see what lies behind the Black Door. What great adventures await you? What wonderful pleasures we will give you. What sacred horrors shall you unleash. She could feel people on the other side. People coming closer. Were they people? Things. Yes. Hideous things. Things with blackened wings and bleeding wounds. Things with pierced eyes and sewn lips. Things with many mouths and things with many thoughts. They came towards the door; crawling, twitching, panting. Shattered, broken, eldritch terrors seeking light and she had invited them.

No, Betty thought. *No, that's not right. This is not what I want. No. No, it's not right. No. No. No. No. No.*

The Black Door opened.

Blissful Hills

ᚾ

Pleasure and pride deceive the sons of men who after money crave;
shining riches at last become a sorrow: many have riches driven to
madness.

- *Hávamál*

Dear Mr. Schnieder:
    I am writing to you today in regard to your recent
absenteeism from my lectures. Your current attendance record
falls far below the expected 75%, and as head of the Archaeological
department at Leeds University, I must inform you that this email will
be proceeding any formal disciplinary.
    My next statement will be in regard to your dissertation. As you
know, this particular assessment counts towards the largest portion of your
credits needed to graduate. The subject you have chosen, 'Mysteries of
Ancient Runes and the Impact on Modern Magic', has not inspired me
with enough confidence to initiate any further action. I would, as your
friend and mentor, strongly encourage you not to continue in this farcical
pursuit of magicka and madness. Although intriguing, it lacks any
academic purpose or conviction. These are stories and fairy tales with which
no evidence, aside from the ramblings of lunatics, has been ascribed. Such
a study will not be accepted for academic writing now, or in the foreseeable
future. I urge you to redirect your focus onto more manageable subjects.

You love the Alfredian wars and have shown such promise in earlier years with your enthusiasm.

Please, Jack, do not throw your studies away with some ridiculous notion of ancient mystical societies, hidden treasure, and strange forbidden worlds. You will not be the first I have met, nor tutored, to undertake this far cry belief, and I dare to say you will not be the last. Professor Day was a brilliant lecturer, theologian, and a good friend. I can tell you, first-hand, that her last few books were transcribed under an unsound mind. I see that you have checked out several of her manuscripts and I urge you to take each of these with more than a pinch of salt.

I hope to see you bright an early Monday.

Dearest Regards,
Dr Francis Meadows. Ph.D. MA Phil.
Head of Archaeology Leeds University

'Eesh, he does *not* sound like a happy bunny,' Lucy turned to Jack with her teeth clenched together, a sign that she quite possibly believed Francis's warnings about this journey they had taken.

Still, they were on the road now. An hour in. No turning back. The extra-shot coffees had been purchased. The playlist had been selected. They were in this for the long haul. Though the sat-nav gave them an estimated arrival time of just under an hour and three-quarters, something about the endless drizzle of rain and the uneven concrete bypass of the A64 made everything louder, longer, and much more tiring. Jack opened his mouth for a long yawn, which took his eyes off the road long enough for the wheels to begin jutting over the cat's eyes. Close enough to the hard shoulder to startle them both.

'Hey. Whoa.' Lucy closed her book, instinctively reaching for the handle above her head.

'Sorry. Sorry. I didn't get much sleep last night. This coffee isn't really doing the trick.' Jack wiped the corner of one eye with the back of his palm and tried to give her a reassuring smile.

'Bad dreams again?' she asked.

She cared. She cared more than anyone he knew. That was why it probably hurt so much to look at her, but he could not help it in the slightest. She looked good. The best. In his eyes. Easy, round features and a smile set to bright even the drizzliest of days.

Jack nodded with a heavy flicker of his eyelids. He felt as if several parcels of luggage had been tied to his cheeks, dragging them towards the frayed, beige car seat. Several hundred yards after the indicator had begun to tick away to the left, the barrage of newly erected maintenance cones diverted them northwards onto a long, uneven stretch of track headed through the hills and trees of an old and forgotten country.

****

This was it. The address. Jack pondered back on Dr. Meadows's words, now seeing the dilapidated asylum ahead of him.

'Arrived at your destination, you have.' The sat-nav said backwardly, in that preinstalled voice of Yoda; the eighties-inspired toad-monk-creature from *Star Wars.*

A fortress. Something from either the twilight zone, or perhaps a post-apocalyptic zombie flick, appeared out of the dense, river-born mist surrounding them. It was a setup. Not like a trap or a sting. More like a movie set. Something created and designed with every purpose to install a feeling of dread and anxiety over whoever set eyes upon it. Whitewashed walls.

Crumbling brick facade. Overgrown ivy clinging to the walls where the world it encompassed slowly died, as entropy regained control of existence. Windows with old, iron bars, rusted almost into the very brick. They stained the edges of the sills with a sickly, coppery taint that made it look as if the building itself was crying. Crying blood.

What a place to house the mentally ill, Jack grimaced. *Survival Rule No. 2: do not enter the haunted mansion.*

It was a throwback to an age before the nationally maintained Mental Health Service, when the best thing to do with a person who no longer held a firm grasp on reality was to lock them away, lest they infect others with their madness. Infesting into their minds like evil weevils.

As the car approached, Jack pushed in the small plastic button by the door release. The window of the Skoda made a whirl, juddered slightly, then came down fast. Jack leaned out and stretched his arm so that the large Kraken tattoo poked out from under his right, woollen sleeve. The button was stiff. After a moment, an alarmingly bright light illuminated above it followed moments later by a crackling voice.

'Blissful Hills. Reception?' the voice asked.

Jack could not look directly into the bright light or the camera inside, but managed to say, 'Please. Visitors to see...'

But before he could say a name, the light went out, and the crackling disappeared. The next sound was that of the huge, twisted metal gates swinging open electronically. Whatever mechanism inside having been installed many years ago grinded slowly. It seemed minutes had passed before the bars disappeared and the gravel driveway was open to them.

'Here we go, then.' Jack smiled, adding quietly, 'I guess.' It was best to maintain at least a low level of positivity around Lucy. After all, he had dragged her out to the middle of nowhere on some goose-chase even he was beginning to doubt.

The reception area opened out with an alarming sense of modernism. Bare walls, with the odd, psychiatrically inspired paintings from residents. Colourful trees. Blue hills. The odd painted quote lining the corridor with words such as, *'Positivity is the Key to Happiness'*, or *'Talking is the Best Medicine'*.

It made Jack shudder at the thought that he was perhaps only two prescription-less weeks from succumbing to this place himself. A fish tank, clean and full, gurgled away in the corner. The reception desk was set back into a small alcove underneath the stairs. Just a phone, some folders, and an Apple computer. The feeling of decrepit entropy had left and been replaced with a cold-warmth; a feeling he did not fully understand. Sterility and heat.

'Hello?' Jack knocked on the desk and as he did a small, younger woman appeared, knocking the folders to one side and flapping about as if he had rudely interrupted her.

'Ah, yes, hello,' she said, rubbing her elbow, whilst leaving the folders scattered over the cream carpet. 'Blissful Hills, who have you come to see?'

Lucy was cringing at the tiny girl, so lost behind the desk that it seemed comical and perhaps a little cruel.

'Erm. June. June Day,' Jack finally replied, collecting the folders from the floor and half-heartedly stacking them back on the desk.

There had been a constant alarm ringing somewhere in the background since they had arrived. Soft but constant, like having tinnitus. It was clearly a call for aid which was being ignored either due to lack of staff or most likely, lack of care.

When Jack turned back to the small woman, he saw that she was wearing a look of...shock?

'Miss Day?' she asked, pushing out her lips like one of the aquarium-cased animals just feet away.

Jack nodded, smiling again. Smiling too much. 'Yes. That's right. She is still a resident here I take it?'

Moving her lips without sound, the girl finally answered, clearly stunned, 'Of course. It's just that, she hasn't had a visitor in like, well, forever as I hear it. I just started like last year, but people talk. You know. Poor woman just has no one left. Could I...ask, why you wish to see her? Are like you a relative?'

Stop saying 'like,' you idiot. Jack clenched his teeth, watching her blister through the conversation.

Lucy sighed next to him, biting her upper lip, knowing exactly what he was thinking before he even gave her a roll of the eyes.

'No. Not relatives. Just, fans. I guess.' Jack was trying to explain something he did not grasp to a woman who had no idea. 'I'm from Leeds. I'm a student. I was wondering if I could, possibly, pick her brain for some help. Ideas. Help. Help for me, I mean.'

Why don't you like, say help, like, again? Jack wanted the ground to open wide and swallow his pride.

Behind the desk, the custodian to this fortress of insanity appeared to mull the notion over a few times. Jack could almost see the idea rolling from one side of her brain to the other, then back again, before she widened her gaze, fluffed up her faux-hospitality smile and said, 'Of course'. Letting the droll blue chair swivel away from them, the receptionist stood, no more than five feet, and began to walk.

'I guess?' Jack shrugged his broad shoulders as Lucy nodded towards the miniature custodian, trundling away towards a newly refurbished elevator. After a moment of awkward silence, the lift doors opened, and they entered.

'Four floors.' Jack remarked. 'Big place. I bet you're fit going up and down the stairs all day?'

The small woman gave a brief, forced smile and took in a deep breath.

Idiot. Jack looked away, hoping that perhaps the lift would shoot them high up into the sky or crash far below to avoid the obvious and failing flirting. He did not want to look up and see Lucy's wide-eyed grin. He knew she never wished to see him shoot and miss, but perhaps she just found it too hilarious to ignore?

Finally, the lift stopped its vibrations and the small light indicating the third floor illuminated. Doors opened smoothly onto a white-washed corridor, devoid of grime, stain, and life. There was not even a poster or painting up here to relieve oneself from the monotonous and clinical confinement.

On the third floor, they no longer pretend to save you. Jack was unsure why he often thought these things. It had seemed from birth that he would have one mind, split into two. Horrid, outside notions and intrusive thoughts would suddenly ping to the forefront of his mind. Usually when he did not wish for them and almost always when he was on edge. These were not always thoughts, in words. Sometimes, they came in pictures. Gruesome, grotesque graphics which would come and go within the blink of an eye. Right now, he saw death. A skeletal figure, holding the sands of time between his bony claws. The sands, which were almost empty.

Jack and Lucy trod the linoleum floor all the way to its end, around the corner and into the carpeted, but no less oppressive foyer of the visitors dining area. No quicker than Lucy was about to ask just how long they had, or indeed what

Mrs Day even looked like, the small receptionist had gone. Vanished into the evening's grey light with the press of a button, and the 'ding' of an elevator door. They were alone.

That was a lie. They felt alone, because there were no other visitors. No other 'normals' around. Only those who dwelt here, amongst the fortress of the damned. Forever. Jack could call them inmates, but supposed that perhaps the term should, instead, be *patients*. Whatever the word, it is always hard to hide fetters and chains.

Around the room, which was just the same as any other room on the third floor, the patients sat. Unmoving. Unflinching. Not even mumbling to themselves or whispering to each other the secrets only the mad possess and the genius envy. Jack stepped over the metallic strip of the threshold and bore witness to the staleness of modern care. As long as everything was clean and sterile, everything was good. Acceptable. Auditable.

Five patients. Two visitors. Each of the bland tables and bolted chairs in the room had been organised so that patients were sat, unable to alter their perspective. Only allowed to face their visitor for the allocated time, in the allocated way, just a step away from the nurses holding placards behind them in place of any real thought. Four of them sat waiting, ever so stoic, for families and friends who might not come; who might never have been. Perched on their seats, as uneagerly to greet their old lives as they were to greet their own reflections. That was, except for one. One of the patients did not sit at a table. She was not waiting for anyone. She was as new to this room as Jack and Lucy. So, she did not fall into line; instead, sought her comfort in the world she had come to know well; the green grass of the gardens just below the third-floor windows. Her eyes falling out over the green-grey wash of the British countryside, almost empty. Almost.

Jack looked from table to table. There was a man, closest to him, perhaps aged around his grandpa's time; eighty-four, maybe eight-six. The octogenarian drooled a little as he waited, immersed in a land elsewhere. Perhaps not even in this same time. He could have been back in and amongst his youth. He might be happily dancing at his wedding or standing shoulder-to-shoulder with his brothers in arms, each of whom had passed in honour so long ago. Wherever he was and whatever he was doing, he showed little care. Just the slow, soft declination of age.

Jack moved his eyes past the man, towards another table, where what remained of a once prolific dancer sat. She danced no more. Merely rocked from side to side, front to back, in a vain attempt to imitate the way her aged feet would tap, shuffle and sweat. Jack glanced over her. She looked nothing like Mrs. Day, though the photo he had was some fifteen years old. But unless she had darkened her skin and grown a full head of hair, this was not her.

The others at the tables were men, and so he judged the lonesome figure in her wheeled seat by the window, yet he could not see her face, to be June. It had to be. The web of fate was rarely as difficult to un-weave as we might think. There are always signs, if one knows how and where to seek them.

Jack turned to Lucy, his teeth chewing against the inside of his lip. Hands fumbling together in front of him, the way she knew they did whenever he became anxious. It was his fight or flight response kicking in from remnants of that reptilian-primate brain. Possible danger had washed over him, and he wished to turn and run.

Lucy gave him a stern grimace and shook her head towards the window. 'Go, you idiot, we've come all this bloody way.'

Jack stepped into an aura of composure, rubbing his palms against his beige jeans, before breathing deep and walking. A haunting reflection of Mrs. Day became larger and more detailed in the glass as he approached from behind. Her hands sat folded across her lap. Her lost hair folded and combed to give the illusion of a typical aged perm. As grey as the skies out over the fields. Her eyes stared hungrily at the world just feet away, yet further than the deepest ocean. Her lips twitched gingerly as though she were speaking to a lover.

'Mrs. Day?' Jack posed the question, adopting the hunched over perch of a man speaking to the infirm or a child. Lucy stepped a little closer, but kept a distance back, just so that she might hear the conversation and not be dragged into it. Behind them, doors swung and shut. The lift pinged and just as she expected more visitors to arrive, no one did. The halls remained silent once more and the patients sat motionless.

'Mrs. Day? June.' Jack asked, speaking her name in a way that suggested she had forgotten who she was many years past. 'I'm Jack Schneider. I'm a student researcher at Leeds University.'

Mrs. Day remained transfixed on the garden. Unblinking. Motionless, except for the twitching of her mouth, as though she recited something soft and delicate.

'June. I'm here from the University. Where you used to work.' Each of Jack's sentences ended with an inflection, so that they could be taken as questions or statements. It was the way people often spoke to small children or pets.

He looked back at Lucy and she saw the same look she had seen a thousand times. It was the look he had worn when searching for a new pair of jeans and found the perfect pair, if only the hem was a little tighter. It was the look that told her, *I am going to give up now. This was a waste of time.* So she urged him on with her hands. After relieving himself from an audible sigh, Jack decided to take another approach.

'June. My name is Jack. Just like the hero in Norn's Fate. Remember? It's why I'm here. I wanted to speak to you about your writing. I'm a big fan. I enjoyed the fiction even more than the historical accounts. You have a way with words, June.' *Had*, he wanted to correct himself, *you* had *a way with words.*

Something stirred inside the old woman, if only for a brief moment. Her face lightened from grey pallor to an almost human and lifelike colour. Her lips had stopped twitching. Now pursed, as if she had a note to add and had forgotten what it was.

'I wished to talk to you about Runes. If I may?' Jack asked, politely.

Mrs. Day astonished him by repeating the word, 'Runes', expanding the vowel, soothingly. Caressing the memory with her tongue.

Jack's eyes flashed wide, 'Yes, yes. Runes. You are an expert…were an…no, *are* an expert on Runic translation. I'm hoping you can help me with a subject for my master's dissertation, June?'

When she did not resist, or revert to her twitching, he pursued his game, 'Francis, remember him? He wants me to give up and pick another area of study. But the Runes, I know you found something. Something you haven't been able to share in writing to anyone. I found your old manuscript from the library. Your last work. Do you remember?'

Mrs. Day flickered a small smile. Jack caught the sight and turned to Lucy, beaming with joy. 'June, please. I have to know. What…is The Black Door?'

Outside, a low, rumbling echo of thunder rolled across the hills of Yorkshire, interrupting the conversation. Before it passed, the lights inside the visitor's room expanded their brilliance, before fulgurating with the synchronised flash of lighting beyond the pale windows.

It could not stop Jack. Fate had handed him a glimmer of hope. 'Mrs. Day, please. I know it must be difficult. I would go mad myself in this place. But, please, what do you know of the Black Door? It would help me immensely and confirm my suspicions about the Volga, the Seidr and the old gods of England. It has something to do with *him*, doesn't it? I've seen him, too, the Wanderer. In my dreams.' *In my nightmares*, he corrected himself again.

Another two-pronged attack of thunder and lightning swam over the horizon. Lucy felt her arm hairs raise with the static and dance on the edges of her skin, electrifying her soul with anxiety and caution. For some strange and unknowable reason, she wanted to grab Jack's arm. Grab it and go. Escape this place. Forget about Runes and witchcraft. Just for one day. Forget it all and escape. But why? Why suddenly the fear? Is this why Francis was so harsh in his email? What was it about this fragile old lady that now put her so on edge?

'Black.' June said. 'Black. Black. The Door. Black.' The words barked from her mouth as though she had transformed into an anthropomorphic terrier, as the fingers on her right-hand clasp at an unseen object.

'Yes, June.' Jack watched her fingers in awe. He was finally getting the answers; he just knew it. Soon, his work would have merit. It would have sustenance and founding. Evidence, it was all he wanted. 'What can you tell me?'

Mrs. Day's fingers clutched together. Clutched so tight that the knuckles turned white. That they trembled, before the index finger flung out like a spear and jutted towards the window.

'What is it?' Jack followed the finger down into the garden.

'He won't leave me alone,' June said, chocking a little on the words she dared not say. 'He follows me. Everywhere. He won't leave. He won't leave. Leave. Leave. Leave.'

In the garden of Blissful Hills, there was a man. A man like any other, from all outwards appearances. A gardener, Jack assumed, watching the gnarled and crooked finger poking down at him so accusingly. He shuffled about the garden from hedge to plant, collecting litter and leaves into a large plastic bag that blew hesitantly beside him in the wind.

Jack let out a mournful sigh, *Perhaps she has gone mad. Truly. And I was so close to the answers I needed. Poor thing.*

He debated against it for a moment, but slowly clambered to his feet. The arch of his back cracked along with his knees. Another sigh let Lucy know that it was time to leave. This adventure had been folly. This whole idea had been nonsense.

As the young scholar turned to leave, he heard a curious word escape from June's mouth.

'Grim,' she muttered to herself, or perhaps to Jack, though he was so thrown by the word that his lips parted but no sound escaped. 'There he is. Old Grim. Come to watch me as I wait.'

A glint of a shiny object forced him to close one eye. It was almost as if the sun had flashed, just in the corner of his sight. Down below, where the gardener still stood, collecting the dried and decayed foliage of Blissful Hills. Stooping then standing. Bending then scooping. Over and over again, whilst June rested; watching.

There it was again. Something glimmering from the old gardener. Jack was about to curse, before a curious and altogether dreadful realisation clicked in his head light a lightbulb. Just like a cartoon, it was an almost palpable and physical shape of an idea. His heart raced, and his stomach dropped at the same time. It was not reflection of light. Not some rogue sunray refracted by the glass of a wristwatch. No. There was no sun. There had not been sun since it rose, sometime this morning, behind the thick layer of permeating English cloud. *What had made that radiant brilliance?*

'He likes to watch me,' June said, as the flash of white aurora appeared again, sheltering the entire garden from view. She seemed not to care. Not even to blink. 'He likes to make sure I'm safe. That I don't go wandering again. Not to that place. I'm too old for such a place. Too old for old worlds. Too old for kings and monsters.'

Lucy had moved a little closer, ever since the lighting had first flashed. The storm, it seemed, had passed now. Rolled over onto distant hills. She could not make out exact words that June was uttering but kept catching odd phrases. Very odd phrases. What she could see, however, was the gnarled, arthritic fingers, scrawling across her knee, writing her invisible novel. Lucy leapt off the chair and disappeared.

Jack saw Lucy dart out of the room but judged that she must be bursting for the toilet, so he pressed June further. 'June. Could you tell me more about—"

'Here.' Lucy had appeared again, quick as a flash. In her hand, she held a small biro and a scrap of paper she had found.

Half-torn with something blue across the back. Lucy gently eased the biro into Mrs Day's right hand, before sliding the torn plasticky paper between the pen and the old woman's knee.

'Lucy.' Jack barked and for a moment, with his overbearing scowl, she thought he would scold her for treating an elderly woman so. But he did not. Instead, he added, 'You're a genius.'

They waited patiently, as Mrs. Day began to form most elegant sketches with her hand, without ever once having to glance down, as though she had done this a thousand times before. Or, as if her limp arm was being manipulated by some unseen, guiding hand. Whatever was happening, it was working.

'It's...' Lucy began.

'Blissful Hills. Here.' Jack finished, staring down at a fairly well detailed depiction of the world. The world from Mrs. Day's eyes. Right here. Down to the shape of the clouds. After the last hedgerow had been sketched, June dropped the paper on the floor, quickly, before returning to her freehand wavering.

Jack mouthed the word, 'another', to Lucy. She nodded and disappeared again to her secret treasure trove of paper.

The next sketch was a portrait. It was close. Too close to be seen from here. *Surely? But, perhaps*, he was right. A quick glance below the ledge of the barred windows, let Jack catch a view of the gardener again. She was drawing...him. He had to squint to be sure, but yes, it was him alright. Not a doubt now.

The gardener, at least the drawing of him, had long hair, which came below his shoulders, oddly patterned with knots and small braids. It reminded Jack of a pirate from a movie he saw many years ago. Next came a sharp, square face. Strong.

Almost a caricature of an ogreish, semi-Tolkien fellow. Big, bulbous nose and high cheekbones set above a thick jawline, which disappeared under a sprawl of fast-drawn squiggles. These soon became a thick, long, ducktail beard.

Again, the picture was finished and discarded, as the hand continued.

The next drawing was of the gardener again, and Jack let out a small sigh, thinking that this repetition had become another dead end in his investigation of…whatever this had turned out to be. The picture was identical. Down to a single thread of hair. Until, Mrs. Day began to cover up the right eye with a thick, shaded circle. Above and below which, a three-dimensional scar was drawn.

'I guess she forgot the eye-patch last time,' Lucy offered.

Jack might have accepted that conclusion, if he had not decided to double check that; no, the man below the window did not have an eyepatch. Not even a scar on his face to obscure it. Blemish and patch free.

The third drawing was the most obscure of them all. This time, this fantastical re-imagining of the grounds keeping gardener, wore a dark, wide-brimmed hat. He had three large beads woven into his beard, several more in his hair, and a medieval torque around his neck, just above where the sketch faded into blank paper. A torque was unusual apparel to give, well, anyone outside of dark age British mythology. It was much like a woven or platted armband, except much heavier, thicker and impressive than one you might find in York Museum. What was more unusual than that was the fact that instead of shading in the eyepatch this time, Mrs. Day had depicted the patch with a very specific symbol.

'What's that on his eye? Looks like those things you hang on your wall.' Lucy asked, eyes focused on the odd imagery, just as Mrs. Day dropped the piece of paper and let her fingers rest on her lap, still quivering slightly.

'Vegvisir,' Jack muttered. Lucy watched his eyes frown, flickering over the drawing again and again to every strange detail it conveyed. It was as though he knew something but could not quite puzzle it all out.

'What's…' she did not have to finish.

'It's a compass. Of sorts. A Norse compass.'

'Norse?' the word was familiar and unfamiliar at the same time.

Jack sighed, 'Viking.' He hated using the word out of context. 'Viking', or to be more precise '*Vikingr*', was not a people or a religion. It was a word simply meaning 'pirate'. Those who raided the old English shores and integrated themselves so deeply into these isles that we cannot go more than two days in the week without mentioning them. Norse was more apt. Or even 'Dane' he would have preferred.

'What does it mean, though?' Lucy pushed.

Jack was about to explain the mysteries of the Viking age and how so much had been lost in time that we cannot always be sure. That, Norse peoples, or Danes, did not tend to write their migrations or religion down. Instead, they passed down much of what we know by oral history. This is why it had been so hard to study them, and why Francis had tried push the 'Viking-age' studies far away from his class. What we knew of the Norse was limited mostly to old English interpretation, and after several decades of being slaughtered by marauding Danes, history had not looked too kindly on them. Only now are we beginning to see a revival in the interest of the Northern Germanic peoples and learning that their culture was far richer and diverse than we could have imagined. Yes, he was about to explain all this to her, when something tapped hard against the window.

For a split second, looking up, Jack expected to see the outline of the gardener at the window. Furious at the constant gawking and spying he had been subject to. But there was nothing there. Not at this window.

It was when the tap came again, louder, that Lucy spun around to peer at the next window along. A large bird, perhaps some twenty-five inches high, was cocking back its neck and thrusting its black bill against the window. The sound ricocheted around the visitor's room and even the half dead patients began to turn around to see the commotion. The blackbird knocked at the window again. Louder. Stronger. So strong that an inch-long crack broke in the thick, double glazing.

Lucy jumped back and ran around Mrs. Day's wheelchair, curling her arms around Jack's. 'What the hell is it doing?' her voice was shaken.

Jack lifted his arm and pulled her a little closer to his chest, as the large bird snacked the window again and again. Luckily, the window, though cracked appeared to be holding well.

It was a raven; he was sure of it. Bigger than a blackbird. No white for a magpie. He remembered seeing some large ravens in London. At the Tower. Legend had it that they had been placed in captivity by King Charles II's command in the 17th century and that should all the ravens die or flee the Tower, Britain and the Crown would fall.

The raven, *Corvus corax*, was an intelligent bird, often capable of rudimentary speech and cognitive skills. It seemed that this specimen was just as cunning as its genus allowed. Perhaps more so. For the bird hopped back a little on the ledge, cocking its head to the side, seemingly assessing the damage, before tipping its beak skyward and cawing.

'Oh, Jees, it sounds like laughter. Horrible laughter.' Lucy turned away, backing up behind Jack.

Slow, drawn laughter it was not. For within seconds another raven appeared, just as big and broad as its brother. The pair began to hop along the ledge, peering in at the denizens of Blissful Hills, before bending down towards the lower pane of the window and pecking vigorously.

'Right. I'm out of here. Come on.' Lucy grasped Jack's arm but try as she might he would not budge. He just held up his hand.

With a splintering of wood, the two ravens managed to pry their way below the window flick the glass upwards. One by one, the ominous fowl hoped under the glass and sat on the inner ledge of the sill. Jack almost felt the air being sucked out of the room, as Lucy gasped, and the surrounding patients began to lose control. There were screams and wild giddy bouts of clapping. One of the elderly men kicked his chair aside and clambered onto a table, beating at the sides of his head with open palms. Jack had to do something.

He stepped forward, possibly thinking he would shoo the birds down the hall or scare them back out of the window. They were clever little animals. One of them hopped to his left. The other, his right. The one by his right looked past him, back to Lucy. Its black eyes steeped to the side, peering with curious intent. It worked. Jack saw the glance and moved straight back, using his shoulders to shield Lucy from view. Behind him, she covered her head in her hands and hid, shaking.

They had not noticed the raven on the left. Unattended, it flew onto the inner ledge, just in front of Mrs. Day. A horrid, intrusive thought of blood flashed in Jack's mind, before he shook it loose. But the bird did not attack. Instead, Mrs. Day smiled at the animal, reaching her shaky arm out in a gesture of friendship. The bird, anthropomorphically, seemed to consider this move. Its beady, glassy, black eyes followed her hand, but at the last moment remembered what it had come to do. It fluttered to the floor, alarming everyone in the room, before scooping up the sketches Mrs. Day had drawn; one by one into its beak.

'Munin,' Mrs. Day *popped* her lips together after greeting the bird, the way a child might as it first learned to imitate those around it.

It...no...it can't be here for the paper? Surely what madness is this? Jack felt his legs inch forward slowly without intentionally acting.

This stalking disarmed the raven, who snatched at the papers before flittering up to the window and pushing itself out into the darkening world. The second one hesitated for a moment, keeping as glaring eye on Lucy as if to say, *Just try it,* before it too escaped with a flurry; leaving the patients utterly discombobulated at the whole event.

Not knowing how much he wanted to, Jack sprinted past Mrs. Day and over to the open window. The cold air hit him like a shield. Not hard enough to force him away. He squinted once more into the garden and saw the event that would change his perception on reality until the day he passed from this world.

The raven, the one holding Mrs. Day's sketches, had glided down over the hedgerows, where the corner of the next annex connected with a small gravel path which led around the back of Blissful Hills. The light had faded somewhat in the hour, but he knew what he saw. The large bird came to a fluttering stop right onto the arm of the gardener. That simple old man tending to his foliage had brought the bird. Shaking the papers lose, the raven dropped them into the gardener's open palm. There was brief moment of contemplating the images before the eyes of the gardener rose to meet the figure staring at him from the third-floor window, Jack.

Something in that gaze made his blood turn to ice. Jack felt as if a pack of wolves was watching him in the night. Every hair on his body stood erect. Every inch of skin electrified with fear. Every fibre of his being telling him to run. But still, he did not look away. Not just yet.

Survival Rule Number 17: *Curiosity kills the cat.* His mind baulked laughter at him, as his body froze in place, turning Jack into a living, breathing sculpture of fright.

The old gardener balled the papers into his hand with a thick, coarse grip. Crumpling them into a rugged ball of white and blue, before there was a heavy glow in the air, the sound of metal on metal below and an inferno of flame engulfed the man's hand. The flame stayed for some time. Long enough to burn his skin and clothes. Yet, it remained controlled, as if by…*magic,* Jack's jaw dropped.

Slowly, the gardener opened his fingers and released the contents, what was left of the drawings. Tiny flecks of ash and ember rose from his palm, caught in the wind and floated away into the evening air.

Then, the old man was gone.

Door on a Henge

þ

An offer-stead to me he raised, with stones constructed;
Now is that stone as glass become.
With the blood of oxen, he newly sprinkled it.

- Hyndluljóð

-

I t was almost as if watching he were watching a play. There stood an actor on stage, portraying him, yet he could not understand the motives of the character. The thespian stood, as if to give his opening soliloquy, motionless. Lights dim above and the theatre turns to a dark, ethereal place which exists outside of time and outside of the world surrounding it, even outside of itself. A place created for one purpose and one purpose only, to tell the story. Nothing else mattered in life, at this junction in time. Only the events that were soon to unfold.

Jack watched himself in the reflection of the window. Unmoving. Shaken, but still paralysed, staring down at the garden where the most curious thing had occurred.

'Jack.' It seemed Lucy had been calling his name for some time. As if being dragged from the water, Jack was suddenly enveloped by his senses into the real world.

What was...

'Jack,' she called again, with a fever of fear in her voice. A different kind of fear he had never heard from her.

Turning, he saw his friend leant over the back of the wheelchair, holding one hand under Mrs Day's chin.

'Jack, she's not breathing. Get some help.'

There was nobody around. No one on the corridors or the hallway. The lift was below on the second floor, but unmoving. Not sure why he thought it might work, he slammed his fist against the 'call' button. It flashed green and died. He needed to try anything, A phone? An alarm?

What the hell am I supposed to do? Jack looked high and low, searching for help and finding only bare white walls and empty rooms.

The patients had come to gather around June, as her legs went limp and Lucy struggled to hold her up in the wheelchair, 'Jack, hurry. For God's sake.'

Turning the handle, he swore, frantically. *Why is it locked? Why is it locked?*

The handle snacked and snacked against itself, but the door would not budge.

Under her palm, Lucy felt a cold rattling breath depart from Mrs. Day, and her eyes seemed to lose something. A spark. A light diminished inside.

Footsteps. 'I can't get help, everything's locked down. Lucy. There's…' His voice trailed as he saw the tears in her eyes. She still held the body upright, but had given up hope. Mrs. Day's pulse had receded to a whimper and then ceased to be.

'She's gone, Jack. It's too late.' Lucy's mouth quivered a little. She eased herself upright and slowly let the body slump to one side of the chair, before turning away to hide her tears from the gawking patients.

'Bollocks. Bollocks.' His eyes squeezed tight as his fist, before he bent down to look at once infamous woman of academia. It was a tragedy, really. That she had to die in such a place as this. The world would see one less madwoman and think all the better for it.

Never even had a chance to redeem her name, poor lass. Jack felt the instinct to touch her hand.

It was as quick as a flash what happened next. As soon as Jack's fingers touched the fragile skin of the old, dead woman, she screamed. Then, Jack screamed. Then, everyone in the room began to scream in terror. Mrs. Day bolted right forward in her seat and with the strength of fifty women half her age she threw her palms against Jack's cheeks, still screaming.

'Find him.' The voice that spewed from June's mouth was not hers. A powerful, drawing voice of rasping, ominous intent screeched at him. The lights around burst in their sockets. A sudden crash of electricity sparked in corners of the room as the fuses blew and shattered in their casings. 'Find him. Find that old bastard and follow him through the Door. Give him a message from me. Tell him…the Hidden-One knows.'

Another surge of power across the room dashed the remaining lights, before a long whir rattled over the ceiling and an empyrean green glow showed Jack that June had once more slumped back into her chair.

The skin where the crazed, zombified woman had touched him seemed to burn. Cold. Like nitrogen canisters from a warehouse he once worked, hot ice. An odd tingle of heat and cool breath both prickling his face. Jack fell back against the window, losing his footing. Lucy was ready to hold him up. He looked down at her and saw the lips moving yet heard nothing. Patients around him were frantically throwing chairs and dancing mad jigs of excitement and he heard silence in his head.

The silence continued almost until they reached the door to the stairwell.

'... ... Are we going?' a voice called behind him. 'Jack? Jack. Stop. Where are we going?'

It was Lucy. Jack turned and saw that he was gripping her by the forearm, so tightly that her skin had already started to bruise beneath. Tears still clung to her cheeks.

'We have to go. Come on.' With the strongest kick he could muster, Jack slammed his boot against the door. Nothing. Again. Nothing. Again. Metal clicked. Again. Metal snapped. The door flew open, slinging into the wall behind, the handle leaving a long indentation in the wall.

Lucy could do almost nothing. He had a grip so hard on her forearm that she thought it might break. Still, she let him lead. Perhaps she was curious. Or perhaps she just wanted to get as far away from that nightmare above as she could. She might have jumped into fire if it meant an escape from that horror.

Every now and again, Lucy would call, 'Jack', or 'please', but she still followed, even after his grip has loosened. Even after he had let go. She still jogged after him. Down the stairwell. Through the fire door. Out onto the landing. Past the nurse.

'Hey. There is no runnin—''

'No time.' Jack almost shoved the woman to the floor as he barged past, headed for the main doors.

The automatic sensors were not fast enough, and Jack slammed his shoulder into one of them, catching him off guard. The pain became just another obstacle. He needed to reach the gardener. That weird old man. He needed to get to him. He did not know why exactly. He knew pieces of information. Some 'things' which Mrs. Day had somehow imparted on him in those terrible screams. Horrific sights of blood and battle. Demons and monsters. But nothing would stop him from what he had seen in her last moment. The Door. The Black Door. Just as he had imagined it when first he read those words, so many months ago. Beautiful. Magnificent. And…here. Somewhere. And that gardener knew where it was.

Cool autumnal wind seemed to push them further into the trees. Jack had spotted the old man just as he had crossed over the road leading to Blissful Hills and trudged off into the wood. His stride had been heavy and persevering, so theirs had to match. Lucy had questioned him many times, but he could not give her any answer she might have understood. He needed to catch this man. He needed to know about the Black Door. In all his wildest dreams, it had never looked as beautiful as it had in the reflection of Mrs. Day's dead eyes. Despite the concurring, opposing thoughts in his mind, telling him to turn back, he pushed on. Even though he was exhausted from the events in Blissful Hills, and even though the mud and the leaves had ruined his brand-new, eighty-quid boots, he pushed on.

Skies had truly darkened now. October light that touched the horizon faster and faster each day, as the long night approached. Trees changed in this light. They became sentient. Twisting spires of appendages that could, if they wished, and at any moment, snatch one from the floor; dragging them up into their realm of bark and shadow. Ahead, the silhouettes of the wood broke just slightly, with ever so much light as to show the gardener reach the top of a small incline and disappear over its peak, some two-hundred yards ahead.

Jack began to wonder something else at that moment. *What if he knows we are following him?*

Regardless, he would see for himself this wonder. Lucy had decided this would be the perfect time to stumble and slip in the undergrowth. Cursing her and himself, Jack lifted her upwards, but would not stop, even as she stood, cut on her hand and mud across her face. He would not stop now. Not so close to his answers.

What answers? Did he even know what he was doing?

'Find that old bastard and follow him through the Door.' The wraith's voice permeated this mind. He could still see the rotting teeth of Mrs. Day as she leaned towards him, screaming.

'Can we turn back, Jack. Please. For God's sake.'

He ignored Lucy's pleas. 'Just. Come on.'

They reached the sparse opening at the peak of the brow and saw that the wood had ended abruptly just yards ahead. Nothing but an open field lay ahead. Several acres wide. Surrounded by hedgerows. Just another field in England. Except for this field had a feature not every field had. True, many had them. Many more had them buried beneath, lost to time. Many people passed them every day and cared not one bit for their meaning, because they had always been there. This field had three standing stones. Right in the centre.

Standing Stones such as those, though leaning and small as they were, were a common sight in Britain. Relicts from a time when religion had been the very lifeblood of the soil and men would spend their lives erecting a single pillar to the gods. Monuments to the firm belief in every man, be they modern or Neolithic, that things other than ourselves thrive beyond our knowledge. Menhirs they are sometimes called, just like Stonehenge, the most famous of such erections. Just as the Danes kept their history and culture oral, so did Neolithic man and so we can only guess as to why, just outside of Blissful Hills, on a small patch of grass, we had decided, so long ago, to drag large megaliths from all corners of England and Wales and stand them upright facing one another. How we did this as hut-dwelling heathens was one question. Why we did it, well that was another entirely different one. Still, stand amongst them, even now after so much rock and ruin and it is not hard to see and feel the answer. *Why would we not?*

Ahead, the figure of the large gardener stood. The strange old man who had somehow conjured fire from his bare hands. This mysterious silhouette who had called to ravens and entrapped the mind of Mrs. Day. He was just standing there, between the megaliths, hands held out in supplication to the sky above. Jack needed to get closer. He stooped a little to a mid-crouch, just in case the old man turned. He wanted to see, no, *know* what was happening and he did not wish to startle the coming event. Whatever it was.

Lucy whispered, 'Jack.'

He turned and gave her an odd flicker of the mouth. Almost a grin. Almost. Waving his hand to beckon her to follow, the pair of them slunk towards the Standing Stones and waited just yards behind, watching the gardener drop to his knees and cry.

'*Mímir. Ymir. Oþið.*'

They waited and watched. Jack's breath drew soft clouds in the cool air. Lucy's hands sunk a little into the earth as the old man yelled and yelled to the sky. Still, they waited.

'Yggdrasil.'

Tingling. A little electricity in the air again. The nape of Lucy's back flushed with sweat as her neck bristled and her body told her that danger was close. Electricity she could almost taste, like old coins. Wave by wave the air above them seemed to push down. Heavier and heavier. Then lighter again as the electricity returned. Lightening over every inch of her skin.

'Lucy. Wow.' Jack had turned to her and was agape…laughing.

Her hair had been touched by static, so much so that nearly every single hair stood towards the heavens, dancing above her head, the way children do with rubbing balloons and cotton clothes.

With a thunderous crack, all light vanished from the world. Gone. No distant sunset. No stars above. Nothing but the three megaliths and the curious gardener. The feeling of utmost isolation and emptiness left before their next heartbeat. When light returned, it did so from one place and one place only; between the three Standing Stones. A brilliant, cascading light whose source remained unknowable. Only the shadowy dawn of brilliance in the centre of a field in England.

Lucy felt Jack shuffle back on his hands and knees and grasp at her palm with his. They crouched, hand tightening, until the rest of the light of the universe flooded back. Still the radiant glow shone brighter before them. its luminosity did not diminish, but seemed to be obscured momentarily by a small figure, who stood briefly against the light, before vanishing out of sight, completely.

Jack's words caught in his throat, 'he's…g-gone.'

He was gone. The gardener had vanished.

The glow of the object between the megaliths started to ease and fade slightly so that the world around it became visible. It appeared, to Jack as if it resembled…

'A door?' Lucy offered.

'A door.' Jack lifted himself up, releasing his hand from hers, running as fast as his legs could through the muddy grass, towards the Stones.

Looking back, it would have been hard to explain just what they had witnessed. An oddity so outside of the world as a radiant door appearing suddenly in a mediocre a place as this. Yet the Black Door did not feel 'outside' of the world. Instead, it felt inside of the world. Deep inside, as if the Door had sprung forth from the naval of the earth, of the cosmos, and been birthed by it. Right here. Right now. It felt like…creation. Renewal. Rebirth.

There was something akin to this wondrous an unexplainable sensation that Alfred had read many years ago. It was in a comparison of literature, in which the author tried to explain many unexplainable events in the history of man as being explainable by proxy of ancient alien civilisations. He cited Ezekiel's Inaugural Vision, in which the prophet of the Old Testament is visited by an almighty vision by the Kebar River. Ezekiel describes the vessel of the Lord and His angels as being 'wheels within wheels', 'Spread out above the heads of the living creatures was what looked something like a vault, sparkling like crystal' and 'awesome''. It was that word 'awesome' that Alfred thought of as the only way to fully describe the Door in a way which had not described it at all.

A Black Door. Blacker than black. Infernal. Hellish. Stygian. When it ceased to expand on its radiance, it was clear to see that it was a door. A very old door. The sort of door one might expect to see leading into the crypt of a Norman Church or a medieval tower. Several long planks of what might have been oak, laid together, with a single, iron handle at the rightmost side. The handle itself was cast in the image of an ouroboros; a snake which eats itself continually. A symbol seen throughout the ancient world and one attested to many alchemical formulae. Though *this* snake *did* eat itself, as though it were *living*.

Upon the face of the door were many images, which Jack and Lucy had no time to fully inspect. They only glimpsed upon the main featured engraving. In dark, almost burned etchings, a figure of the Allfather had been carved. An old, one-eyed man, hanging Christ-like from a towering ash tree. A long spear gouged his side and beneath him; twenty-four Runes danced magically.

Gingerly, Jack placed his foremost foot inside the Standing Stones and felt a low, quivering hum of music. It came from everywhere and nowhere. An earworm that did not aggravate, but merely calmed his mind. Thought the music was soft, almost nostalgic, as if the notes had been played before, but he had long forgotten the sound and with just a few touches on his soul, the sound had dragged him back to a time before life and sorrow. Yet, the music itself was sorrowful. It was a lamentation. Jack immediately closed his eyes and felt the vibrations of the Stones imbue the music with strength and power, drawing him closer.

Drawing both of them closer. Lucy had been caught in its weave of siren song also. Her bygone years at the seat of her grandmother's grand piano had left her feeling as if she could reach out and simulate the song with her slender fingers as she moved her hands over the vibrations. Minor key. The odd subtle change in tempo before the release of long, drawn melancholic chorus, and then it began to quiet. Either decrease in strength, or whatever form the music had taken through the Stones, the pair had started to attune to its nature in a sort of symbiosis. It was no longer other. Even the Black Door felt homely and warming, like a crackling hearth on a fresh winter's evening.

'Jack,' Lucy began, eyes opening again, voice softer and free from anxiety, 'what's on the other side of this door?'

A breeze of cool air swam from beneath the lintel of the Door and kissed his cheek with an affectionate pull, 'I don't know,' he answered, but I need to find out.

'Is this what you came here for? Is this what you needed from June?'

'Yes.' His eyes were still shut, but behind his lids, the radiance still burned with fear and wonder.

'Jack, maybe we should move away.'

'Yes,' he said, but his feet moved closer towards the Black Door.

'Come one. I don't like it. Jack. Please.'

'Yes.' The fingers of his right hand were almost touching the iron handle, that swam around and around as the carved Ourobourus ate itself in perpetual rebirth.

'Hey.' Lucy's hand gripped tight onto the hem of his jumper, a single thread unravelling, caught in her nail.

'Yes.'

'No. Jack.'

'Yes.' The handle was ancient and a little rusty, taking several turns to twist its weight around and feel the bolt click back from the frame of the Door. And then it was open. It was open and behind the mysterious door was…nothing.

Cool mountain air gasped, breathing the soul of untouched lands into their lungs.

Darkness.

Wyrd Wood

ᚠ

I counsel thee. If thou knowest thou hast a friend,
whom thou well canst trust, go oft to visit him; for with brushwood
over-grown, and with high grass, is the way that no one treads.

- Hávamál

-

Jack awoke in a place of darkness. Into the depth of night,
so thick that his eyes could not penetrate the shroud for
more than a few metres. There was foliage here. A forest
floor, teeming with the sounds of insect life. Slithering,
crawling life. Every brush of leaf or undergrowth against his
skin made him startle and shiver. Jack began to fumble around
in the dark, searching for Lucy. Hands groped over moss
covered stones and a path so overgrown that he was not sure
how many years it had been since it was last trodden. With an
open palm, Jack finally found something. The clammy touch
of cold skin grazed his hand and he started back on his knees.

Please, no. His mind pleaded to an unseen deity above.

Thoughts of broken limbs and twisted spines filled his
imagination. The thought of Lucy's warped face, lying on the
cold ground, staring unfocused into the trees overhead.

But it was not her. It was not even human. The remains
of some animal cut down in the forest or run down on the

road and come to the darkness of the woods to die. Hairless and large as it was, it was not her. Still, as his fear for her grew, his fear of the shadowy realm he crouched within grew larger, so that he dared not scream her name out loud.

His breathing was loud enough. Loud enough for some beast to hear his thumping heart. His laboured breaths. His trembling hands.

It took some time for the fear to become manageable. Perhaps an hour of shaken, unblinking stares into the night, before Jack managed to climb to his feet and start walking, inch by inch along the forgotten path through the trees. Sounds of foxes baying made his blood boil and his neck freeze at once. Reminded him of his childhood, when he would lay awake at night after a 10:00 p.m. horror film of Channel 5 and listen to the long, high-pitched wails of the wildlife in the trees by the train track. Horrid, bone-tensing sounds he believed could only come from one source, monsters.

He began to march. Not sure why. It was a thing he did. Not a goose-stepping frogmarch through the desert, but a straight-kneed stomp. Something that made him seem calmer. More uniformed. It was a little like the 'Hero-Pose' his therapist had taught him,

'Put your hands on your hips,' she explained, showing him the movement. 'Place your feet apart and look strong. It gets the testosterone flowing. It will help will the exam anxieties. I do it before every presentation, just to give myself a boost. Try it. Go on. Don't be scared.'

He did. It worked.

As he marched, trundling over the forgotten path with its canvas of rotting leaves and skittering creatures, Jack felt his hands begin to sway by his hips. As they swayed, they

brushed his trousers. And as they brushed his trousers he felt
…*hey. What was that?*

He was an idiot. A stone-cold idiot. Better than a stone-cold dead idiot, but still, all this time in the darkness and he had failed to remember Survival Rule Number 14: *Check your goddamn pockets, lad.* The voice that called through his memories was Bomber's; a grizzled ex-Para who had served enough time in the desert to officially call himself a *SandSnake.* His real name had been Richard Lancaster III, like the King, although the nickname 'Bomber' had stuck since childhood, for obvious reasons.

Slipping three fingers of his right hand into the jean pocket, Jack felt them grasp around the cool, metallic object. He drew it out, gave it a quick shake to stir up the chemicals, and clicked the stiff button. First, the soft whistle of gas. Then came the inevitable, small glisten of a spark, and before he could ask it to be quiet, the TurboFlame lighter hissed out a blue jet of fire from his grip. He had bought the gizmo three weeks earlier from Go Outdoors; camping and supplies shop. It was not a lighter. Not really. It was a goddamn lightsaber.

The TurboFlame made limited use of the darkness. His eyes saw no further, it only increased his knowledge of what he already knew. Trees and mud. Yet, although Jack was no Bear Grylls, he had never had to survive for their teen days in the Amazon drinking his own piss, he was not a complete civilian either. Two years of training with the 299 Parachute Squadron Royal Engineers. It was child's training. Basic. Very basic. Something to tick off the list so that he could inform his superiors in the Duke of Edinburgh Award Scheme that he was competent enough to pass and claim the coveted Gold Certificate. One Tuesday night a week. That was all he needed to get by.

Jack let the lighter fade to black and dropped to one knee. He reached into his back pocket, retrieved his car keys on the orange and black carabiner, before fumbling for the thing he wanted most; his half-inch foldaway knife. He took the blade and auspiciously hacked away at the lower six inches of his left jean leg. Fingers trembling and sweaty, Jack searched, almost maniacally, for a suitable branch with correct width to length ratio. Unspooling the wire cool from his pocket tool, Jack wrapped the torn trouser leg around the lump of wood, shearing away all the excess twigs and foliage.

Survival Rule Number 3: *Never leave home without the pocket tool*; spooled wire, screwdriver, flint, paracord, tiny compass and mini cloth. Luckily, he always had these tools attached to his carabiner, which in turn was attached to his car and house keys. He never once thought he would need them, but like the old gun-loving American saying goes, 'Better to have and not need, than to need and not have.'

Though he had given up smoking many years ago, Jack clicked the lighter and felt a moment of small anticipating delight as the flame roared. As though he were about to light his very first cigarette of the day.

Without our care for the wind, the TurboFlame ignited the bundle of denim and twigs and suddenly the primal dread of the forest became a waking nightmare.

One hundred twisted, screaming faces lunged out at him from the darkness. Each one more insidious and deformed than the last. With a rodent-like yelp, Jack stumbled back, planting his fear end onto the mud. A shockwave of pain momentarily forced bile to shoot into his throat, as he struggled to keep the torch upright. If that landed in the mid and went out, then it would be moments before the faces engulfed him.

And, it *had* been moments. Eyes flickering open, Jack winced at the torch-lit visages all around him. They stared but did not move. Motionless in their horror.

A wave of palpitations faded from his chest, as Jack realised what they were. Trees. Carvings in the trees. Hundreds of them. Several in each of the trees of the forest. Perhaps thousands. Maybe more? As he moved the torch from left to right, he saw a wooden army of sentinel terrors, every detail of horrified screams and wails delicately etched into their skin, their bark. He wanted to leave, now more than when the darkness had been his home. Ahead, the path seemed to meander endlessly into the dreamscape of petrified masks. Totems of the damned.

Which is precisely when the noise came. A heavy noise. A not-so-distant rumbling, as if a Sherman Tank had decided to make its march of war through the forest of faces. But no vehicle make sound like this.

One, two. One, two. Rhythmic. Concussive. Untimed. Natural. One, two. One...two.

It was an animal. A beast. A creature from the nightmare woods, lumbering its way towards him. Jack realised just how large the creature must be. Overhead, the winged animals fled in unison and the treetops quivered, dropping their seeds and buds as the sounds grew larger, longer and closer.

A brief glimpse in his mind's eye flickered to a childhood memory, watching the small plastic cup of water on the television ripple and ripple and ripple, as Lex and Tim Murphy waited for the inevitable approach of the T-Rex. Maybe that what was coming? A dinosaur. A reptilian throwback spat out from some primeval forest realm. It had caught the scent of something it had not tasted for many aeons; human flesh.

Sweating, shaking, terrified human flesh. What a morsel he would be.

Jack was so overcome with the utter panic, that it never occurred to him to, put the damn torch out, or, throw the damn thing.

The eye did not appear first. There was something ahead of the eye, but in the dim orange glow, it was the huge black eye that glistened against the torch's light. An eye large enough to see the agitated form on the ground below it. It remained there. Pupils dilating and contracting. The creature did not stay for long. With a snort of what may have been revulsion, the black eye turned from Jack and followed the concussive, lumbering feet, away into the nether regions of his nightmare, where he prayed to God it would remain.

Overhead, so far above, he did not recognise the heavens. An alien, distant sky. So much brighter and fuller than he ever had seen. Someone had cast a handful of sugar over a dark blue canvas and let it hang there for eternity.

Ahead, in the clearing of the woods, the dark outline of a shack blotted out the treeline. *Safety. It must be.*

Jack did not have it within him to look back. Not out of some existential philosophy on following his current path, but because he was afraid, he might see something that would petrify him in place. Leave him stranded here like a Medusian statue, frozen in eternal horror. No, he ran. Straight for the shack. When it closed in, he felt a pang of relief, which uneasily mixed inside his bowels, with dreadful anticipation, as to what grotesquery could possibly have awaited him on the other side. Not realising the extent of his fear, the rope handle felt prickly to the touch, slipping against the clammy sweat of his palm. The door swung open with barely a murmur of appreciation, having been standing here all these many years without a guest.

Jack entered, slowly, cautiously eyeing the now-low and dim dance of the torch. He needed light. But it would be morning soon. All he had to do now, was wait. It was the smell that discouraged him at first. A sickly, bittersweet smell he had not known before. Something rotten and growing. Month-old eggs mixed into a batter of tinned tuna.

One last glimpse into the strange outside and the door shut.

He spotted something in the corner of the room, though the shack was void of any furniture. Something crumpled up in the far corner. Covered over with a rough sheet of what may be tarp or may be cloth. He did not investigate the form; however much it appeared in his mind to resemble something human, at least bipedal. The torch was leaving him, and it was all he could do to slump by the wall and curl into a womb-like state.

Minutes turned to hours and Jack lay hunched in the warm night, dreaming of a Stygian Door. What stepped through the shadowy light was not an old man. It was not he or Lucy, but the Devil himself.

It shook him awake, panting relentlessly. He turned his hands over, twice, just to bring his mind back to reality. Whatever reality had become. When he strained to see his fingernails, a shuddering nausea overcame him. It was still dark. It was pitch black. He had slept for, what? Several hours at least. He had been exhausted and still the sun lay waiting. Opening the door, without a care for what could be lurking in the beyond, Jack gazed up and saw what he had feared; nothing had changed. That is when the tears came like a Biblical deluge.

Jack had not realised, due to the lightless abode he rested in, but just behind where he had sat, scrawled in thick, stained blood had been the words that would become his mantra. The latest edition to his collection of travelling tips.

Survival Rule Number 666: *Don't step through the fucking door!*

Riot

ᛦ

To the chest they came, for the keys asked; manifest was their grudge,
when therein they looked. Of those children he the heads cut off,
and under the prison's mixen laid their bodies.

- Völundarkviða

"**N**o, I don't need any fucking support and I certainly don't need a...what did you call it?"

"Care and Rehabilitation Strategical Specialist,' the man said, in a monotone voice that suggested he did not care if one was provided or not.

The man was younger than Don, much younger. He wore the same pastel blue polo shirt, with the distinguishable SecuCor logo, a white eagle resting on a golden cage. Symbolic? Maybe? Looks as if it was designed by a seven-year-old? Most definitely.

'Do you know who the fuck that is in there?' Don asked, waving his hands around and almost chucking his papers down the corrugated steel steps. 'That is a grade-A fucking monster. Rehabilitation? What are you guys, dumb? Is this a joke? I'm going in there to get that motherfucker to sign eight sheets of paper. Got it? One document. Then you can fry him or freeze him or stick him in a fucking virtual reality helmet until he rots from the inside. I couldn't give a fuck. Now, open the door, and let me speak to him.'

Don was wearing his second worst suit. It didn't fit entirely all that well, sagging in places it should not have and growing tighter in places he had forgotten about. It was beige. The colour of his grandmothers Oldsmobile. If it had not been for the occasional meetings with his client, Mr Grayson, Don would have thrown the suit in the garbage. But who wants to wear a nice three-piece to a damn prison? Filthy place. No, it would *suit* the purpose fine for today. Don was aging faster than he wanted. Faster than he expected and the thought that he was not yet living it up on some British Island, where the weather was warm and the beaches plenty; thank you climate change, depressed him greatly. He would soon celebrate his half-decade and had only half of what he wanted to show for it. Now, on his birthday of all days, he had to spend his afternoon with Mr Grayson.

The officer flicked open his palm and held a two-inch metal rod to the edge of the plastic door. There was a moment of hesitation, as though the database failed to recognise: ID 6714, Officer Keel. But then the device whirred, made the recognisable three-bolt lock clunk and Don was able to slide the door across into the aptly named 'Care and Rehabilitation Centre.'

'Thanks, buddy.' Don offered a bruising smile to the officer, elongating each vowel with distaste in his mouth.

A *centre*, it was not. Not even the size of one of the plusher cells up on Row 64. A centre implies that there is generally more than one room and the mind conjures up images of coffee and food. This was just another cell in a fortress of cells. A hive of humanities worst nestled in the heartland of New America. Just how big it was, Don was still unsure. The size of a small town? Likely. The size of a city? Possibly. It grew every year. More arms, wings, and appendages were added to the Frankenstein's Monster that was the New American justice system. That might have been one of the underlying causes that forced Don to recoil in disgust so much at the word, 'rehabilitation'. It was an ugly word. Ugly because it was a lie. Another fat lie sold down to the masses so that we forgot about the riots. Forgot about the deceit and the chaos that led to the great burning fire of NYC.

Don closed the door behind him. The three-bolt lock whirred, and he was trapped once more with Mr Grayson. The room smelt of ten-dollar aftershave and musty ball sacks. Mr. Grayson saw him wince, curling his nose, and slowly raised an eyebrow.

'What's a matter, Donny? Don't like the smell of cages no more?' Grayson shook his head and lifted his shackled hands as though he were offering Don a seat opposite him. As if he could offer up anything in his state.

'I don't like the smell of week-old ass, as all.' Don slid the chair out from under the metallic table with a whining, hissing screech.

Grayson recoiled a little, 'Jees, man. Easy on the upholstery. Some of us gotta live here.'

Grayson had a thick southern accent. Louisiana. It had been the only state that he remembered, in which he had not committed a single crime. 'Never shit where you eat,' he liked to say. He wore the typical grey jumpsuit of a federal inmate. His hair had been slicked back into a ponytail, but still had its greasy, unwashed blonde straggles. His face had three-day old stubble and it was apparent after he spoke that he was missing several new teeth. A small blinking patch by his ear gave him the hearing he had lost in the infamous shootout at the De'Mon Hotel. How apt a name.

'Here.' Grayson reached onto the table and tried to throw a small, folded note over towards Grayson. The shackled hands let it fall short by a fair few inch.

Don looked at the note for a second, then at Grayson, then back at the note.

'What is it?'

'Take a look.' Grayson shrugged, smiling coyly, like a child.

With one hand, Don lifted open the letter that read, *Happy Birthday Donny*, in almost perfect calligraphy. The literary art was marred by the fact that just below; Grayson had drawn a crude impression of him sexually assaulting Don, who was still wearing his beige suit.

'I'll put it on my fucking wall,' Don sneered, dropping the paper to the floor.

Grayson watched it fall all the way, like a cloth in breeze, before Don managed to snap him back into reality.

'Hey, look at me.' Don lifted what he had brought into the prison. It was a see-through, plastic briefcase. The only way things could *be* brought in now. Everything made nice, neat, and clean. Don had never been sure if it was for security reasons, or health. The great flu had changed almost everything in modern life.

'You gotta stop it with this shit, Grayson. What are you doing? Huh? Stalling for time? Prolonging the inevitable? You're done, man. A *dead* man. No jury on God's green earth is going to let you walk. Least not on a fucking technicality. It's a small error in a tapestry of fucking terror. You're America's Monster, kiddo. Mothers would rather see their daughters marry Ted *fucking* Bundy than hold your hand for one minute.'

Grayson shrugged again, as it he did not have a care in the world.

'Worth a try,' he offered. He had the voice of a southern gentleman, with a coyness and sweetness to it that almost felt as if he were coming on to you every time he spoke. Maybe it was his sociopathic mind trying to engage. Trying to butter people up and feel sorry for him, before him clubbed them to death with a claw hammer and...went about his work.

'I ain't that bad. Hell, I never raped no one.'

Don stared wide eyed at the killer sat before him. 'You have been found *guilty*,' he emphasised the word by tapping twice on the metal surface, 'of sixty-three counts of murder.'

'But—'

'Sixty-three counts,' Don continued, cutting him off, 'that's only the ones they found. You ate a fourteen-year-old kid. A kid. Crafted a toy town from fucking corpses. Made a fucking mince-meat pie out of a one-hundred-and-seven-year-old.'

Grayson mouthed the word, 'chewy' towards Don with a scrunched face.

'You shot and killed the oldest woman in New America.' Don gasped for air, 'and her dog.'

'No.' Grayson almost stood and slammed his palms onto the table.

Don turned around and saw the officer move to his sidearm and close in on the room. Don waved him away, shaking his head.

'I ain't never killed no dog. Never. I love animals.' Grayson slowly sat back in his clear plastic seat. 'It's just people I ain't so fond over. Look outside, man, worlds burning. I was just trying to have a little adventure before the spark went out.

Gunna lock me up for creating jobs and food for people, huh? Worlds gone crazy; you see?'

'It's over, Grayson. No more *technicality* bullshit. No more *judge* hearings. No more *interviews* and press conferences. It's over. Let America move on. You're history, man. And, you always will be. Take some fucking solace in that. You made it to the newspapers. Even Hollywood.' Sighing, Don began to drag out the papers from his briefcase. It was an awkward and fumbling exercise. The plastic buckles never closed right and when they did, they never opened right.

'Damn Jet Whittle.' Grayson sulked down in his chair.

'I didn't mind him in True Blue Warrior.' Don said, without looking up. When he finally did, he dropped the small stack of papers between them both.

Grayson eyed the manuscripts with curiosity and contempt. 'This what's gunna let 'em alkali me?'

Silence clung to the edges of the plastic walls. Outside, there was the usual ruckus of the jail. From the clear plastic centre, it was possible to see over into the visitor's reception area. It was surprisingly empty.

Huh, Don thought. 'No visits today?'

He caught a glimpse of Grayson's face in the clear plastic reflection and he did not like what he saw.

'El Jefe told 'em all it was cancelled.' Grayson smiled, playing with his fingers, scooping bits of fluff and something red out from under their long, yellow edges.

El Jefe? Don searched his mind, 'The Czar?'

It was only a nickname. One of several nicknames Bartholomew Gusev had been given on his rise to power in the late 2060s. His impressive connections with those in the higher echelons of New American society had allowed him to ascend almost unnoticed as the Kingpin of Inner Chicago.

Inner Chicago soon became Illinois. The Czar, or El Jefe as Grayson called him, claimed to have more money than Old Fort Knox. But, what did that have to do with prisoner visits?

'Tick-tock, doc,' Grayson finally looked up and spat out something bitter tasting he had found in his nails.

'What?' Something did not feel right. A cold sweat began to pool under Don's arms, and he was unsure just why. As though the air in here felt funny today. Or maybe it was the unordinary quiet of the maximum-security prison?

'Tick-tock. You want me to sign those papers, or not? Got a busy day, you know. People to see. Things to *eat*.' One wink set the hairs on Don's neck on edge.

With a sarcastic reply just waiting on the tip of his tongue, Don opened his mouth, spat out a consonant, but was cut short by the high-pitched wail of a siren just outside the door. It was ear-splitting. Don instinctively threw his hands up to the sides of his head. Furrowing, he could feel his forehead already ache from the strain of trying force his ears closed from the inside. He looked up. Grayson was still. Smiling.

Not heard by the wailing metal-banshee outside, Grayson improvised a poor imitation of a hundred-year-old cartoon, 'Eh, what's up, Don?'

Even if Don had recognised the pale impersonation of Bugs Bunny, he could not hear it. It was not that the siren cooled off or lowered in tone, but Don felt the sting dissipate a little. It had been enough to allow him to remove the palms from his ears and assess the situation. No, the siren had dissipated a little, he had not gone deaf. Grayson's voice was the same as it had been minutes before.

'It doesn't last long. The guards have a personal alarm in their earpiece.' Grayson nudged his head towards the door, watching the prison warden tap rigorously at a small, wired earbud dangling by his chest. 'That first few blasts are just to wake everyone up who's sleeping on the job.'

'What's happening, though?' knocking the chair over in an almost teenagerly-clumsy manner, Don stood peering out over the floor below.

A handful of guards had come and gone, sprinting towards the next wing. Turning back, Don suddenly realised that things inside the maximum-security walls had taken a turn for the worst. His personal guard had vanished from the landing. *Fuck.*

'Told you, Don; tick-tock.' Grayson gesticulated his eyebrows in a sordid and lustful way, while he tongued the roof of his mouth. 'I'm kidding. I don't got a clue what's happening. Seriously. I thought El Jefe just wanted a little alone time with that funny-looking Mexican guard on India-Wing. Looks more like a riot to me. *Smells* like one, too.' With that last remark, he lifted one butt cheek from the chair and made a wincing, straining face, before sinking back with a smile across his face.

Don tried to give him a look of disgust, but all he able to manage was a pale expression of panic at what might be occurring in the rest of the prison, 'So what the fuck do we do now?'

Grayson shrugged. No one was coming for them. He had been left all alone with only steel shackles preventing New America's most virulent monster from doing unspeakable who-knew-what's to him. Which is why Don jumped and let out a tiny little yelp when the door behind him swung back on its heavy hinge and screeched through an unoiled layer of metallic corrosion. The chair was already overturned, but his spindly legs would have sent it over once more had it been up righted. Grayson found every awkward movement hilarious, or so he sounded to. In the doorway was a new guard. A different guard. One shaved head, down to the scalp. One long platted goatee tied up with several bands. One right eye that wandered around the room and one left eye that seemed to lay fixated on Don. With only a singular, non-vernacular grunt, the guard gestured towards the door.

'Thank the Living Lord.' Don almost spewed with gratitude, but felt the emotion lay best where it was, in the pit of his churning stomach.

He left the room as quickly as he could, though when he expected to turn and thank the guard, realised that he was alone on the landing. The guard had left him and entered the visiting room. With a set of only three keys, the guard unshackled Grayson, did not re-shackle him to his own arm or even his hands together, before letting the murderer walk clean out of the room like a free man. Grayson looked down at his hands, stretched them apart as wide as he could, and Don heard a low clicking sound from the shoulders.

As they met eye-to-eye, Grayson winked again. 'Ready, partner?'

One by one, the doors opened and closed as the two men followed the prison warden across the upper floors of the super-max. Every few feet a gunshot would echo with a high whoop, or a guttural scream would make its way up from some clandestine depth of the prison. Don was just about to piss his pants. Behind him, his client, Mr. Grayson, did not help the situation; he acted as if it were Christmas morning, yipping and hollering like a rodeo clown. Ahead, the clang of feet on metal slowed, as they began to approach a new set of doors. Ones that led to very high-security function.

Don't Play with Dead Things

❮

Surt from the south comes with flickering flame; shines from his sword
the Val-gods' sun. The stony hills are dashed together, the giantesses
totter; men tread the path of Hel, and heaven is cloven.

- Völuspá

A s soon as Don started to move, Grayson grabbed him by his shirt collar and held him for a moment. Before Don could call for help, Grayson leaned in close and whispered into his ear. His breath was foul with the stench of rotting gums.

'That,' Grayson muttered, 'ain't no guard.'

Not to cause any alarm or suspicion, he moved Don onward but kept him close and kept a small distance between them and the guard, so that they could speak in private. They entered through another security door and waited.

'What do you mean?' Don whispered back, trying to turn, but Grayson flicked his head forward.

'His eye. I seen it close when he grabbed me,' he said.

'Right?' Don urged him on, edging around to peer at the guard.

Grayson gave him another flick on the ear. 'Don't give the game away, Donny. Take a gander when he's peering. His left eye. It's fake. I mean the tattoos would have been obvious fifty years ago, now they all have 'em. But the eye. It's one of them implants.'

'So fucking what?' Don's voice broke under pressure and raised enough for the guard to give a quick glance over his shoulder.

'Ain't *no* guard allowed *any* implants.' Grayson was sneering behind Don's back, 'Fucks with the security coming in. With the machines. No way he works here. Only inmates are allowed implants, like mine. Implants make it harder to get through certain doors. Why do you think they chip us all when we come to stay?'

If Don had been terrified before, there was no word for what he was feeling now. At any moment, he could have collapsed into a ball, loosed his bowels and bladder, and cried in a corner until the military arrived. Why did he not? Just slink away and hide.

Grayson shoved him forward, saying quietly, 'Just walk. I'll take care of it.'

What did that mean? Don shuddered. *Oh, God, what did that mean?*

With the sound of the magnetic keys twisting in their lock, Don turned towards the door, terrified. He expected a dozen angry cons to be waiting behind every nook and cranny. The cranny's especially. When the guard was able to stand in the doorway and look out without harassment, his heartbeat lowered, just slightly.

'Come on, Don, for Pete's sake.' Grayson shoved again.

Don felt like a small child. Scared and outnumbered by the adults in the room. The real men. They seemed to tower above him. Guards and killers, and here he was; a shaken little lawyer from New Jersey. Maybe this was survival of the fittest?

Weed out all the unnecessary elements from society. Leave only the ones strong enough to survive the dog-eat-dog reality. Don had been pampered by his Aston Martin, Bermuda breaks and fine dining. His leather suite, cinema room and fancy shoes. It had all made him so pudgy and weak. It crossed him mind more than once that he should have done something more. Joined the military. Become a martial arts expert. No, then he would have just been Don. Dead Don, buried in some mass grave over in the desert with a thousand of his fallen brothers. It was life. It was death. It was coming for him sometime. Why not die here on your feet, rather than fat and old in your five-thousand-dollar bed.

'You ain't gunna die here, Don. Not here. Move.' Grayson said, and Don for a moment thought that with all this man's unnatural abilities, that perhaps he could read his mind. But this was not true. Grayson could not read mind's any more than he could levitate.

Oh, God, what if he can levitate? It would explain a lot. Don gulped down a burning sensation from the back of his throat. it stung all the way into his empty stomach. He was not sure if he could wretch again. He had lost his breakfast and lunch now over the hallway. What was left?

The guard, if he was a guard, looked back and Don noticed what Grayson had meant. His left eye did not move in synch with the right. It was delayed. What was more unnerving, the tiny red glow far in the recess of his pupil. The man did not say anything, but angrily flicked his head towards the doorway and took a step to one side.

'Naw, naw, man. Ladies first.' Grayson offered up his hand towards the door and a broad, if sarcastic smile.

Sweat rolled behind the shallow crevasses of Don's knees. It had soaked through his undershirt now and left a wide wet patch under his 'man tits'. More forcefully, the guard flicked his head again, but not before he reached down by his left leg and drew something out. At first, Don assumed it was a baton. Like the police used years ago in the sixties. Looking more closely, he did not know what the hell it was. About a foot long. The plasticky mould of what might have been an extendable handle, disappeared into the end of a nasty looking arrow head. No, it was not an arrow head. A spear head, more like.

'Well,' Grayson sighed, 'that sure as hell ain't standard issue.'

Don turned pale. He turned paler as he and Grayson walked past the guard and out onto a long, open walkway which stretched around the length of the visitor's area. It reminded him of something he saw in middle-school drama class. The secret stage above the real one that was lined with ropes, pulleys, and lights. Except this was no play. This was real life. And instead of ropes and pulleys, there was tactical disarming equipment pointed below into the visitor's area. What if he…could he turn one of the machines around and fire it at the guard? Or Grayson? Or both? Maybe it was one of those electrical shock guns he had seen on the internet? They were illegal now, but who the fuck cared in here? Could he do it? He was well aware that he did not have the courage to do so, as the machines seemed to pass him by very quickly, and his hands barely moved towards them. Grayson and the guard were fully in charge now. He would do whatever they said and knew for well he would offer no resistance. What would Grayson have called him, a 'pussy'? That fucker was from a different time. The only man Don knew that still asked for a pack of cigarettes on his birthday.

Something about the way the guard opened the next door sat Don on edge. He had noticed it just for a brief moment. An odd hesitation in the man, as though he had sensed danger behind the steel and plastic. It almost reminded Don of the old Spiderman cartoons he watched as a kid. The way Peter Parker had his 'Spideysense'. A supernatural ability to know just when an enemy attacked. There would be an alarm, some tinnitus, and then Parker would get that same faraway look in his eye, feeling subtle changes on the air. Ignoring this twinge, or playing into it, the guard spun the magnetic key and the door reminded them where they were; it creaked and swung on heavy, double bolted hinges.

'Aww, fuck.' Don jumped back out of his skin, feeling his posterior brush up against Grayson, who promptly pushed him aside without seeing the image in the doorway.

A prisoner. It had to be. All white jumpsuit and what might have been the small smatterings of blood on his collar. But the man was facing away. Not even turning when the door swung open and crashed into the desk. He would have been completely motionless, if not for the gentle swaying of his shoulders.

'Hey, princess.' Grayson craned his neck forward and received a lash of red optics from the guard's electrical eye.

'Grayson, stop being a fuckhead.' Don muttered, but it came out as, 'f-f-fuckherd.'

He was laughing. Not Grayson, no. The guard. And when he turned around and held up his hand, Don realised it was the prisoner in the doorway who was chuckling. Cackling like a madman. Of course, the level of mental health issues in inmates was higher than GenPop, at least sixty percent had some underlying deep-rooted crisis. This was different.

Eruptions of giggles and chortles became high shrieks and literal convulsions of hilarity.

'Ooh, hehehe.' Waves of rippling howls broke the prisoner's words apart, like some delusional, homeless lunatic on a public bus. 'Fjolnir. Hehehe. You are a slippery one, hoohoo, who knows where you've been h-h-hiding. But weeeeee found you; hoho, we found you.'

The last image Don saw of the man was just as he turned around, still shaking with that maniacal laughter. From the feet up, the prisoner was ordinary. Maybe a little shorter than the three of them, but in his prison issue whites, nothing struck him as more or less dangerous than your average killer who, when behind bars, seemed to lose that illustrious vigour of theirs, the way a lion's eyes grow dull and placid in a zoo. Except this one had no eyes. Nothing sat in those empty sockets bar two bursts of bright-blue flames. Each remnant of optical flesh was wrapped within the bulging, crackling fires of some magical, ethereal, cerulean blaze. Don felt no other word could describe how he felt, other than simply, 'upsetting'. It wholly and completely upset and distressed him to see the man standing before them who had been given searing coals where his eyes once sat. Enough distress to cause the light to fade from Don's own eyes, right as he crumpled like a soggy newspaper and hit the deck with a silent thud.

In his dreamlike state, Don tried to waft away the animal that was slapping its tongue against his cheek, over and over again. The animal carried a strong, sweet smell that made his throat burn. As the world started to return around him in bright flashes, he saw that it was Grayson, knelt over him with that sly, cocky grin of his. It was an animal, in a way; Don just prayed it was the creature's palm against his cheek and not his yellowed tongue.

'What happened?' Don felt pulled to his feet by New America's Public Enemy Number One, and was surprisingly glad to see that he and the guard were still standing. He needed more information to process what had occurred. Had the blue-eyed man been real? No and yes. The information was there, but wrong. Blue-fires, not blue eyes. Or had he dreamt that, too?

'This guy right here,' Grayson skipped over to the guard and slapped a heavy, crunching hand on the broad-man's back, 'is a bonafide, *certified*, genuine superhero. Wasn't for him, I might have thought we was in trouble back there.'

Back there? Don looked around. *Yeah, back there.*

This room was different. Subtly. You might expect almost every room in a prison to hold some semblance to the other. Cameras. Security feeds. Lock. Bolts. Doors. It was darker here, though. The windows must have been fitted with *Shade-Encrypt*. It was relatively new, and Don had only seen it a handful of times, usual in vehicles. With the swipe of a finger, the windows would tint to varying degrees of opacity, allowing privacy, mostly for nefarious and clandestine relations, he had thought.

'Seriously, man, this guy just threw that monster about like a ragdoll.' Grayson was jumping and skipping about the place like he had just met his childhood hero.

'So, we're safe? Was that real? What I saw?' Don was slowly massaging the back of his head, noticing that a small, sore lump had started to grow by his left ear, where he had most likely hit the ground first.

Grayson was nodding and grinning, 'Sure as hell, man. I mean, it was real, yeah. But, we ain't, metaphorically speaking, safe.'

That's not how you use the word, you fucking moron, Don winced.

'What do you mean? Are there more of those things? What happened to them? What's the situation outside? Is help coming?' Don fired his questions at Grayson like bullets. He wished they were bullets. Real *Full Metal Jacket* ones. He looked at the guard once or twice, but all he got was that strange reflecting red glow back.

Creepy motherfucker.

Grayson did not answer him in words. Gritting his teeth, his client moved towards the rear window of the room, just above a series of dull monitors and slide his finger across the window, ever so slightly, from right to left. The opacity of the shading dropped, and the light poured inside with an unnatural quality. Light should not behave like that. Shadows on the outside of the window slowly started to form into shapes. Moving shapes. They bustled and shoved against one another, and before Grayson un-tinted the glass, Don already knew what he was about to see. Dozens of inmates. Each one more vicious looking, more scarred and more disfigured than the last. Every one of them part of New America's growing surplus of rapists and murderers. Now, they had been given a horrifying new element to add into their résumé's. Sapphire infernos clung to their surveying organs. Every eye had been melted into an ultramarine bonfire. These searing sockets dripped with the flesh that had rendered in the heat, letting sizzling, blue chunks dribble down their faces so that they might have seemed like angelic tears; if not for the wild, hungry rage drawn across their faces. Their teeth chattered together almost in unison, as their hands slapped and eagerly pawed at the glass. This room, was luckily, fully soundproofed. Don thought for a moment that he might have been at home, watching an old zombie movie on the TV, except the sound was muted, and instead the undead just silently clawed at his flat screen, like playful kittens, trying to escape their plasma-embodied existences.

'Yeah,' Grayson sighed, 'not entirely safe, given the circumstances. But with Thor here, I'm sure we can hold them off.'

Don looked around, and furrowed his face, 'Can't we just sit here and wait for rescue? Have any of them made it in?'

The guard, who clearly understood English, just refused to speak it, nodded at Grayson. Giving a 'Sure, why-not?' shrug back, Grayson moved towards one of the monitors by the window. He touched the screen lightly and Don saw the image that convinced him that they could *not*, in fact, remain in the room for long. The monitor was split into four sections. Each showed the security room from a different angle. Two just illuminated what Don had already seen, flame-eyed inmates thrashing against the glass. The other two were showing the room from both above and below. A handful of the prisoners had managed to get hold of weapons. One even had an HK37 police-issue sub-machine gun. They were very, very quickly dismantling and 'flat-packing' the security room, from the outside. Every few seconds, one of them would manage to dislodge a panel, or rip out a series of wires. And what was worse, the three of them were beginning to hear them. Soft, hollow bangs and scrapes, both overhead and beneath. This horror show was not enough to satisfy Grayson, it seemed. He lifted his yellow-nailed digits to the top corner of the monitor and pressed on a small image, a microphone with a white line through its centre. When his finger left an oily smear behind, it was as though Don had been given the gift of hearing for the first time. Sound reverberated and echoed at such an alarming and disarming volume that he immediately threw his palms upwards to shield his ears. He wanted to give the gift back, exchange it for something he could cope with. Something he wanted.

'Tear their flesh apart,' a voice screamed through the constant gnashing of teeth and smashing of bone on metal.

'It's time, Fjolnir. The bitch is dying.'

'You'll never see her again. She sleeps in Sickbed tonight.'

'All hail the All-Father. Keeper of none.'

'Your bones will snap. Your eyes will boil. Your tongue will stretch.'

So many horrific sounds and words that Don had to stable himself against a desk to keep from falling again. An orchestra of harrowing cachinnations constantly echoed through the prison. As though ten-thousand demented clowns were performing some unspeakable show all around him and he could not escape, not even for a refund.

It's a nightmare. A goddamn, fucking nightmare. Don clutched at his hair and pulled. His palms slapped and slapped at his face, until just like that, the sounds disappeared, leaving only the high-pitched ringing of his own ears behind.

Don looked up. Grayson, surprisingly, was offering him a look of what seemed to be empathy, if not just pity, as the killer drew back his finger from the monitor, before dragging his hand back across the window, to shade Don from the grotesque theatre on the other side. 'We gotta leave, Don. Now.'

He knew they did. He just did not want to move. Thick, never-ending quicksand had taken hold of his feet and cemented them to the floor. By the rear of the room, the guard seemed to be studying a basic imprint of the prison layout, which had been photocopied so many times that it was hard to tell what the images meant. It was hard to believe people still used paper, but perhaps it was a remnant from an older age, something sketched up hastily during a power-outage or a riot. Don eventually found enough courage to join Grayson and their protector by the map. It was definitely old. Don was sure that this room was twice as big as the crude blueprint suggested. And fire alarms had been defunct in government outfits for almost five years now. No need. Every particle in the air could be displaced and soaked with ionised water at any time. No moon-buggies for Don, but at least the future meant he would never burn alive in an office.

The door beside them, which led onto the next landing, began to tremble slightly. The inmates were running the asylum now and they were almost fully in charge. Don saw the door on the map and noticed that the next landing ran almost to the edge of the building. Whether or not that had changed over years, would have to be seen. He fingered the drawing, following the lines and looked back at Grayson.

Grayson sucked air through his teeth, 'I dunno, Don. I ain't never had a visitor, so I rarely come this far through. This blueprint is old, real old. Might be just another doorway into someplace worse. There're nearly six-thousand inmates here. There's maybe a hundred round about us. What's Thor think?'

With a waving finger, Grayson tried to spell out what he meant to the guard as if the man was deaf and dumb. But he could hear, just chose not to talk. Eventually tired of Grayson's fumbling on the blueprint, the guard lowered the man's hand, forcefully enough that Don was worried the riot would kick off right here, between these two fuckers. And still, Grayson, Public Enemy Number One held a level of utmost respect for his own guard that he backed away gracefully and waited to see what the man did next with a patient smile.

What he did next was surprising, to say the least. He knelt down. Straight to his knees, the guard was immediately overcome with a glimpse of serenity over his face. He closed his eyes and placed both hands on his knees, breathing slowly and deeply. In and out. In and out.

Below, the coming slaughter picked up pace. Don could nearly hear the laughter of the madmen as they tore and shredded the room apart. Still, the guard just sat and waited, like a perched, nesting bird.

'Fuck. Fuck.' Don began to pace the room. 'What now, huh? Is he waiting to die?'

'Just…' Easing him away, Grayson watched the guard with a strange fascination.

When the guard's eyes opened, the red glow of his optical implant glowed so fiercely it might have burned a hole through the plastic shielding of his cornea. He leapt to his feet just as a heavy, probably important, sheet of metal was torn away from below. Don heard it clatter all the way to the floor of the visitor's reception, breaking something far below. He had not noticed the guard move towards the door. He stood silently, then without looking drew his finger towards the map and tapped on the image showing what they had assumed to be a door leading to either an old fire-exit or some failsafe escape into the outside world. Maybe even an engineer's hatch; it would lead up or around, not to complete safety, but it would at the very least be *outside*. Drawing his hand back, the guard traced that same finger in several jagged lines over the door, which might have been a symbol, if Don had kept up with the movements. Then again, he need not have. Strange black lines started to burn without fire into the door. Wherever the guard had run his digit, the lines appeared, slowly, searing a scorched sigil into the metal sheeting. Then, the door began to tremble. *Oh, fuck,* Don screamed to himself. *Oh, fuck. What the fuck? Oh, what the fuck?*

Every fibre of the door shifted and shook apart, ripping bolt from hinge and screw from handle, culminating into a single, fiery explosion, which blasted the door from its frame, sending it rocketing across the landing.

Don felt the surge of an earthquake rattle his bones. Muscles he did not know he had ached with surprise. He tensed and let go, dropping to the floor. Shaking the ringing and the flashes from his head, he turned to see that even Grayson had been brought down. His client was punching a knuckled fist into his right temple, no doubt trying to shake the aftershock away. Then the screaming began. All around. Maybe a hundred agonised voices shrieked in the bright light of the prison. They scrambled and clambered over wall and glass, until Don saw their faces appear by the door.

Don saw the blue-fires of their eyes as the demons crowded over the remains of their fellow inmates on the landing. The door had splintered into shrapnel and torn the fucker's limb from limb, leaving blood, guts and matter across the walls. As Don began to retreat, the guard moved forward. He once more drew the strange baton from his side, with a quick flick towards the floor, the metal extended into a spear, perhaps six feet long. Without a moment's hesitation, the spear lunged forward and sent one of the demonic inmates shorting backwards, a deep hole in his gullet spurting blood. Another flame-eyes creature crawled across the roof like a tarantula, and dropped onto the landing, baring its teeth. The spear took this one between those brown and yellow gnashers, as the rear of its head erupted into a sanguineous fountain. It happened again and again and again. They came and they fell. A goddamn, fucking superhero, Don thought and when he looked at Grayson, saw something glisten across his face. Jealousy. Don could have seen what happened next. His client, famed-biologist-turned-mass-murderer, ran forward behind the guard, no weapon in hand and began to fight his own battle. His own demons. The two of them sliced and diced punched and kicked, until Don, like an idiot, finally understood the game. Run, you fucking moron. Above them, on the landing, arachnid-like monsters clung to the rafters, following their movements. Every few feet one of the inmates would clamber up from beneath the steel or drop from on high. Sometimes, they screamed things such as, 'Never seen again', or 'She'll bring the end, Fjolnir', onto to be dispatched by either Grayson's bare hands or that supernatural spear. Other times, they shrieked in a language Don had never heard, and managed to draw blood with a finger or a bite. They did not stop though, even as they sent bodies over the edge. Just kept going and going, until something glimmered at them from ahead, bribing into their souls like a heavenly choir. Sunlight.

Grayson whooped behind him. Daylight. It seemed to sing to them both. Dazzling freedom and safety all rolled into one beaming glow from a one-foot square window. Don was smiling, actually smiling, and he saw that Grayson was grinning inanely, too. With a swift nudge, the guard ushered them forward, but grasped hold of Grayson's neck with a tight squeeze as he did. The killer's face turned from glee to awe. Don could see him struggling against the grip with all his might. With every ounce of that fucker's brute animal strength, he could not move his neck an inch. Don was half sure that the guard was about to snap his neck like a twig. Possibly toss him mover the edge like a piece of crumpled trash as he had done to the others. But he just seemed to stand, staring into Grayson's eyes with the fixed, haunting expression of a vengeful spectre. Maybe this is what he wanted? He just needed Grayson to make it this far. The fucker was collateral? No. they were speaking. No. Not speaking. But they were conversing. Somehow. A killer's tongue that Don was unable to translate. Not in his wildest nightmares. The firm grip loosened, and the guard thrust his closed fist towards Grayson.

There was something in Grayson's eyes that struck Don with more petrification than a thousand rioting cons could have. It was fear. Fear in the eyes of Michael Grayson; New America's most prolific and sadistic serial killer. The image burned into Don's mind. Grayson held out his hand, shakily and allowed the guard to drop an old, rusted key into his palm. The object was distorted, Don thought, but soon understood that it was because Grayson's hand was quivering so much. Before wither could say a word, the guard with the mechanical-eye spun on his heel and stormed off towards the last door. The blood and the flesh of his victims still clinging to the spear in his hand and the railings by his side. A warrior, wandering back through his battlefield, victorious.

'Well,' Grayson sucked back air, 'we'd best be leaving, I think.'

The killer's eyes focused narrowly on the departing man, and Don would have given every penny he owned not to know what was going on in that mind of his. Instead, he knew a gift from God when it came. Without a word he walked towards the exit and stepped aside to allow Grayson the pleasure of earning his freedom. The key was ancient, it seemed, and it appeared to both of them that it could not have possibly unlocked this highly-technical bit of machinery in front of them. But as Grayson moved the iron closer, the lock of the door began to change. Mesmerised, they watched, as if time had slowed to a snail's pace and what they saw as some trick of the eye. Ana illusion. The lock, which was more of a thin hole, surrounded by a series of lights and alarms, began to crack and reform, until it no longer resembled anything it had before.

The transformation leaked outward from the lock, altering the texture and shape of the door itself. Don could see Grayson's lips moving but failed to hear what he said. The world had become a silent orchestra, with only the beating of his heart as the overture. Don slipped back onto his heel and saw that he was looking, still at a door, but one that was jet black. The colour of matte steel, with the textures, knots and grooves of an oaken aperture. Where it had electrical wire across its top, there was now a heavy lintel, beneath which lay the ominous and portentous words: 'Gjöll's Bridge.' Accompanied by some weird occult symbols Don did not recognise: ⴼⵎⵔⴲⴼⵚ.

'Grayson, I don't think this is a good *fucking* idea.' Don was sure he had said. He could have sworn he screamed it at the top of his voice. But Grayson did not hear or did not care. The key sprung into the lock like lightning. A heavy rumble echoed like thunder through the visitor's area along with the slow, creeping noise of an old hinge folding on itself. The last thing Don remembered hearing was a laughter like that of a thousand maddened and crazed children. It sang through the prison as if the world were full of tiny lunatics, each rambling a nonsensical rhyme which had no note or rhythm. The laughter continued in his mind long after the door opened and long after he saw the vast open blackness on the other side.

Haunted Trees

X

She there saw wading the sluggish streams bloodthirsty men and
perjurers, and him who the ear beguiles of another's wife.
There Nidhögg sucks the corpses of the dead;
the wolf tears men. Understand ye yet, or what?

- Völuspá

What struck him first was the thought that this was it; *the end*. He had died. He had trusted that damned guard and he had fallen so hard and so far, that his body was broken. He lay there, motionless, for what seemed an hour. It had not been an hour. Not even close. He was just trying to make sense of it all; death. Why here? Was this Hell? The Inferno and the lake of fire? Because if it was, and he was sure as anything that was his final destination, Grayson did not seem to mind it. It had a cool breeze. A dark night filled to the brim with sugar-coated stars. Trees that swayed overhead.

Hell, he chuckled to himself, *I could be in Oregon.*

Sweet resin poured from the pines and was picked up by the winds, soaring into his nostrils and filling his lungs with the scantly pine-fresh feeling of sensory illumination. His soul soared. Maybe there was no Hell. Not really. Even after all he had done. All the killing and the necromancy, that did not earn him eternal torment? Or perhaps, like some Dante-inspired punishment, he would be forced to remain here, with only himself for company and the soft, singing pines. God must have got Himself all turned around somehow; this was Heaven. Maybe this place even had life. Little bugs he could study. Animals he could observe.

Still, he thought, pulling his arms from the mud with a long sucking *smack, I should probably get up.* Grayson arched his back and leaned forward, easing up onto aging bones. *Man,* when had he gotten so old?

He supposed if he had an eternity here, there was no use in rushing about the place like some lost soul. He could take his time, comprehend the ins and outs of his new home. Firstly, he gathered as many dry twigs as he could. He was unsure how long the nights were here, and he might have to make a fire. Strange that Hell would be cold. He wandered, aimlessly but with direction, see if he might just stumble upon something out here. When it struck him how existentially oddly, he had taken his own death. Of course, death had been one of the few things Grayson had ever feared, but he thought when it came, the afterlife would be different. *More...*he wanted to say...*Egyptian,* but he did not know why.

A not-entirely-concrete feeling drew over him, beneath the spilled yoghurt of the overbearing celestial abode; the strange desire, that weird compulsion, that had followed him since he was eight-years old did not seem to imprison him here. Grayson was finally free. If it would last, only time would tell. Perhaps it was the universes cruel trick. He no longer had to become the Angel of Death, as there were no more souls to reap. Or where there? Was he alone in the afterlife? All these thoughts were distractions. But from what? Grayson felt that his mind was overthinking to compensate for an irrational feeling which crept up on him like an assassin in the dark.

Ain't nothing to fear. You're dead, idjit. Grayson laughed out loud. His throat closed like snapping turtle as the laughter echoed behind him with a giggling, childish voice.

A quick snap of a branch by his left. A low panting breath not too far behind. The hairs on Grayson's neck electrified towards his hairline. When the first breath of air, not from the forest, no, from a mouth, graced his ears, he dropped the twigs and ran full speed into the night. Infantile cachinnations followed his every footstep. A long, felled pine, by hand or storm, lay ahead. Grayson leapt up, almost reaching the precipice. His fingers found only notches and knots to hold. Old and not the young wolf he once was, Grayson slipped back down to the mud, dropping so deep, his foot smacked hard beneath the surface and his right knee buckled. Smatterings of fresh, wet earth dashed his face. Mammalian, his neck flitted back and forth, back and forth and saw nothing but the trees and the night. No one there. Then who was still laughing? And where the hell was it coming from?

'All right. That's enough. Why don't you show yourself, young buck?' Grayson yelled at the pines. 'I ain't got time for these games.'

The forest called back, laughing, 'We do.'

Aww,= hell, Grayson snacked back his foot, and with all the strength his age could give, leapt onto the fallen hardwood. *Come on, you old bastard.*

When he managed to reach the apex, Grayson saw something flash not far from where he stood. Only for a moment, but enough for him to gage the bearing and direction. He had tracked enough prey through the forest to have gained a level of frontiersman-like advantage over the common man.

That what he called them, prey, never anything else. If these kids wanted to play a game, he could show them real fear. The *real* game.

As fast as he could run on his aching knee, Grayson sprinted on, seeing the light flicker again and saw he was right on track. The giggling in the woods had ceased, but every few yards he would hear what sounded like animal growls in the not-so-distance and the padding of paws on the soil.

Just don't think about it, he told himself as many times as it took to stop the urge to scream. Had he ever screamed before? What would it be like? He imagined he might have screamed when they fried him or split his skin with the Alkaliser or whatever it was called. *The hunter becomes the hunted*, and that thought did not fill him with any form of remorse or guilt, only terror.

One hundred or so yards through the trees, Grayson made out an odd arrangement of wood and because of where he was, or had thought he was, his mind would not allow him to believe it was man-made. Only when the light flickered again, through what was quite obviously a window, or door, Grayson realised he was running towards a small shack in the forest. There was a clearing ahead, too. The pines broke before the building, leaving a wide, open pasture.

Open killing fields, he mused, before easing up on the throttle and letting his feet glide into a slow jog. Grayson dipped a little lower, letting the ground absorb the noise of his slowing feet, before finally he dropped low to the ground, just in eyesight of the shack. *Could be a trap. Or a lure.*

New America's Public Enemy Number One knelt in the mud, as he used to do in those hunting days, watching the shack from the safety of the treeline. The noises of the forest had dwindled into hushed voices, faraway. He was almost ready to believe he had escaped the horrors, when remembering how he would have done just the same. Lull the prey into a false sense of security. Let them believe the hunt is over, and in that last second, when their blood is coursing with anticipation and reprieve, strike, like a trapdoor spider.

The light glowed past the window once more. Definitely a window, not a door. Grayson was sure he had seen a figure, holding a torch. But the light was too dim. A lantern? Overhead, the heavens gave out only a pale light. No moon here. Or a new moon, behind the trees. He assumed the door must be around back. Or front, depending how you saw things. He had to move though, whatever had been silently stalking in the far recess was getting closer again. Footsteps this time. Small ones. several of them. He just hoped they came from separate entities. Grayson did not want to imagine the demonic grotesquery that had more than one pair of human feet. His mind drew back to his own creations; what the press had called 'abominations'. *Well, at least they were dead.*

When the laughter started again, not so far away and to the right, Grayson decided to run. All at once. Everything he could give. His first footstep sloshed against the mud and sowed him greatly, but when he felt nothing close in, he breathed out and carried on, faster. When the treeline broke, a thing, a dark thing, a hairy, black, charging thing erupted from the woods with him, just another hundred-yards to his right. It bolstered from the pines with a long-droning howl that reminded Grayson of a Loon. They sounded more like wolves than wolves did, which was why it was always a Loon on the silver screen, not a canine making those sounds. Yet, this looked very canine.

Grayson had not time to stop and admire the biological monstrosity, as much as he would have loved to dissect and analyse it. This was not the time, nor place. He needed at least a gun. If not several, judging by its hideous howl and the ferocious way it tore through the trees.

Almost there, Grayson turned the corner of the shack, feeling his hand brush up against the hardwood, raising his heartbeat in delight. *Safety?*

There it was, the door. The backdoor. With an almighty crash, Grayson did not stop to try the rope handle and instead barged through, forcing the timber to clatter into the wall and the figure inside to yelp with a horrified, feminine scream. Grayson managed to get one good eyeball of the figure, before the light in its hand dropped to the floor and smashed, leaving them in darkness.

'Don?' Grayson hunched over, holding his knees with his hands and trying to suck back as much oxygen as was humanly possible, before his lungs burned to a crisp. 'what the…hell…are you…doing here?'

'G-G-Grayson? Is that you?' Don ran forward and actually threw his arms around the killer, embracing him like a long-lost brother. 'Aww, fuck, am I glad to see you. this place is a fucking nightmare. A nightmare. I-I-I woke up, freezing my ass of in some swamp. I-I-I ran through the woods. And, oh, fuck, Grayson there was this little fucking girl. She was all, fucking, rotten and her hair, aww man, it was, aww, fuck. Fuck.'

Easing the lawyer away from him, as if he were a small, needy child, Grayson took a step back, flicked his head out of the door and saw that the beast had gone. For now, at least. He took a long look before closing the door.

'Where's that light?' Grayson demanded, as though he had not heard anything Don had said.

'W-W-What? Oh, it's my torch,' Don stuttered, fumbling on the floor until he found the small device given to him by the Prison Warden. 'They give it to us for self-defence when we come in. As well as the pepper-spray. Or CS spray, whatever it is, I never used it.'

'How the fuck is a torch self-defence?' Grayson snatched the metal tube from his hands.

Politely, Don took it back with little resistance, 'Here, look.'

Don had to smack the tube against his palm a few times before it began working again. When he did, he first switched on the torch light, aimed it at the wall and began clicking through a selection of different modes on the buttons.

'So, they showed me once, ah.' The torch flicked from permanent brightness, into a red, LED light, back to an even brighter full-beam, before finally becoming a rapidly flashing mix of blue and white strobe.

He pointed the torch at Grayson and the man understood completely, bringing up his hands as shields, 'turn that damn thing off.'

'W-W-Works better in the dark, I guess,' Don said, dropping the torch to the lowest brightness and setting it on the window facing in.

Now, they could see each other again.

'Jees, what the fuck happened to you?' Don asked, looking Grayson up and down.

Grayson did the same to himself. He was in far worse shape than his lawyer. His prison issue whites had become a Jackson Pollock painting. He was not sure where he had bled from but knew where the mud had come from. What the strange, almost translucent green stuff was, well, he had no idea. Don looked in good shape, comparatively. A few small grazes on his face and some mud on his knees, but that was about it. He had been crying though; a lot.

'I dunno. Weird place this is.' Grayson tidied himself up as best he could, leaving droppings of mud all around the small shack as he paced around.

'Yeah, say that again.' Don moved and peered out of the window over the clearing. 'Any idea where we are?'

Hell, Grayson thought, but could not bear the thought of Don's reaction to his theological discovery.

'No idea. Oregon?' he said instead.

'Oregon? Fuck.' Don stayed, staring through the window pane. 'How the fuck did we end up in Oregon? Where's the supermax? Did that guard drug us? Did he drag us out here and leave us in some fucking nightmare woods to be picked off by wolves and…oh man, what the fuck was that little girl? Jees, you should have seen her, Grayson. L-L-Little fucker snuck right up on me. I put the strobe on her, and it did nothing. Like fucking *nothing*. She just kept laughing.'

Grayson sighed, 'You gotta stop swearing so much, Don. It ain't gentlemen like.'

'Oh,' Don chuckled, 'coming from the serial killer?'

Grayson shrugged. But Don might be right. Not about his etiquette, but about what had happened. Maybe he had *not* died. Maybe that weird superhero guard *had* captured them. Hogtied them up and dragged them a thousand miles away to some ritualistic hunting ground for his own amusement. Made sense, in a way. It was all probably just for him. Don was just collateral. Some sick bastard who wanted to get his rocks off by hunting Michael Grayson through the woods like a pig. Still, that did not explain the creature. Or the haunting children. Or the stars. Or the smell of this place. Sickly, sweet and rotten.

'Don't play with dead things,' Grayson said, but he was just spit-balling, not actually meaning to say the words aloud.

'Huh?' Don turned back to him.

'Just,' Grayson sighed, and Don saw a look of solace, maybe even sadness in those monstrous eyes, 'something my momma used to say. Don't play with dead things. Not sure why I thought of it now; just seemed fitting as all. Something about this place, Don. Just feels dead. Even the air feels like it ain't alive no more.'

'You're a creepy fucking guy, you know that?' Don shook his head, seeming to clear away the bad thoughts. 'Guess even then, your mom knew you to the core. What a fucking thing to say to Michael fucking Grayson.'

Grayson snapped, 'Hey, enough with the swearing, especially around my momma's memory, all right?' It was a demand, more than a question to be answered, which is why it shocked Grayson so much when Don returned fire.

'Hey, no. Fuck *you*, man. I wouldn't be in this fucking mess if hadn't been to come see your hillbilly ass in jail. Nah, fuck this, and…and, fuck you.'

Seeming to see himself in an out-of-body episode, Don realised he was thrusting his finger at Michael Grayson; serial killer extraordinaire.

'Y-Y-Yeah,' Don had seen the surprise on Grayson and decided to follow through with the tirade, 'You know what, you fucking asshole? Huh? If it were up to me, I'd have those family's rape and butcher your ass. How's that for some fucking legal clarity you—'

Don's words turned first to shocked screams and then quickly descended into violent, shaking choking sounds. Grayson had not even heard the window break, let alone see the hairy, shadowy arm sling its hand through the glass in one quick motion, wrapping its paw around Don's neck. instinctually, he ran towards the fight. Whatever it was, it was large. Over seven feet, with coarse fur all over its body that had been matted by a mixture of blood, mud and sweat. Tiny dreadlocks amassed into a shag so thick that Grayson only saw two bright red eyes under the coat. When the creature spoke, it did so in a voice so low and so animalistic, that if it was peaking words, they were of a language older than time itself. Grayson had watched enough sci-fi and old *Star Trek* reruns to know some sort of messed up Klingon when he heard it. Which is when the second idea of his came floating right into the centre of his mind, aliens.

Don struggled with the bicep of the arm, trying to clear his throat, but very suddenly had turned a violent shade of purple. His legs kicked out frantically. Grayson had to push them back with his own feet to get at the fight. He had no weapon but himself. With a flick of his head, Grayson flung his jaw forward and sunk his yellowed *chompers* into the creature's arm. Another violent howl emerged. Blood started to seep in rivers down Grayson's chin, meandering through the stubble on his neck. with his hands he dug nails into the upper and lower arm, deeper and deeper until the howling began a yelping.

With one strong swoop the creature released its grip on Don, and it all happened in the blink of an eye. Don's feet found the floor. His eyes and lungs opened, sucking in one huge gulp of air. Just as the lawyer's chest swelled, five long black nails protruded from the creature's claw. They drew back with the arm, but not before piercing the flesh on Don's right breast and cleaving their bloody way across his chest, opening him up from nipple to neck. The cuts were deep. With a screech, the beast left. Grayson heard its feet patter away over the grass and eventually, the leaves. Back into the nightmare woods.

'Don,' Grayson cried.

His lawyer fell forward. Grayson caught the man in both arms and let him slide gently to the floor. He was trying to speak. Trying to open his mouth for words, but all that escaped were torrents of stygian sanguine essence. It was clotted in parts already and collecting on the floor in small molehills of blood. It was impossible, and yet everything so far had been impossible. Don died there on the floor of that shack, in Grayson's arms. He felt the last death-rattle expunge the man's soul from his body and the muscles cramp tightly, before finally going limp for the last time.

Unsure just what to do, or how even to feel, Grayson decided that it would not be long until the monster returned. He might not even be able to put up much of a fight this round. Something in him had died. For some bizarre reason, some subconsciously inspired illumination of gothic literary terror, Grayson dipped his hands into the pools and lumps of blood. He left them there for a few moments, to get good and dirty. He had never done this before, not for so long. He knew that he would not desecrate this body. Not Don's. Instead, the blood-soaked man placed his blood-soaked hands up against the back wall and wrote something of importance over the hardwood.

Fall Rot

ᚠ

An ash I know, Yggdrasil its name,
With water white is the great tree wet;
Thence come the dews that fall in the dales,
Green by Urth's well does it ever grow.

- *Völuspá*

I
t had been a curious spring. As the solstice closed in, so
had the invaders. An unconscious mind had brought
Aishling to settle here, at this particular moment in time.
It was as though the cards and the runes and the blood had
weaved her path through Europe, across the ancient continent,
to rest here, in Paris. She had been only once before; to see the
Siege of what was now known as the *'Île de la Cité'*; by a most
bewildering raider by the name of Ragnar Hairy-Breeches. He
and his Danes had sacked Paris with only five-thousand men,
stringing up the Parisians by their own ropes and burning large
swathes of land in honour of the Hanged-One. Another
curious name for *him*. There were other Gods men called the
Hanged-One; Christ being one. Prometheus another.

    Synchronicities, Aishling wondered, as she sipped her tea
and felt the roar of twin engines from the Luftwaffe push the
heat of a burning city back down from the sky. She dreamt a

great many philosophies that spring. Reasoned with all her reasonableness to fathom the unfathomable nature of men against the simplicity and delicacy of his life. Still, Ragnar, that pious and defiant young fellow did set things into motion that may well have provided for the setting she saw today. His army had sailed by longship and now this new Heathen Army came by airship, burning, hanging and looting all they could find. Both armies driven by what they might call expansion, but Aishling knew it meant only greed.

'Sit well?' a familiar and unwanted voice climbed into her ears.

Aishling seemed to appear over the ledge as a lone, disembodied head. Her look was one might expect from a head without body; resentful, frustrated and perhaps finding existence a little tedious. Repetitive.

'Grimnir,' she sighed, turning away from the man below her, back to her table. If she had not expected company, why had she felt the need to set another chair? Or place another cup by the teapot?

An old man, beaten and worn down by his years climbed slowly to the top of the stairs and up onto the veranda. He looked only briefly, at the orange glow of the burning city, as though it simply marred his view of the land. Not a care seemingly given for the souls perishing in the streets below.

'Tea?' Aishling held out her hand and the old man nodded, before lowering himself with creaks and cracks into the woven chair.

They sat in silence for some time. Other than the pouring of a thick, green liquid, the only sound to be heard from the rooftop had been the old man's groans as he twisted and turned in his chair.

'You've aged *very* quickly, Grimnir.' Aishling did not look at him, her gaze was concentrated on the Champ de Mars, and the wrought iron monstrosity looming above it. She hated that landmark. Had hated it since the day its construction began. An eyesore on a once picturesque slice of heaven. Though these years had changed much, the ancient city still looked and felt *ancient*, until that steel giant was erected. Man's phallus standing tall, as Paris's guardian. How very French.

The old man simply said, with a broken voice, 'Rag…na…rok.'

'How's the tea?' she offered, still facing away and ignoring that revelatory remark.

Smacking his lips, Grimnir pursed a faint smile, 'helping. Forgive the age since last we met. I have been *uting*.'

An hour might have passed. Slowly, the pale, liver-spotted complexion of the old man began to fade. The long wisps of hair, like spider's webs, filled and darkened. What were just minutes ago paper-thin, his hands returned to their former glory; perhaps even able to hold his precious Gungnir once more. The heavy sandbags beneath the eyes toned and shrunk. In the centre, his left eye began to notice again, to see in real time what was happening.

'My, my. Look at that. Such a dreadful colour.' Grimnir blinked again and again, almost believing that the orange glow of a city could be magically transformed by his own will. 'I never imagined the end of the world to look so…ghastly.'

'You sound different this year.' Sucking at the last remaining drops of tea, Aishling peered at the now-much-younger man over the edge of the porcelain.

Grimnir made a coughing acknowledgment, '*humph*, I have returned to England. Well, I *had* returned. Until all of this began. I do *love* the English. So, like us. Calm, if not a little bitter. Makes the sunshine taste all the much sweeter when it breaks through the rain.'

'Like you, maybe.' Aishling scoffed, 'I'm a different breed.' Her thick Irish accent had remained in tone for this past millennia, unscathed by time and passing winds.

'Of course. Of course.' Grimnir also drained his cup and sat it down beside his chair, on the floor. Not on the table.

He wants me to read, Aishling had a kind to think this already, Grimnir was merely cementing her suspicions.

'You know, there's a bunch of wee little hellions down there claiming that ye gave them this power o' theirs.' She had not posed this as a question, but a statement of fact. An accusation.

'Of course. Of course.' Grimnir watched the eagles of iron twirl between the smoking clouds. 'These *Deutchesvolk* are curious entities. All their history I have watched them worship the Aesir, until like,' his fingers clicked, 'they become most devout followers of Christ. How two ideas must clash in their minds, like wolves feasting over the same bones. But I am no creator. Never was. I have actually created very little but stolen much. No, it is *The Architect* who creates. The One Above. I simply weave. How I love to weave. The Germanics are a proud people of heritage. It is man's nature to strive for love, war…'

'And gold,' she offered.

Grimnir shrugged the retort away, 'Don't we all? Even us immortals? What do you think *he* wants out of all this?'

Aishling smacked her lips, 'Loki?' When Grimnir did not answer, she said, 'not gold. All that bastard wants is death. I have heard from the things that crawl in the darkness that he is known now as a demon? Perhaps he is behind this madness after all?'

Smiling, Grimnir nodded, 'But why? He is free. Has been for some time now. An age. Why wait until now to exact his revenge?' then added, in a broken voice once more, 'Rag…na…rok.'

'What happened, Grimnir? After I read the stones for you? What happened to everyone?' her voice had changed, altered slightly. She sounded curious, if not a little empathetic. She knew the tale, by other tales. It might be different, to hear it from the Raven's mouth.

'Everything,' for a moment, Grimnir watched Paris burn and pondered on what he always suspected. 'I believe that Ragnarök has come, not as you predicted, but because it was done as such.'

Seeing her face twist and the fires of her eyes begin to ascend, he waved a hand, adding, 'no. No. What I mean is that perhaps we listened to your words all too well. The future is not a certainty. Not at all. Look at us. Here. Now. No. Nothing is certain. Maybe, in listening to the future, it was our fear that caused it to manifest and become real? We each feared what Loki would do if he ever escaped his bonds. That fear drove us apart. It broke our power. That is how he broke his fetters. But we had to chain him. It was right and it was just. This is his vengeance. His story to tell, now.'

A thundering cannon-shot ricocheted somewhere down below and the teapot on the table rattled. The loud, whining ring of the tank's shell hitting the road beneath.

'Is it too late, Grimnir?' Aishling asked. 'What about the girl? We just left her there, to rot in that awful place. What was yer bastarding plan, anyhow?'

With one good eye, the now-younger man sat and let the smell of gunpowder and flames fill his lungs. Never had he smelt a thing quite like it. So demonic. So powerful. A dark taste in the air.

'Did I ever tell you of how I found this key?' Grimnir dodged her question, almost. 'It began with Loki. Always the trickster. He had caused the death of my *kjæresteson* son, Baldur. We were gods in those times. And gods cannot be seen to show weakness. Loki had to be punished. Perhaps we went a little *berserk* in our demand for vengeance. Using the entrails of his own son, we bound Loki to a cave. Within its hollow walls we left him for an age and more, all the while a viper dripped its venom overhead. The agonies ensured that none would dare to offend the gods, for each thrash that Loki gave in pain sent shockwaves across the world. Small reminders to these *volk* in Midgard that we are not to be trifled with, by they or *other* gods.'

'Then ye came to seek my help?'

'I was scared. We all were.' Old Grim nodded, unabashed. 'Your visions spoke of our end. The Twilight of the Gods. Ragnarök. So, I decided I would begin again. create a new world. A secret world. Devoid of curses and blood-feuds. I met a Dwarf once. Name of Dvalinn. Tricky one to catch. Always wore a Tarnkappe; a sort of cloak that made him invisible to the eye.' Grimnir then tapped at his left pupil, with a hollow, wooden sound emerging, 'but not from me. I found him and I captured him, as we were longed to in that age. A very clever Dwarf. Gifted with the Runes, as I. Eventually he succumbed to the hunger and I promised that if he made just one item for me to take home, I would provide him with a feasting plate that would never empty. So, he fashioned me a key made from the heart a dying star. Upon holding the key in my hand, a bright Silver Door appeared, and through it I was taken across time and *verdensrommet* to a world more ancient and forgotten than the oldest of the gods. I named her *Altheim*. The old world. Inhabited by a small populace of rodent, like I felt it would be safe to begin the *utvandring*. The exodus. I used my Silver Door to bring them, one by one, into Altheim. There we would be free from the end of the world. From our twilight. From Ragnarök.'

'And when was it that ye first heard of Loki's escape?'

'I didn't.' Old Grim offered a small, clearly forced, smile. 'One day, inspired by a dream, I decided to return to Altheim. Which by now, after lifetimes, was flourishing on its own. Humanity had thrived. They had built cities of their own. Others had heard of this new haven. Elves and Dwarves and so new doors opened and from across space they came to escape the prophecy of Ragnarök. I held the key in my hand and by some unholy curse felt the iron burn with the heat of the underworld. Then it came to me, expanding from the aether as a Stygian, reflection of my deepest fears. The Black Door. my creation has been cursed, tainted and befouled. What existed now was an abomination. I was dragged through that place into Helheim, the world of darkness and bones below. Using all the powers left in me I escaped that dread place and returned to Midgard. That is when I came to see you once more.'

'To ask me to find ye a princess.'

'Yes.' It was not lightning that flashed overhead but the sky lit up the single eye of Old Grim with a brilliant flash. 'I needed a descendant. An *Ildsjel*. A Skulla. One who could watch over Altheim. Blood of my blood. Kin of kin. They would ensure the survival of my world, long after the gods had fallen, and Midgard burned to ash. Then I could destroy the key, ensuring none could find Altheim. Life would carry on. I would defeat even prophecy and wyrd itself. But, one by one

Loki found my descendants and one by one he cut their lines. Till only one remained. A small girl in Oklahoma. The rest, as they say, is history.'

'But how?' Aishling shook her head. 'How did Loki take her? How are ye so blind to his power ye could allow her to be taken so easily?'

'There are more magics than even I know. And I have sacrificed much in the pursuit of knowledge.' Lifting up the metal spoon from his tea, Old Grim tapped the cloth bandaging his right eye and there came a hollow, tin sound. 'I cannot say how. All I know is why. Loki is set upon vengeance. No longer is he the god of trickery and deceit. Those years alone in the darkness have changed him into a monstrous demon. He has allies now from those places we thought long gone and those hidden valleys we thought existed only in fantasy. Ragnarök is coming. I fear there is nowhere in the great cosmos free from the fires to come. The Wolf is hungry and soon his monstrous jaws will devour everything. Unless we act. Now.' Adding to his punctuation, a German fighter plane whistled above, tearing through the air, before dropping its payload onto the conflagration already overwhelming Paris.

'There is enough will and strength within these bones for one more fight, my dear.' Grim's face gave an alluring grimace, 'enough to open this door just a few more times. If it is *Helheim* he wants…then it is Helheim I will give him.' Newly youthful fingers lifted up what was once a sight of wonder, and now an object of dread. A deep-black key, inscribed with miniscule images of damnation and torture.

'How, then, do we stop this?' Aishling knew what would be required and before the man answered, had cleared the table with one hand and thrown down her cards with the other.

Grimnir nodded again, 'This is a three-sided game, Little Ash-Tree. First, I need you to draw for me five cards. Place our princess, Beatrix, at the centre. Draw four around her that will protect her. They might be spaced far apart, in time. It matters not. We still have the key. I have had Dvalinn add some runes. We can go anywhere we want. And any-*when*.'

'And, eventually, *where* is it that we want to *go*, Grimnir?' Aishling knew the answer, it was why she hesitated on drawing the final card, she was waiting for the word to appear from the darkness of that ancient throat.

'Helheim.' Grimnir said, adding, 'but you need not join me. I merely need to find my four.'

With a reflex as quick as lightning, she gave him a look that could have petrified the man in place, 'you bet yer arse I'm coming with ye.'

Beyond the city, the sound of rolling tyres, roiling flames and resistance had been begun to die down. Paris had fallen. Tomorrow would be a new day. A dreadful day. The beginning of the end.

Aishling flipped the first card over, 'The Magician. Hard to catch a scent on this one. I'll be no help here. You'll need another to trap this little mouse. I can point ye towards him, but I cannot see a future ahead.'

She turned over the second, 'The Philosopher. An old soul. Wrought. Bent. Broken. He's running from something alright. Something inside he can't escape. He'll be trouble, if ye can't tame him.'

Flipping over the next she took a moment to catch the scent, 'Ah. The Valkyrie. She deals in death itself this one. Knows her fair share of the afterlife. When yer not afraid of death, you become lazy. Clumsy. It'll not be the dead this one fears, but life. Careful she doesn't grow too attached down there.'

'And the last?' It seemed as though Grimnir had been taking each card with good sense. A fair assessment of a plan not yet formulated. It worried the fortune teller. Troubled her deeply. As though, like his youthful self, he was playing with a fire too dark for him to extinguish.

'The Necromancer. Be careful of this one, Grimnir. I can smell more than death on his soul. Oh, Grimnir,' the tears returned, 'not this one. Please. Let me pick another.'

As her hand moved towards the deck, he thrust out his own with a strong, but calming force that emanated out across the veranda in waves of unseen light.

'No,' Grimnir warned, 'this one will suit our cause just right.'

The tea was turning cold in the pot. Turning cold as the flames began to die over Paris. It had been a long day and an even longer night. A resistance had fallen over the city, as it had fallen in Aishling's heart. Her desire, driven by guilt and by shame, to return the young one from the bowels of that hellish domain far outweighed Grimnir's need to quash the coming Twilight of the Gods. She cared little for Gods. Had seen so much blood spilt under names she had long forgotten. But a journey into Hel, to save her own soul, that was a ride worth taking.

Driftwood

ᚺ

Easily to be known is, by those who to Odin come,
the mansion by its aspect. A wolf hangs before the western door,
over it an eagle hovers.

- Grímnismál

Jack awoke, sometime into the endless night. Waking with a cold sweat, his heart trebled its beat. Something was outside. What it was remained to be seen. Grapefruit heard two feet, shuffling through undergrowth and dried, dead leaves, approaching the door. He tried to act quickly but found himself frozen. He had merely leapt to feet, only to stand petrified awaiting his inevitable horror. The rope of the door let out a small groan, which was repeated and amplified by the hinges of the old shack door.

When the hardwood swung wide, Jack let out a noise that was neither a gasp of shock, nor a yelp of relief. A figure, garbed in a multi couple red jumpsuit, did not enter. They caught each other's eyes, and both were for a second, disarmed. Jack saw the man. A five o'clock shadow over his face. A windswept ponytail dragging along behind his scalp, carrying with it clumps of earth and small slivers of foliage. His jumpsuit was not multi-coloured, either; it was white, with closely kept patches of mud, grass stains and what was clearly blood. What Jack might have believed, if only objectively, was that just the sudden appearance of another person, here, just the physical image of a man, dressed in blood in this shack, this isolated cabin in a forest of horrors, would have shocked him to the core. But it was not the image of the man, but what he was doing that made Jack's spine tingle with panic. He was smiling.

'Well, hi, there,' the man had an American accent. A sort of southern state drawl you would expect from an old Dukes of Hazard rerun. 'Looksie here, not at all what I was expecting. Who the devil are you?'

'But—' was all Jack managed to blurt, though his lips kept moving without sound.

The American eyed him, raising one brow, 'sa'matter? Cat got your tongue?'

Jack weighed up the options of both leaping through the small window to his right and using all the strength he had left to barge passed the American. Neither option left him with the sense of decent odds. Something g about the newcomer filled him with a primal urgency to back down from the fight. As if the shack belonged to him, the American stepped across the threshold and moved passed Jack; obviously not sensing any equal threat emanating from him.

'Well?' The man sounded annoyed, 'Name? You can call me Grayson. Pleasures all yours, though.'

'Jack.' And before Jack could take the time to come to some, at least soft, acquaintance with this American, there was a long, slow rasping knock at the door of the shack.

The two men turned on their heels. They had both spent enough time in this realm of nightmares to know they whatever stood on the other side of the hardwood, was likelier than not to be foe, not friend. When neither of them moved for some time, the knocking came again. Long, slow and drawn. Grayson nodded towards the door, as he stopped and placed his back to the wall beside it.

He wants to open the door? Jack felt a twang of renewed panic turn his face a pale green. It was too much responsibility.

Grayson gritted his teeth and nodded again, moving his hands into two tightly clenched balls.

Jack moved cautiously, noticing in great detail at the level to which his hands were shaking. If he were holding a can of Coke, it would have been wise to let the liquid settle for several hours afterwards. The rope handle once more chaffed his skin, tickling the sweat-drenched palms. He gave Grayson one last look, and saw the crazed-eyes staring back and the lips mouth the word, 'quick.'

It happened faster than Jack's mind could piece together. A knock of wood on wood and the door swung open, violently. Before he could step back, Grayson had shoved him into the corner and lifted a figure out from the darkness with vein-pulsing hands, dragging the cloaked biped inside and thrusting it so hard against the rear wall, that the whole shack quivered in excitement.

'Who the hell are you?' The American, Grayson, had almost lifted the man's feet off the floor, before letting them slide back.

They were staring at the worn, wind-scarred face of a man in his late sixties, possibly early seventies. He had a long black cloak wrapped around his unusually muscular form. Atop his head sat a brown, wide-brimmed hat. Over his left eye, hung a patch of black leather, and when Jack saw the curious symbol painted onto it, he knew exactly who the man was. He also knew why he was here; in a manner. On top of all this, Jack also knew, this man was the only one able to release them from whatever infernal dimension they had been sequestered to. But there was only one question on the top of Jack's tongue that he needed answering.

'Where is she?' he barked, moving in on the man, so that both he and Grayson had him pinned so tightly against the wall, not an ant could crawl between them. 'Where's Lucy? Where's she gone? What did you do to her?'

The man's breath was rancid. 'I do not know who Lucy is. Now, please, release me and we can continue our conversation in a polite manner.'

Grayson did not let up on his grip. His knuckles whitening around the scruff of the man's cloak. 'I know this son-of-a-bitch. This is the prison warden who dragged us here.'

Prison warden? Jack's eyes widened, *jees. Seriously? It explained the white jumpsuit. Who are these guys?*

'My name is Grim. And I brought you here, ah-ah-ah,' Grayson was leaning into the man's thigh, burying his own knee in place. 'Enough. Please. I am an old man, what harm can I do?'

'Bullshit.' Grayson twisted his knee tighter, until Grim winced.

'Let him go, just, keep an eye on him.' Jack wanted answers, and torture was no way of getting the right ones. He had heard enough war stories to know that much.

Grim dropped an inch and began to, carefully, wipe down his cloak so that it was free of any remnants Grayson might have left. He did this as though the American was infectious; keeping his distance.

'I mean neither of you harm,' Grim began, 'I have brought you both here because I need something from you. There is a job. A job that requires certain...skills.'

'What job?' Grayson spat. 'What skills? Who the hell are you?'

And Grim explained. It took several tries to overcome the furious stonewall of 'fuck-you' attitude Grayson had built up around himself, which had also started to form around Jack. Though, the younger of them kept some vague notion of an open mind. After all, this is what he wanted. He had sought these answers for almost a year. Nearly driven himself to the point of madness in pursuit of the words which poured out of Grim's mouth like a waterfall. He explained that the place they were in was called...

'Helheim? Hell?' Grayson added, 'I knew it. I knew it. What is this? Huh? Some sort of random cognitive interference before my mind finally goes dark? We fell—' Grayson remembered who 'we' was. It had all been so real. The monster slicing through Don like butter. The laughing demonic children. But the brain did that did it not? Made everything so real?

'Helheim,' it was Jack who spoke next. 'I knew it. It was the Door, right? The Black one? It's a portal. This is real? This is it?'

Grim nodded, though felt a more tactful show of enthusiasm would work better than a smile.

'And this Skulla, is?' Grayson did not sound all that accepting of the fact that he was not, in fact, in Oregon. Not even in the States.

'Let me talk then, and I can explain.' Grim cracked his back against the wall and arched, as though listening for a pin drop. 'You are both from different times. You both were drawn for me, in a way, so that I might find you. From across almost a century, I dragged you both here, now, because I need you. The realms need you. Everything you know and love is in danger. The end of all things. The Twilight of the Gods is coming.'

Twilight of the Gods? Jack blurted, 'Ragnarök?' before his childish imagination could run wild, answers were needed, 'where's Lucy?'

Grim looked at him with all the vacancy his one-eyed expression could muster. His silence over the next few seconds gave Jack a deep-set pang of remorse, running through his veins like wildfire. *She's...gone? Where?* 'she must be out there. I'm going outside to find her.'

Surprisingly, it was Grayson who blocked his path, 'whoa, hey there English. I wouldn't go sneaking around those woods at all. Who knows what creatures you might stir up?'

Why did Jack imagine wolves, after all he had seen? 'I have to find Lucy.'

'No,' Grayson shook his head, so vigorously, that his ponytail caught over one ear. 'No, you don't, kid. If you're lady friend's out there, she's either smart enough to find her way here, like we did. Or she's mincemeat.'

That made Jack want to spew out, but upon retching, realised his stomach was completely empty. A burning bile-froth clung to his throat.

'He's gunna need a minute. As for you, bub, I'm gunna need some straight-talking.' With a thud, Grayson thrust the old man back against the wall.

Immediately, the coarse hands came up to wail in protest, 'Yes. Yes. Of course. Yes. There is a girl, in peril. A young girl. She needs your help. I might assume after all you have done, that your soul could require some semblance of…redemption? I need your gift at the hunt to help me get her back.'

'Kids go missing every day. What makes this one so important. Granddaughter?' Grayson tried to lift the old man's eye-patch with his free hand and found it stuck tight.

Grim bobbed his head. 'In a way. A distant relation. But that is not the only reason why we need her back. If she is not returned to the land of the living, I am afraid, there will be nothing in which to return you. Either of you. The Great Wolf will devour everything you know and love. And the dead will ride the Naglfar into your world, destroying everything.'

'Well, I can clearly see that you're nuts. So, I'm gunna grab the kid and find a way out here. And, I mean, you're welcome to come along, but I ain't saving your ass if there's trouble. I don't believe in inclining my skills to aid the mentally feeble.' Grayson let Grim drop once more.

The old man brushed away a streak of dried mud from his cloak, where Grayson had so uncouthly accosted him. 'Very well, but don't say I did not warn you when you see what is coming. Now, where are the others?'

Others? Grayson slowly peered over his shoulder, 'what others?'

Grim sighed, 'oh dear. They must not have arrived on time. Let us hope the Wyrd Wood has not taken them before their task is completed.'

'Oh, holy hell,' Grayson barked, through gritted teeth, staring at the door to the shack which was wide open. 'Kid's gone.'

Cold as the Grave

✝

A cowardly man thinks he will ever live, if warfare he avoids;
but old age will give him no peace, though spears may spare him.

- Hávamál

Miss *Safiya Meadows, Funeral Director, Embalmer and Manager*

That is what the sign read, but what Safiya saw was just one single word, success. Sixteen years it had taken to reach this point. Sixteen long and patient years. In her more philosophical moments, Safiya felt that she had lost more than she had gained. Two marriages. Three houses. Three cats. And a host of second-hand cars. If she looked outside, she would see another empty show of vanity. The personal licensed plate on her brand new 2018 plate Volkswagen Tiguan. It read, *SM20 OFD*. The last three letters had been instituted for her business. Her own, privately run, business: Osiris Funeral Directors. It was not much to look at from the outside. Just a small building set back from the main road that led from Derby to Matlock, the A6. Inside, though, Safiya had formed something not seen in this world for many decades.

She had chosen 'Osiris' as a name because she had been utterly enamoured by ancient Egyptian lore and history as a child. So much so that her mother had spent nearly every Christmas and Birthday from ages seven to ten, buying various archaeological knick-knacks and treasures for her to 'discover'. The idea was to place a hidden object under a thick cement of clay and chemical composite, therefore giving the child of the illusion, using tiny tools and brushes, that they were uncovering something not seen since Sekhmet herself walked the undying lands of Egypt. Of course, being that her family were devout and borderline fanatical Coptic Christian believers meant that Safiya almost had no choice than to completely rebel against anything with wooden floors, stained-glass and icons of the hanging saviour on the cross. Safiya's mother, Mariam, had fled persecution many years ago and run across oceans and borders, into the arms of a Methodist greengrocer from Birmingham; Kevin Meadows. They would have wanted nothing more than their beloved daughter to have married and produced a litter of children by the age of thirty. The fact that Safiya was single, living alone and no longer practising her mother's religion had caused what some might refer to as a 'rift'. Still, they called as soon as the funeral home opened to wish her well. Osiris Funeral Directors has been unveiled for the first-time last month, under the headline of: *A MORTUARY TOO FAR?*

It seemed that there were more than a handful of protests to her hauntingly beautiful aesthetic choices. Black marble-looking walls. Tall golden-topped pillars. Strange hieroglyphic carvings. Faux-candle lights. Black leather upholstery. No mummification though, however. She had been keen to quash that particular rumour. It was just about the sensation and the feel of the afterlife. No need to go scooping out brains through the nasal cavity. Still, it seemed the English had an aversion to anything surrounding death that had not been plastered over in cheap 1960s garb and only whispered about when the time was necessary. For a country so enamoured by its National Health Service, it was curious to think how little was spent on the deceased. Keep calm and ignore death - that might have made for a better welcoming sign that her golden weighing scales.

Nevertheless, within the first six days, she had received eleven pre-payment plans and a handful of corpses to dress. On plan to overtake the local conglomerate one village over. Safiya opened the front door, pressed the small button on her key fob and waited, as the metal roller shutters curled above her, revealing a cold, frost bitten morning. The sky was an English grey. Different to other greys, it was familiar, comforting and necessary. The clouds were the only think keeping the air above negative Celsius. That moment, another car swung speeding from the road, hitting the slight bump leading into the car park with a plastic scraping sound that made Safiya wince. An '03 Ford Fiesta. Scraped to hell. Wing mirror missing. Leaking oil. Puffing out a thin smog of pollution as it ground to a halt. The driver sat less than a foot from the windscreen, which had not yet managed to fully clear itself from the early morning freeze. Although Safiya could tell by the way the cigarette smoke billowed, that the heating had been turned up all the way.

'Morning, luv.' A tiny figure slammed the car door behind her, letting it crash against the untidy seatbelt. She slammed again. Then opened the door and flung the material inside. She slammed again, fulfilled. 'Ah, bit nippy, int'it?'

'Morning, Maureen,' Safiya laughed, watching the woman who might have looked seventy-three, but was only sixty, skitter across the icy car park. Lunch in one hand, keys and a Tesco bag filled with goodies in the other. 'It were a nightmare getting in this mornin'. Ooh, I'll never be 'avin' a tipple on a Wednesday again. Feel like death warmed up. Morris popped round and well, you know, he likes a drink.'

Safiya shook her head but kept smiling. Maureen might be old, losing her head and so sunburned that her skin resembled finely tanned leather, but she knew her business and had a kindly, elegant manner. It was welcoming to customers and clients. Even if she spent half her time chatting on the work's phone to friends and family. She was the best Safiya could find. One of a rare breed of administrative assistants who could find her way around an Apple Mac just as easily as a typewriter.

'What's up, luv? Look like you've seen a ghost. Eh, get it?' Maureen giggles with her dry, dark humour. It was much needed in a working environment such as this. Everyone had it. Managers to drivers.

Safiya almost felt as if she had. All morning, she had been wondering just who they were and why they had been following her. It was curious to use the word 'who', as what she was referring to, was the presence of two large, jet-black birds. She had seen them at first light, at home, more than sixteen miles away. Then again on the road, overhead. Now, they were perched above the houses opposite the funeral home, eyeing her as though she were a juicy rodent.

Safiya considered herself a good judge of character, and, at the pub, would usually see the following situation arise, as people recognised her, or, found out what she did for a living through passing.

'Do you like, actually dress the bodies?' 'Don't you get scared?'

To which Safiya would concretely answer, 'Yes, obviously', and 'No, what sense would it make to be fearful of a dead man? The question itself is a paradox.'

Not the most tactful way to speak to a working-class Northerner, perhaps, but until today Safiya had bolstered her career on the attitude that, *Dead men stayed dead.* It was just good business.

****

Sliding out from the fridge, the stainless-steel tray made a series of *cathunks* as it hit the adjustable trolley. Most times she could get the height's accuracy down to a millimetre, allowing the tray to slide smoothly across. Safiya felt a little off tonight, which caused the deceased's arm to shake and rock over the edge of the surgical steel bed. She huffed, wiped a gloved hand over tired eyes, and walked around to stuff 'Mr Borrsson's' arm back under the near see through, white sheet.

What a peculiar name, she thought, reading it again, from the hospital tag around his wrist. Borr-sson. *Too many repetitions in it. Not seemly for a name. As though someone had just plucked it from a hat, before bringing him here.*

Safiya gently rolled back the sheet covering the cadaver, to see a man in his late sixties, with heavy white beard, thick neck and almost pristine face. Only a single blemish above the left eye; a scar. The eye itself was not hollow either, nor sunken back. She took the aneurysm hook in hand, using it to fold back the eyelid and found a solid mass beneath. She tapped the surgical steel against the eye and heard a soft *ticking* sound.

Fake eye, she smiled, *don't see many of those anymore.*

Then, when she tapped on the material a little harder, the lid of the eye closed with such force that the hook slipped from her fingers and clattered onto the tray. Safiya let out a small yelp of surprise, *get a hold of yourself*...No, best not to think about it. Not here.

Funeral homes were curious in the way they materialised themselves into our reality. A place where the dead sleep. Almost everyone who has worked in one would have at least one, if not many, small tales to tell of things going bump in the night. This remained but another occupational hazard, alongside the formaldehyde, medical waste and sharp tools. It was not wise to apply oneself to a career with the deceased and admit to a nightly fear of them; it simply made no sense. Ghosts, like the unmoving dead, were just another customer, though unlike the corpses, these had likely paid their fee in full already.

Safiya grabbed the small toolbox from the white cabinet and readjusted her pencil, pinstripe skirt with the other. Inside the black and yellow box where the implements to provide the deceased with their 'First Offices':

- Needles (curved, several sizes)
- Aneurysm hook (looks like it could be used in the process of mummification)
- Superglue (needle and thread do not always hold)
- Eye caps (to give that small impression of life)
- Cotton wool (for...well, everywhere)

What was utterly strange about this corpse was not what it possessed, but what it did not:

- Lack of a coloured pallor (green or yellow would indicate illness. Green usually for the cancerous and yellow for the kidneys, liver and blood-borne diseases).
- Lack of mobility (not that they walk around much, but Rigor mortis usually only lasts for a few hours. This guy held tight to a lifelike quality of muscle structure.)

- Lack of 'skin-slip' (what is the body's largest organ? That's right, the skin. First thing to decay after the eyes sink. Ends with a lot of too-rough-embalmers ending up 'degloving' their clients)

- No semblance of damage or a physical wound that could be seen (stab/gun/other)

- Real eye intact (too lifelike. The liquid in the eyes disappears very, very quickly – a good sign to check for life)

- Gums/Lips/Nails all without change, almost as if...

****

Safiya dropped the arm. A soft but very noticeable pulse swept once through Mr. Borrsson's wrist. Then the eye opened. Safiya threw her hand up to her mouth but was not fast enough to stifle the loud scream. With a monster-movie quality, Mr. Borrsson slowly raised from the tray, pushing the headrest out behind him, so that it tipped over the edge, breaking the now silent ambience of the room. The sound of the plastic block hitting the linoleum matched in near-perfect synchronicity with the groan Mr. Borrsson exhaled.

'Oh,' was all Safiya managed.

She had worked inside a prison for three months after university, in the healthcare department and the instinct to rush towards that big green button when panicked still remained. But there was no distress button. Nobody to come running to her aide. Nothing but bleach white wall by the four-man fridge. As though awoken by the dead man, these temperature-controlled-units began to brim with life. Coughs, splutters and cries emerged. One of the inhabitants of TCU 2 even let out a ghastly ear-piercing shriek. As if watching Arnie, in his greatest role, Safiya watched the cadaver of Mr. Borrsson slowly twist its neck, until the one good eye was bearing down on her.

Bursting into the corridor, Safiya did not look back. Only when she heard, 'ey up luv, you alright?' did Safiya stop and yell at Madge to 'run. For god's sake run.'

Ignoring her conscience and ignoring Madge's calls, Safiya broke out into the dark obsidian coloured foyer she had designed. Her work coming back to haunt her. So to speak, she had leapt headfirst into the fire. Littered about the funeral home entrance, were four, no, five rotting, stinking corpses. They shambled about the place, bumping into one another, knocking over objects and knickknacks and tripping over the furniture, seemingly unaware of each other's presence. Some wore their own clothes. Others wore the typical white shroud. Others were naked. Mrs Gardner, who wore a blue gown, tripped, snagged the cloth, pulling it down to reveal a deep triangular coroner's scar about her upper chest.

Five corpses, no, six. The hand clutched her shoulder. It pulled hard. Safiya felt her throat swell, as the saliva caught in a knot. He was young, naked and Safiya recognised him at once. Mr. Taylor:

- Car accident
- Died at Derby District Hospital, November 1st, 2019
- Injuries sustained to ribcage, pelvis and left leg.

****

Mr. Taylor hobbled and looked through closed eyes at Safiya. He tried to scream. The thread holding his gums to his nasal passage together stretched. One partial slither of gum tore away, letting a damp, hot breath of stomach acid seep from between those pale lips. Safiya dipped and swung under

-134-

his arm before she knew what she was doing. *Where was Madge?* *Shit. Shit. Shit. The admin room.* Breathing in small, shallow doses, Safiya turned slowly from the door she slammed behind her, releasing her fingers from the lock. Except…this room had no lock. Never. She had found her eyes scanning a handle, frame, door and lock she had never seen before in her life, let alone issued to be installed. The entire door was…she did not know.

- New frame (ash or oak, with a dark colouring and near ancient texture. Scratches on the surface – look to be made by hand, or claw, and not age)

- New door (Stygian black. Most likely ash. More claw marks in places. Not painted – same colour as the door. Strange cuneiform letters dotted non-sequentially with no obvious arrangement or relation. Nordic? Whatever lacquer or varnish used gave off a sulphuric, 'eggy' smell. Judging by the age – possibly medieval?)

- New handle (silver. Strikingly contraposed to the obsidian wood. Forged into the shape of a coiled snake)

- New lock (complete with rusty, iron key)

****

The outward breath made her spin about, buttock to handle. Mr. Borrsson sat as naked as he had been upon the tray. Life had returned to his body with almost supernatural pallor. The greyish tinge to the flesh now a soft, pale pink. The corpse, or whatever it was, drew a long, exacerbated pull on the churchwarden's pipe between his right fingers. Its cherry glowed, as the light of the room seemed to lower around them. Mr. Borrsson simply sat, paying her no heed, with a lungful of smoke, gazing at the rear wall. Safiya felt as if her heart would not explode from her chest, but rather heave and cease to exist. Grey smoke trickled out of a slither between Mr. Borrsson's ribcage, high up below the armpit.

So that's how he died, she realised, wondering how her skills of perception had failed to see such a wound. *Now was not the time to be figuring out injuries or causes to extremities. Now was not the time. Nor the place. Or, maybe it was the most ideal place?*

Not for Safiya Meadows. Perhaps some might have stayed. Pulled up a chair and conversed in great detail with the dead:

- How are you?
- What's it like?
- Is it painful?
- Is my grandfather there?
- Do you need anything?
- Are you at peace?

Not for Safiya Meadows. She spun. Turned the handle. Pushed. Nothing. Pushed again. Nothing. Saw the key. Turned the lock, click. Turned the handle once more and push and...breathe.

Never Reveal Your Secrets

I

Heidi they called her, whithersoe'r she came, the well-foreseeing Vala:
wolves she tamed, magic arts she knew, magic arts practised;
ever was she the joy of evil people.

- Völuspá

She came and sat down beside him. Alex had watched her waddling her way down the aisle some time before, having first seen her poke through the bright entrance of the cargo door. He had prayed, actually prayed, that she would not come and sit down in Seat 4B, Row C of United Airlines Flight 715. And, of course, she had. Previous to this, Alex had clocked the gargantuan, sweating Yank make her way through the airport lounge, knocking over a child's glass of pop, before forming her own individual queue at Kentucky Fried Chicken. Alex kept inferring to himself that she was a Yank, American. But she was so much more than this to him. She was America itself. The flag of individuality and libertarian do-as-I-shall freedom, forcing her way across a sea of international faces and cultures. In one hand her Sony Walkman, made in Taiwan. In the other, her oversized cola, made with the finest ingredients harvested on stolen soil, by stolen people. Even her sweatpants bore the dewy mark of a flying American Bald Eagle, across a stained, dark crotch. Her hair, the bleached blonde of a white washed political campaign, hiding the coloured roots beneath. Alex watched her push past women and children, holding their meagre belongings and come to place her large derrière next to his; which was placed, of course, in First Class.

How very American, he thought.

Flicking the in-flight paper open, Alex gave the woman his typical, sarcastic, dry and utterly British succession of grunts, tuts, and sighs whenever she moved and he found himself compelled to scream at her, but forced instead to bite down on his stiff-upper-lip.

Finally, the colossus spoke, with a high upper-east-state voice, 'Ayuh, looks like we're sharsein' tonight. What's your name, sweetie? I'm Dayna. First time in the air. Can ya tell?'

Dayna had what Alex came to notice as a New England accent. Which was sort of ironic, in that, for all intents and purpose, it was he who had the 'New' England accent. After all, he was not speaking in Shakespearean soliloquy, as much as that would have allowed his mother to die with some semblance of pride in her son. The stage was his and all in it, but it had become anything but Hamlet. Macbeth, maybe, in some of his more Gothic productions, but nothing mother dearest would have paid to see, even with her son as headline act.

'Comin' or goin'?' Dayna asked, slurping down a long, gritty straw-full of the extra-extra-large cola.

'Going,' Alex replied, thumbing the magazine, 'home.'

'Ooh, wicked spooky. You're a Limey,' Dayna wiggled the fingers of her left hand at him. 'My psychic said I'd fall in love with a handsome Englishman. Now I know she wasn't talkin' 'bout those fellas to the nawth, or those Massholes, either. Must be a real Brit. Shame you ain't handsome.' Dayna snorted a long chortle, elbowing Alex until he gave in and uttered a soft, unlicensed laugh.

'You know, I kinda recognise ya,' opening a packet of strong-scented sweets, Dayna turned and eyed Alex curiously, 'You ever been on the TV?'

And just as Alex was about to brush her away, fate intervened, in the form of another British man in his late forties, who huddled over towards Row C, brandishing paper and pen.

'Mr. Wormwood,' he said grinning, pushing out the pen and paper.

Alex tongued his teeth before feigning a grin and scrawling his signature across the paper.

'Ah, this is great. My wife adores your shows, Mr. Wormwood.'

Waving his hand, Alex said, 'Please. Alex.'

'Alex. Wow.' The man seemed to blush and, staring at the returned autograph, gleamed, huddling back towards his own seat.

… *Like a real British fan*, Alex thought, *didn't outstay his welcome.*

It took almost another minute for the clockwork critters inside Dayna's head to click into place.

'Alex Wormwood,' she spurted, dribbling a small amount of cola down her chin, wetting the six or so small hairs that were sprouted there. 'Oh, golly. I saw your live show last week. Well, I caught a rerun on the TV, but I watched nearly a whole segment. I thought you looked familiar. Didn't you do the Houdini trick last time, with the water tank?'

Alex had already grown tired of the drawn-out vowels and unduly added 'r's' spewing from Dayna's mouth. In fact,

Alex Wormwood, born Alex Krieger, believed he might actually have hated *all* Americans. He would never come back, if it were not for the money. Maybe that *was* America?

'You know where you should play next? Huh?' Dayna continued, 'Fenway. Imagine if you could make the Green Monster disappear, like you did to that Big Ben.'

Alex gritted his teeth, nearly chipping one, 'That, was James Hyde, and it was all smoke and mostly mirrors. He even said how he faked it on BBC One a week later.'

'Oh,' Dayna said, but it sounded like 'oooh', 'gotcha.'

Most members of the human race would have seen the nerve they tugged on in Alex's temple rise, but not Dayna. No, she kept on, all the way through the safety announcement, only ceasing her sugar-induced relent, once the engines roared and the Boeing 747 started to shoot across the tarmac of McCarran International Airport, Las Vegas, Nevada.

Alex Krieger had begun the journey home; a three-bedroom luxury flat, in one of London's most affluent areas. With views of Tower Bridge and a sunrise that could make the Queen herself envious, Alex had believed he had truly 'made it', in whatever modern terms that meant. He supposed, in London's heyday, its history, to 'make it' might mean one simply had roof over their head, four walls and a hot plate of food. How times had changed. Even in the thirty-four years he had been alive, rolling around on this planet earth, he had seen change to marvel. The Iron Curtain had fallen. Video game revolution. The Spice Girls. Television's golden age. And now, Alex Wormwood, magician extraordinaire. In just five short years the world would celebrate as it never had. Almost six billion people, set to bring in a new millennium. Would Alex Krieger still see his name in Vegas lights? Or could it be Hollywood to call home?

As Alex watched the dizzying lights disappear into a long, unyielding, lifeless desert below, he felt eyes on his back. Turning, past Dayna, having to lean slightly he was seeing a curious looking fellow in a flat cap and tweed jacket watching him. Instinctively, as people do, Alex first turned away, then had a sneaky look back. He was still staring across without a hint of social grace. Alex noticed that not only did the man wear a perplexing smile, but also a grotesque two-inch scar over his left eye. Putting the man out of his mind, Alex allowed Dayna to broker a peaceful barrier between himself and the gazing weirdo, before closing his eyes to the gentle rock of the plane, easing him into sleep.

It was not the turbulence that awoke him. Nor was it the spilt cup of coffee over Dayna's lap. Nor was it even her New England cursing. It was that same feeling of being watched.

'Bah,' Alex let out a quick yelp of surprise, when he found himself confronted, eye-to-eye with a large black bird, clinging itself to the side of the window. The bird gave him a cock-eyed stare, before disappearing towards the cockpit, as the Boeing ascended above the rainclouds and distant lightning.

How high up are we? Alex looked down and saw only cloud. *A bird? All the way up here? How fast is it flying?*

Sensing his dream had somehow spilled, momentarily into reality, Alex sucked in a deep breath and closed his eyes, counting backward from ten. Looking across Row C, as Dayna dabbed at her crotch with paper towels, Alex saw that the man with the scar had left his seat unoccupied.

'Ayuh, cripes,' Dayna muttered, 'I need to calm down on the old caffeine. Giving me the jitters. Who knew planes would be so bumpy?'

About to close his eyes again. Alex uttered something that he was, again, not sure existed in dream or reality.

'If you're looking for Mr. Grim, he's gone into the cargo hold to have quick nosey. We're behind schedule, ya see?' she said without bringing her eyes up from her crotch, still mopping up the coffee, now stained.

'W-what?' Alex puffed.

'Mr. Grim, silly,' Dayna giggled at the man in the pinstripe suit by her side, as though he had just asked what colour the ocean below was. 'He's been expectin' you'd follow him. But I suppose you were too busy sleepin'?'

Alex's mouth opened, and he failed to say what he wanted, instead he just blustered, 'I need to use the bathroom.'

Squeezing passed her, he heard Dayna chortle again, 'Okay, so, but you'd be lucky to find a bath in there. Place is tiny.'

What the fuck is going on in this plane? He nipped two fingernails into his wrist. *Nope. Awake.*

Never, in his most vivid, drug-induced, Vegas-hallucinations, had Alex ever seen anything close to what came next. It was back. The black bird. Just…sitting there, on the back of that woman's seat. The avian eyed him, before hopping sideways and tilting its beak, to show Alex the top of its crown.

Did that fucking thing just bow to me? What is…No, this is a dream. No chance fifty people are failing to see this? They have nothing to say about the bloody crow dancing around the cabin. For God's sake, mate, there's kids in here.

And yet, they paid the bird no notice, as if mattered not that the animal pecked at their scraps, tore off chunks of their books, or made outrageous squawks as it flitted about the cabin.

It's happened, Alex sighed, in a come-to-terms attitude that had always seemed to save him from life's great despairs. *I've lost it, just like mother said I would.*

The bird cawed and dashed by wing, past Alex, past the toilet and came to rest on the fold-down tray in front of Seat 4A, Row C. He heard Dayna gasp.

Finally, someone is going to acknowledge the fucking bird on the plane, Alex felt his blood boiling.

'Oh, hey there, Hugin,' Dayna held out a curled hand under the bird's neck. It stared upwards as she did, allowing Dayna's fingers to caress the avian's throat, stroking up and down. The bird fluttered its wings in the same expression of love that a dog wags it tail.

Alex's heart thundered, as he saw the face that Dayna now wore. She turned to him, over her humungous shoulder, and Alex was confronted by a grainy gargoyle's visage. It was, to him, as if Dayna had turned to stone. As though Medusa, in the form of this black bird had gone all 'Mother-Shipton' on Dayna and petrified her flesh. When the new Dayna blinked at him, and the eyelids flickered, not vertically, but horizontally, he turned and fled.

Bumping his thigh into an armrest, Alex coughed out a wince, rubbed the pain but kept moving away, shooting down the aisle. No one seemed to care at all that there was a fucking gargoyle in Seat 4B. That was, until he kicked over a child's bag of toys, and the father yelled, 'Hey, asshole' at him. Alex waved the insult away, headed for solitude at the rear of the plane; a long jog from First Class.

Just breathe. Just breathe. He hunched over the cabin-crew's desk, breathing deep concussive blows.

'Mr. Wormwood?' a soft American accent asked, and he almost broke down. 'Are you alright? Some of the passengers—'

'I'm fine,' Alex felt guilty for shouting almost as soon as the words escaped; lowering his tone to repeat, 'I'm fine, really.'

'Actually,' he added, just as the cute blonde started to leave, 'could you find out who the woman sitting beside me is?'

She eyed him curiously, 'here's nobody sat beside you, sir. Mr. Blackwood, your agent, he was very explicit that you were seated alone. Said you get a little nervous in the air.' Then, she smiled, offered his arm a gentle pat, gleaming at him with bright white pearls under pink, pearlescent lips, before adding, 'By the way, a few of us were wondering if we could get a picture before we land. Got some fans on board. My dad caught your show in Houston last year. Said it was just amazing how you walked through all that fire without a single burn. How do you do that, anyway?'

'Magic,' Alex smiled nervously, and whipped his hand, producing a handkerchief from nowhere. It was a cheap trick, but that was all he had on him. Everything else was in the hold. It seemed to do the trick. The woman beamed and gave him a soft clap, before leaving – as Alex used the handkerchief to mop at the river of sweat rolling into his eyes.

'Come on,' poking her head back through, the woman waved him to follow, 'I'll show you back to your seat. Get you a stiff drink. What's your poison?'

As she had promised, Alex returned to Seat 4A and found Seat 4B was now empty. His mind was not eased as such, but he felt a modicum safer at least.

Overworked and underpaid, Alex closed his eyes and concentrated hard on the roar of the engine to his rear, as the Boeing raced ever onward towards England. Towards sanity.

When caught in an unprecedented situation, one involving imminent danger, there are two options: fight or flight. Alex Krieger felt the immediate rush of supernatural energy course through him, as Flight 715 from Las Vegas dropped two-hundred feet from its cruising altitude of thirty-odd-thousand. Alarms blazed from the cockpit, or flashing seatbelt sign, or over the discombobulated tannoy. They screamed into Alex's head. *Fight or flight.* Alex Krieger almost always chose the latter. As there was nowhere to run to, instead of fleeing from the primal predator, he retreated into his own mind; closing himself off from the world and its dangerous ways. Around him children wailed, and parents panicked. In the seconds of freefall, before Flight 715 'found its feet' again, luggage and toys, plastic bottles and trays lifted into the air, dispersed, and were strewn about the cabin, slamming back into reality. Two of the crew had been thrown from their feet, crashing into the aisle, as their trolley collided with the nearest seat, sending glass over several shrieking passengers.

Alex breathed again. A fleeting reprieve from the horror the brain cannot truly accept. It was near-impossible to convince a human mind it was due to fall from the sky and meet its death – when the body itself was never meant to be there. Flight 715 blared with alarms again. Its nose dipped forward like an arrow, headed into the Atlantic target. Her wings blustered with slipstream, forcing white, streaming jets from her tips. Oxygen masks fell like dead men catching on the ropes of their gallows. After fifteen seconds, Flight 715 bracingly pulled from its death spiral, as the Bald Eagle retreats from its fight.

How very American this all is, was a thought rushing through Alex's mind, captured in stills, images of a life he did not recognise.

'...Err...this is your Captain speaking...I apologise on behalf of...err...all of us up here with United. An unexpected slipstream forced our plane to...nosedive...believe me, it was unavoidable. I...err...apologise again. We have corrected altitude and have what appears to be safe, clear weather on the horizon.' The tannoy failed to cut off before every passenger heard, 'What the fuck happened?' from the co-pilot's mouth.

His arse returned to its rightful place, Alex tried to drown out the sobbing children and stress-riddled passengers, along with angry, clueless crew, by placing the headphones over his ears and tuning into the uninterrupted film; shown overhead, several seats down. He could make out Robin Williams, dressed as some sort of jungle warrior, leaping about a New York mansion, as monkeys and a tiger chased him and two kids. It was just enough background noise to try once more to get some sleep. Mr. Williams and the kids talked in the background to narrate his next dream, when Alex felt a tug on the flap of skin between finger and thumb. It came again, harder. Alex darted back and smacked his head on the plastic wall as the bird tried to peck at him a third time.

'Hey, piss off you little tosser,' Alex shouted at the bird, realising only after people watching him began to mutter, that there was nothing there. *Time for a walk.*

Unsure why the small holding door was unlatched and flung open, Alex felt a curiosity that was new to him. This time, the trigger pulled a different way, and he was drawn towards the mystery, climbing down into the cargo hold below. It was exactly as he imagined. Boxes, containers, luggage, and netting. A wide-open order of disarray. Behind the stack of suitcases,

Alex saw two figures. The first was unmistakable, Big Dayna. Her wide, broad form made the old man with the scar look even frailer and more aged. In all honesty, after everything, Alex had put the creepy old man out of his mind, chalking the guy up to an overactive imagination. Why else would he not be here, with Dayna, in the hold, along with a bird?

'Ayuh, hey, kid, there yar!' Dayna exclaimed, ushering Alex over with both hands, as her rolls shook beneath. 'Told ya he's been waiting on ya. That was some bumpy ride, yeah. Felt my whole body move.' Her face, human again, carried a smile and her palm still grasped the extra-extra-large cola. The old man, however, gave Alex a fleeting look, as though he could not bear to look directly at him.

'Ooh, it's my first time crossing this lake in a very long time.' Dayna slurped down the cola and gave a shameless belch, 'I tell ya, world was a much bigger place when we landed in Skraeling country. I'll tell ya that for a dollar.'

And then, Alex felt he almost understood her. The way Dayna was. It was American. But not American. A façade. A charade. Someone playing the part of an American, allowing most of the 'yee-haw' to scrape through whatever her real identity was.

'I'll tell ya,' she continued, 'I ain't got the body to row all that way anymore. Used to call it the 'Sea O' Worms'. Luckily, the big guy saved us. Tell him, Grim, how your boy calmed the storm. Ah, he's busy. Best no interrupt, if ya wanna make it out of here alive, ay?'

Bloody hell, what? Alex felt a migraine starting to form at the edges of his skull. *Are they, is this a hostage thing?*

'Get back,' Alex shouted, holding his hands up, edging back towards the ladder. 'Get back. I swear. I'll shout.'

'Ooh, ya swear what, ya big goofball?' Dayna laughed a throaty, masculine roar. 'Will ya tell him, Grim?'

'Help,' Alex screamed, climbing into the cabin and belting down the aisle, looking back every few seats as if pursued by an unseen hellhound.

At once, the cabin exploded with uproar. Several of the cabin crew rushed towards him, cornering Alex before he could make it farther than his own seat.

'Whoa, Mr. Wormwood.' A man with seemingly never-used, gleaming teeth approached him. A small, winged badge on his chest read, *Chad*.

'Fuck off…Chad,' Alex whipped a pen from what looked to be thin air, and held it out in front of him, waving it around as though it was fire and they, Neanderthals. 'Something weird is going on and… I…I…there are people. Downstairs. The big one, Dayna. And the old man. And the bird.'

One by one, the crew looked at each other, as their expressions changed from worried caution to apathetic understanding.

'It's all right, honey' a different blonde moved closer, giving Alex a pitying smile.

'Hey. Hey.' Alex brandished the pen again. 'I am not crazy. I'm not. Get back. There are people beneath us.'

'Mr. Wormwood,' Chad raised his voice, 'you are frightening people. You—'

The nose of Flight 715 dove once more at a sixty-degree angle towards the Atlantic. Alarms blared. Chad and his crew fell sideways into the seats. Alex fell into the plastic wall by the toilet, bracing himself, staring, now down, through the cabin. One of the blonde crew yelled at him, but over the rush of air, sirens and screams, Alex only saw her lips move, as the metal trolley smacked into her, dragging her torso down the aisle towards the cockpit. In a burst of sound, Alex saw a spark of flame from an opposing window and realised it was the engine, sending plumes of acrid het-black smoke behind them. Alex closed his eyes but counting and breathing shallow achieved nothing but passing precious seconds. He turned away and saw only one option left. By his right shoulder, the pressurised cabin door stood. Its bright orange handle almost calling to him. Hearing another pop and click, Alex felt the object in his hand alter in size, shape and weight. Ignoring all else, he peered down at the pen, to see it was now, a rusty old key. On its edge, several runes had been etched; one of them glowing with a supernatural aura.

Not knowing just why, Alex brought the key around. Even the door had changed. *Emergency Only* had become an obsidian steel frame. The pressurised edges had become old, blackened and charred oak. Instead of a long, orange lever, a silver handle, forged in the shape of a serpent began to turn. Alex felt the key twist in the lock and a heavy rush of air pull at every muscle and fibre of his being. Alex had chosen…flight.

Gjöll's Bridge

❦

*Many ages before the earth was made,' added Jafnhar,
'was Niflheim formed, in the middle of which lies the spring called
Hvergelmir, from which flow twelve rivers, Gjoll being the nearest to the
gate of the abode of death.*

- *The Poetic Edda*

J ack waited in and amongst the trees. He was not alone. A
dark, hooded figure had emerged onto the path,
illuminated by the torch he had drooped in terror. He had
been running so hard and so fast from what his eyes told him
was a small girl, but his mind told him…he did not want to
think of what it really was. The fire of the torch was
smouldering, weakening on the ground, so that only a faint
orange glow remained. It had been enough for him to make
out the size of the figure. Taller than him, but not overbearing.
Grayson would have probably just leapt out and tackled the
figure to the ground and bashed his brains in. Jack had no such
inclination. He would sit and he would wait in the bush until
the danger had gone and then he would search for Lucy once
more.

'*Kom ut lilla*,' it was with the voice of a man that the figure
spoke, but with the raspy death-rattled cough of a corpse.

From the tips of the figures cloak, Jack saw fingers, like pine branches. Long, gnarled and malformed. When a long plume of air escaped Jack's mouth, he understood how loudly he was panting.

'*Jag kan höra dig*,' there was no emotion in the figure's voice and even though Jack did not understand the words, he grasped that it was himself who was the target of the words.

He's seen me. He knows I'm here. Oh, Lucy, I'm so sorry. I'll never find you now. Jack felt only one option available. He was going to run.

He was preparing his feet to dash forward, when, under his palms, started to quiver. Slowly, a rumbling, like a jet engine roared overhead. The figure in front of him screeched in either anger, frustration or terror and took off with unnatural speed into the woods, away from him. The noise got louder and louder, until Jack had to kneel down and clap his palms to his head. On and on the roaring thundered through the trees. He almost considered grasping at handfuls of dirt and stuffing his ears and his mouth to silence the dreadful noise. Then, with a blast of warm air, the trees bent forward altogether, and the sound vanished across the forest as quickly as it had appeared. The torch went out as if it were electric, leaving the woods in total darkness. At least whatever that was, had possibly saved his life. Then, came the thud and the slosh of mud. A single, heavy *thump*.

With every fibre of his being screaming at him that something new had arrived, Jack picked up his feet and leapt out onto the path. He was not going to stop. He was not going to stop until he reached the shack. And he would have kept going, if not for the body. Jack caught his foot and felt his face splatter with earth as he dropped to the floor. Like a cat, he sprung back on his hands and peered back at the corpse, laying on the ground, face down in the mud.

What the...? Jack kicked the corpse and heard it groan. He was frozen again, waiting for the dead man to get up and reach out with a cold, lifeless hand. But he did not. Instead, the corpse lifted its head out of the mud and blinked, staring at Jack with as much daze and confusion as he had himself.

'… Hello?' the corpse groaned. Corpse? No. It breathed. *He* breathed. A man. Another living, *breathing* person.

'… Hey,' Jack still wanted to run. Nothing here was safe. No one here was safe. Everyone and everything was trying to hurt him. He knew this. knew it as a fact. An everlasting truth. Universal and absolute. So why was he still sitting there, staring possible death in the face?

'… Where am I?' the not-dead man asked with a familiar British accent. London. Possibly.

Jack wavered on his answer and thought of Grayson, '… Hell. I think.'

The man blinked several more times, as though waking up from a year-long slumber. Then, he wiped the mud from his face, as much as he could and rolled over onto his back. Jack looked up, too. It was haunting, how beautiful this place was above the nightmare of the trees.

'Oh, good. I was afraid we had crashed in France,' the man lay there, motionless.

'Crashed?' Jack asked.

'Right,' the man fling himself to an upright position and turned around noticing the man in his early twenties staring back, open-mouthed. 'Guessing you weren't on Flight 715? Is this England? You local? No? Talk to me, mate, I've just had a *Twilight Zone* experience at thirty-thousand feet.'

Jack began to understand. He also began to understand other things. Things related to the world around him. Things related to Grim, to the Black Door, to Grayson and…all of this.

'I-I suppose you should come with me,' Jack stood and offered the crash-victim a hand up.

The mud had covered almost all of his suit, but Jack still saw the image of pin-stripe trousers, waistcoat and colourful pink tie. The newcomer looked as if he had just rolled off a Scorsese filmset.

'*He's* waiting for you, I think.' And Jack started to walk. 'What's your name? I'm Jack.'

The suit and tie gangster, looking like he should have a Nino Rota score following him wherever he walked, replied, 'Alex? I suppose you can call me that. To most people, it's Mr. Wormwood, but we aren't in normal circumstances, right? Can't believe I survived without a broken bone. Wonder how far I fell.'

Along the path, Jack tried his best to try and make some connection to the newcomer. Alex asked him a variety of questions, to which his answers, were either a shrug of the shoulders, a shake of the head, or just a simple, 'I don't know.' It turns out that Alex was a famous magician. Jack had guessed, by his flagrant use of the word, 'boss', that they did not come from the same time. Nor did they come from the same England. Alex was a southerner, and a rich one at that. One of the ones Jack despised, who ate at The Shard and drank expensive prosecco at lunch and drove cars with less than one-hundred-and-seventy-thousand miles on the clock. Alex kept asking where they were and asking how he was going to get his luggage back. It would sink in. reality. Soon. When the horrors began again and the nightmares came out of the woods, he would understand, he was not getting his toiletries back any time soon. Jack thought that there was something egocentric about Alex. He was so wrapped up in his own world, that he failed to notice several important issues at hand. Firstly, where was his plane? Even parts of it? If it had crashed, where were the other bodies. Secondly, the fact that Jack who had been in the woods for some time had not seen a plane. Or fire. Or an explosion. Thirdly, that everything about this world was dead. Apart from the flora. The air was rancid and stunk. The sky was filled with the corpses of a million decaying stars. The earth under their very feet was grimy, rotten and dark.

'So, hey, what year is it?' it was Jack's turn to ask a question. In the short amount of time, he had spent with Grim and Grayson he had picked up enough, from the old man's words and the curious plastic jumpsuit that Grayson was from some point in the future. He had noticed one particular point on Grayson's skin that not many others ever did: a small, coded tattoo, like a glyph, just behind his left earlobe. As his ponytail moved, Jack had thought he had seen a microchip gleaming from the skin, but it was some sort of high-tech imprint, or tattoo. Something related to that word he had used, prison.

'Year?' Alex puffed out a yet of air, 'You a druggie, mate? Cos I'll be fine making my own way, it's 1995. Like...*April*. You missed four months of your life?'

Under his breath, Jack muttered, 'More like you missed twenty-odd years.'

The shack appeared again, and Jack saw that the door was still open, as he had left it. A bright gleam came and went several times from inside. It looked like a torch.

'Oh, here we go,' Alex puffed out an even louder breath of air, 'This your drug den, mate? I'm not spending the night in a junkie's allotment. Just let me use your blower and I'll phone the old bill. Swear this thing was fully juiced on the plane.' The magician tapped at a mobile that was both taller and thicker than Jack's hand; and it even had an actual aerial.

Jack needed a second by the threshold, before he stepped through and saw Grayson, Grim and another new face gathered by the window. It was a woman. A little older than him. Younger than Grayson. She wore a similar pin-striped suit to Alex, and it made Jack wonder whether there actually had been a plane-crash. Maybe he was suffering some sort of hallucination. A concussion brought on by head-trauma. Had he been on a plane? Had Grayson been on a plane? Had...*Oh, Lucy, where are you?*

'There you are kid. Thought the lions and tigers and bears might a' got you?' Grayson was actually a sigh of relief to see. Someone Jack felt might actually have the skills to get them out of this mess. It was something in his posture. So rigid and straight. Made the world around him seem small and controllable.

'This here's Safiya,' Grayson continued. The woman by his side lifted a shaky hand and offered him a dry smile. 'She's British, like you. Don't ask her how she got here, though. I thought my ride was rough.'

'What are you all looking at?' Jack stood behind them, trying to peer through the window, out at the clearing.

'Gandalf here is trying to summon us a way home, but I think the hobbits might have run off with the last of his marbles.' Grayson offered, and Jack saw his reflection grinning back at him through the glass.

Grim turned back, 'the Hidden-One is closing in. I can sense the Wyrd Wood waiting for him. His daughter comes also. They seek to free the Great Wolf.'

Jack could see Grayson making a grand show of rolling his eyes and sighing, 'Yeah, so that's what I've been dealing with. How about you? find your lady friend?'

'No,' Jack answered, ignoring Grim, 'but I did stumble across the Godfather out there. He's trying to get a signal on his 90's looking Carphone. Name's Alex.'

Grayson coughed a deep, gritty laugh. To his side, the woman did not speak. She kept as close to Grayson as humanly possible. Every now and again, she caught Jack's eye and gave him a fleeting smile, then carried on peering out of the window. Grim was busy, shuffling his hands over parchments of notes he carried in his cloak, or weird handfuls of stones that he shuffled obsessively in his pocket. A wiser man than Jack would not have taken the old man at face value, but to him, all he could see was what he had been told. Old Grim. Allfather. Jack was nothing if a little underwhelmed. Never meet your heroes. Whatever and whoever he was, in reality, he was as confused and scared as the rest of them.

****

A crash of lightning without thunder lit the earth around the shack, silently illuminating the clearing for the briefest of moments. In that split second, Jack felt that the world had gotten just a little more crowded.

'He's here,' Grim said and marched towards the window.

Another crash by the door, and Alex stumbled his way in, spitting out words like machine-gun fire, 'Hey what was that? Who are you? Who are they? What the hell's going on? Who are you people? Who are those guys, out there? Mate, what's happening?'

'You must be Alex.' Grayson barged past him, out of the door.

'I wouldn't do that, mate. Those guys just appeared out of nowhere.' Alex had turned as white as the stripes on his waistcoat.

Jack followed the prisoner. Then Grim, followed closely by the woman.

'Safiya, get inside. You, too, kid.' Grayson held his palm back to them, as though protecting them from whatever might leap out of the darkness.

The only one who obeyed him, was Alex, who threw himself inside and closed the door with a heavy thud. Jack stood beside Grayson as the prisoner held up his hand and clicked a small device. A beam of LED light shone out in a small cone. It hovered over the far treeline for a moment, before it started to glide inwards, like a searchlight. Nothing. Just empty grass and...something moved. Another figure was standing in the grass. Grayson inched the torch sideways and another figure was standing there, motionless. Then, another and another. And another.

'Fuck,' Jack wanted to retch again.

'All right,' Grayson elongated the word, 'no one move. Let's not startle the locals now. Grim? What's happening?'

But Grim was not the voice who answered.

'Children, children,' it was an assibilated, crooning voice, slithering out of the darkness with a serpentine tongue. 'Did father bring you along for the journey? That was very naughty of him. Tssk-tssk. Shame on you, Grimnir. The woods of Helheim are hungry.'

Grayson moved the torch back and forth, left to right. Nothing but sentinel, hooded figures in the grass. The light stopped on each one as the voice spoke, but he could not pinpoint its location.

'Come now,' it slithered again, 'let us make this easy. Children, go inside. I shall deal with you later. Grimnir, empty your pockets, and step closer. I shall make this quick. I intend to make a great eagle out of your skin, *old* father.'

'Enough, Loki. Show yourself. No more games. I have bought the key. Return to me its power and we can call this truce, here and now. No more games. No more tricks.' Grim bellowed so loudly, that Jack's ear started to ring again with pain.

Grim held up his hand in the air and thrust out the old, rusted key.

'Oh, good, a gift.' The voice called back and Grim was thrown forward, dashed into the grass like a ragdoll. His fingers flew open and the key shot out, into the darkness, like a bullet, steaming its way over the grass, which bent forward before it.

Grayson followed the object as best he could, when the light stopped on a hunched over figure in the grass. Jack felt sick again. The creature in the grass slowly unfurled itself like a coiled snake. Its arms and legs sliding upright, until it stood taller than a man. Its skin was an obsidian black, cutting out the torchlight like a black hole. Jack saw two red eyes beaming back, piercing though a jet-black face broken only by dripping, white-painted cheeks. It was a demon, in every sense of the word. In every, horrific detail that Jack could have ever imagined. If he were to conjure up his worst nightmare, this was it. The thing which made men weep in fear when they woke screaming from their beds. The demonic eyes that linger in the shadows of their nightmares. Straight, knife-like nails jutted from slender, stygian fingers. The knees stooped so that

Jack imagined that there were no feet on the tips of those slim shanks, only hoofs. It did not speak again, instead, as Grayson followed it with the torch, the figure rose and turned its back on them. The clawed hands curled about the key, reaching out, as if to open a door.

'No.' Grim remained on the floor, watching in horror, as another silent bolt from the blue appeared and gathered around the grass in the shape of a doorway.

Electric currents arced around the figure, before the hand turned. A brilliant flash of light grew brighter and brighter with all the glow of a hundred silver-coloured candles, overwhelming the torch. Grim was still shouting as he clambered to his feet, nearly tripping over the cloak. The silver-light was too brilliant to look at. Jack tried to watch through the gaps in his fingers, but had to avert his eyes. Grayson stood, as if watching a nuclear strike, bracing himself against the radiation wave to come. The electricity in the air had lifted the prisoners pony tail above his head. Jack saw the tiny hairs on his arm stand erect and felt as though he were charging up, like a battery.

The light died, just a little, enough for the torch to see that standing there, in the clearing, was an open door. Grayson dashed the light from side to side.

'They're gone. They done vanished.'

'After them,' Grim scarpered ahead towards the door and turned back, ushering them through the Silver Door.

Grayson put one foot forward, then seemed to shake the ideas from his mind. Safiya clung to his side, her hair billowing like tall grass itself, over her head. A chorus of howls and shrieks began to rise from the trees, growing into a crescendo. Jack was in a horror film. The standard roll of fog was all that was missing. It was the Night of the Living Dead, as a legion of corpses began to shuffle their way through the nightmare woods, into their view. By their feet, hounds and wolves, blacker than night stalked out of the trees. Other things, larger things, shifted the treetops, moving closer. Jack remembered the giant eye on the path when he first arrived. What else was out there?

Grim was still calling to them by the Silver Door. If not for the army of the damned appearing, would Jack have followed him, like a faithful dog? He had followed him before. He looked once at Grayson, saw the man nod and took off into the grass. He did not have to check if they were following. The shambling, rotten corpses were edging closer and closer. Soon they would be...

A scream erupted from the shack. Jack turned, almost at the Silver Door and saw Alex fall flat on his back. A shatter of wood burst over the man's head and something half-eaten crashed across the threshold of the shack. Alex sprung to his feet and called after them, sprinting through the clearing. Jack surveyed the woods one last time and swore he saw tentacles emerging to the left, slimy and slithering. Forgetting Survival Rule Number 666, he took one deep breath of the acrid, hellish air and entered through the Silver Door.

Crash Landing

ᚴ

'The Norns,' replied Har, 'who are of a good origin, are good themselves, and dispense good destinies.'
But those men to whom misfortunes happen ought to ascribe them to the evil Norns.

- The Poetic Edda

For the second time in less than seventy-two hours, Jack felt as though his skin was being torn away from his muscle, into ten-thousand tiny pieces, before being seared back in place with a thousand small soldering irons. This process, though painful, lasted just under three seconds. When it was over, that familiar dazzling light had appeared, filling the corners of his visions with a dancing cosmos of stars. Jack hit the floor with a heavier thud than last time. Or maybe it had been the same pressure exerted against him by the ground, but it was only the surface that had changed? Opening his eyes, the world was different. Not by a great deal in so way as appearances just yet. The sky was clouded. Overcast by a brownish, grey hue that stretched from horizon to horizon. Against his face, Jack felt a gust of sea-air bristle against this skin. Full of salt and minerals. The ground beneath his palms was rock. Tufts of weeds had managed to work their entropic magic through the earth, but not enough to constitute as grass.

And now, where am I? Jack got to his feet with an earful of pressure that forced him off balance. Waves of vertigo came and went for some time after the initial exiting of the doorway. Not so far ahead, there stood the erection of a lighthouse. At least that is what Jack imagined it to be. What other building clung to the edge of cliffs, overlooking the sea? No light, though. Keeper must be on holiday.

A grunt to his left made Jack spin in fear.

'Oh, man. That ride was rough. What the hell happened?' It was Alex. The man had made it. A small part of Jack had kind of wished he would have been swallowed by the horde.

Jack did not answer. He was surveying the area. Not much to see other than the lighthouse and the sea. In the early morning sun, he could only have guessed this, nothing else stood out. Just the tall, leaning tower above them. Safiya had to be somewhere, and so did Grayson. It was curious how he felt a pang of fear to think that Grayson had landed far away, and he was left defenceless. Whether Grayson was any form of defence against whatever lived out here, well, that was another question. He was a convicted…something. Whatever it was, it cannot have been for overfeeding goldfish or failing to stop at a red light. So, if anyone had the ability to take life if needed, Grayson was probably the closest. It was a defence. Sort of. Where was he?

'Here, mate,' Alex sauntered over, uneasily, wiping down his suit of dried mud. 'Where'd that creepy old man go? And the bird? You know, the Asian looking one.'

Jack felt a desire he had not felt in years; it was the desire to turn around and clock Alex right in the nose with his balled fist. He imagined blood pouring from the shattered crevasse where his smeller had once been and it made him shudder with a warm fire in his veins.

'I don't know, *mate*,' Jack gritted his teeth. 'But I suggest we find them. And Grayson. I don't know where we are.'

Except, that isn't entirely true, Jack mused. *I do know. Sort of. But, how do I know?* A word wanted to slither its way out of his mouth, and Jack forced it down. Alt…heim. Curious.

'Heah.' That's what it sounded like, somewhere nearby, coming from an unknown source.

'Did you hear that?' Alex lifted his chin, as if he could see over the ninety-degree angle of the cliffside.

Close to where they stood, a long bridge bobbed and frayed in the wind. It crossed over a small inlay of water channelled into a bay. On the other side, stood the lighthouse. It looked as if someone had brought the bridge out of an old western movie, or maybe an Indiana Jones flick. Struts of wood bandaged in place by rope. Rope handles either side. A hole in the old boards every few feet. Certain death to cross.

Then the sound came again, but it was not 'heah', it was 'help'.

Jack jogged over to the edge of the cliff and looked over. His head swelled with vertigo. It was a long way down. The cliffs were white, and grey washed with limestone crags. Roughly sixteen feet below, laying on an outcrop of chalky earth, was Safiya.

'Hey. Hey.' With the wind muffling the words, Jack clapped his palms around his mouth. 'What happened? Did you fall?'

Safiya was waving her arms in the air as though she were lost at sea, 'I dunno. I just woke up here. Is everyone else up there?'

He was not sure why, but Jack turned around and looked, 'There's just two of us.'

'You have to get me up. I don't like it,' Safiya shouted back.

Well, that would've been obvious. You didn't really have to tell me, Jack thought and immediately began to look around. He wanted to find a long, thick branch, or some rope. There were people nearby. Maybe one of them left something he could use.

Alex was just standing there, trying once again to lift his phone as far above his head as he could to get signal.

'Hey. You gunna help?' Jack spat and Alex ignored him, moving around counter-clockwise as though that were the solution to everything. *Prick.*

Then there he stood. Grayson. Jack saw the dirty white jumpsuit standing out from a small gathering of trees like a sore thumb. The prisoner lifted his hand, in a meaningful gesture and walked over to him in long, purposeful strides.

'Am I glad to see you,' Jack sighed, looking back over at Alex, now bashing his extra-large phone with his thumb. It was a strange device to look at. Roughly two hand widths long, with a long, plastic aerial protruding from the centre. It was either a very cheap phone, or a very expensive one. Maybe a *satellite* phone? Jack had not seen a satellite phone outside of movies and assumed that all modern smartphones had the same capabilities now. Or, what had Grim said about different times?

'Where's Safiya?' Grayson asked in that long southern drawl.

'In a spot of bother, but she's okay.' Jack guided him over to the edge of the cliffs and noticed that there was a huge hole through the material of his left leg. The hole in the white, plasticky jumpsuit was encircled with bright red blood. 'What happened there?' there was not a mark or a scratch on the skin beneath and yet the hole looked like a shotgun blast had torn through it.

Grayson waved him off, 'Later.'

The pair were trying to formulate a plan to rescue Safiya, who looked entirely too pleased to see Grayson, when Alex stormed over and thrust his hand over the edge of cliff, laying down.

'You don't think, if we thought we could reach, we mightta tried that?' barked Grayson.

Still, Alex tried a little harder to lean over. He was only thirteen feet away, surely another stretch would do it? Grayson shook his head, was about to turn away, when he felt something. They all did. Jack watched, as small chunks of the chalky cliff began to crumble away from the edge and begin...working their way upwards. He stared, entranced. Alex kept heaving and stretching, somehow unaware of what was happening, until the strange feeling of vibrations on the skin began to grow and grow. He must have been concentrating too hard, because just as he was about to give up, Safiya's hand leapt out of the air and *grabbed* his.

'Whoa,' Alex almost let go, 'what the hell just happened?'

'Ho-ly hell.' Grayson muttered.

Jack kept blinking rapidly, still in disbelief that whatever had happened, had happened. *Had he really just caught her? Or, levitated her?*

The moment passed and Jack and Grayson reached over, dragging Safiya to safety. She stood, shaking and pale, staring at Alex, who in turn was staring, unblinking at his hands.

'Seriously, guys, what was that? Did you guys spike me? Eh? What's going on? How did I do that?' Alex looked at each of them in turn, as if they could explain.

Grayson shrugged, 'That's not all.' He pointed first at his trouser leg, where the fabric had been punctured and ripped, then he pulled up the hem to his knee. There were long lines of dried blood, running away from where the hole had been. Yet there was nothing but skin. Scarless, hairless skin. Before any of them could ask, Grayson knelt to the floor, gritted his teeth and jabbed into his skin with a small rock, twisting it until the blood began to pour.

'What the, hey, what?' Alex made a retching sound and turned away.

Grayson drew the rock, carving a small incision into his flesh. Jack and Safiya watched in utter disbelief. He dropped the rock, then took a deep breath, and rubbed his palms together, before placing them gently over the newly made wound. Again, that curious feeling of vibrations covered Jack's skin and before he could open his mouth, Grayson had removed his palms and wiped the blood away. Nothing. There was nothing there. No wound. No scratch. No more blood.

'I hit the ground badly, back there.' Grayson began, 'might have touched a tree when I landed this time. Woke up with a branch halfway outta my leg. Stung, but nothing disastrous. Would have slowed me down though. As I was tending to it, I realised that wherever we are, right now, I got a superpower.'

Jack opened his mouth, but no words escaped. Safiya was still staring down at the leg before turning her attention back to Alex, who was turning in circles, rubbing his face with his hands, and muttering under his breath. They each needed a moment. Grayson started to make some adjustments to his clothing. The weather was warm here, even though the sea drafted up a salty breeze. Jack even removed his hoody. Underneath he wore a t-shirt which read, *Amon Amarth*. He had recently purchased the latest album and had actually been listening to it on the journey to Blissful Hills. When he caught sight of the logo, a sudden feeling crept over him; he might never hear the music again. Then, he thought about Lucy. If she was still stranded in that hell-dimension back there? Poor Lucy. If he made it back home, what would he say? To the police? To her parents? That she…what? Went missing? Not suspicious at all.

Safiya turned back slowly and was the first one in the group to speak again, 'guys. Erm, could you check something for me?'

Grayson eyed her curiously and nodded. She looked worried. Extremely worried. It was readable that she was the kind of strong, independent woman that was not quick to show her emotions, especially in a situation like this. Now *she* was pale.

'What's up?' before Grayson could ask, she grasped hold of his hand and held it to her wrist. He gave her a look of astonishment, like a fox caught in the headlights. 'What…'

'Can you feel anything?' Safiya asked, her lips trembling so much that she had to bite down them.

Grayson shook his head, 'Nothing, why?' and then he realised, 'Oh. Erm.' Without asking, he moved his other hand up to the side of her neck and pushed ion slightly with two fingers. If anyone knew what he was doing at this moment, it was him. At this, Grayson was a professional.

'Hell, kiddo,' he finally said, almost laughing, 'you ain't got no pulse.'

Clearly, Safiya needed a minute. Then, Jack thought that come to think of it, she had looked extremely pale since they landed. It was warm, she was scared, and she was not sweating. Not at all. She looked… clammy.

'Am…am…am I dead?' Safiya uttered, leaving her mouth open wide enough to catch flies.

Grayson wanted to respond. He wanted to say something sarcastic, make her laugh, or smile. Nothing happened. He looked at Jack. Jack shrugged.

'I…guess? Who's to say we ain't all dead.'

And Safiya just replied with, 'Huh', and that was that. Safiya Meadows had accepted death with all the grace that she had her entire life.

'All right, all right, come on. Gather up.' Grayson called them all in. Standing in a circle, he felt it was time they get moving. They had shared some strange experiences and the time had passed. They were not going to get it back. The sun was rising on a new day in a new world. They needed a way home.

'We gotta get moving. I get it. Some messed up things been happening. Okay. But we need a plan. A direction. Anyone seen the old man?' When they all shook their heads, he continued, 'That's fine. I'm sure he'll pop up. I'm not sure if we got drugged, or this is all some sick reality show and we ain't guessed it yet, but we gotta follow some sort of plan. I gotta feeling there's more monsters and ghouls out here than we seen so far. Ya' ll got any ideas what to do next?'

A sea of vacant expressions.

'Right. Me neither. I guess we head north. Dunno why, just feels right. If that's the rising sun. and considering this place works the same, then we cross the bridge and head that 'a way,' Grayson pointed to the lighthouse, 'might even be a soul up in that tower what can help us. I figure sooner or later Gandalf will appear and show us the way to Mordor. As for now, we got Lazarus here,' pointing to Safiya, he then looked at Alex, '…And Harry Potter over there. And I'm clearly Wolverine. That's enough firepower to keep us safe right? Chins up. We're gunna be alright. What about you, kid? Any hidden talents suddenly emerged?'

'I,' Jack looked out over the bridge, 'know where we are. I mean I haven't been here before. At least, I don't think so, but I know this place. It's all in here,' he tapped his forehead with one finger, 'like a map that's slowly unfurling. There're places nearby and people. I can see pictures of people and their names, but, ah, it's all jumbled up.'

'Okay. Might be you hit your head hard, but we'll keep an eye on it.' Grayson laughed.

'No.' Jack grimaced. 'Seriously. So, see that lighthouse? It's called…*Storm's Rest*. And, and, like fifteen or so miles that way, there's a town. With people. And food. And, and…' A sharp bolt of pain drew across his temples, ricocheting with fire around his brain, before Jack stopped trying to picture anything at all. What was the worst thing about being trapped in another world, far from home? No paracetamol. Slowly, the fire eased, and the pain started to subside.

'Okay, then,' Grayson smiled and clapped his hands together, turning towards the bridge, 'let's go to, what did you say? Storm's Crest?'

One by one, the group edged their way over the side of the cliff and down onto the rickety, shambolic bridge. It wavered and sank with each new member.

'Hey,' Alex called from the rear, trying not look down through the cracks, 'Who's Harry Potter?'

Storm's Rest

ᚱ

Clever thinks himself the guest who jeers a guest, if he takes to flight.
Knows it not certainly he who prates at meat, whether he babbles
among foes.

- *Hávamál*

-

There would be a taboo now around the opening of doors. None of the group wished to be the first to step through it. One small foot over the threshold and poof, who knows where they might end up? Grayson looked back at Jack, as if their newly found walking dictionary knew what awaited. The only reply Grayson got was a heavy shrug, as though the questions had already become tedious. The kid had a gift; they all did. It was time to utilise whatever they had if they were to escape this new prison. Grayson stepped forward. A hot breath of air warmed him through to the bone. Shuddering, he suddenly felt a modicum of happiness well up inside of him. Sea air can be a nice getaway from the tedium of everyday life, but it sure did work its way into the joints quickly. He looked up and saw a trawling spiral staircase wrap its way around the inside of the tower like a stone vine.

Alex was the last to reach the top. Grayson wondered about the man's health. He seemed to be panting as though he had run a marathon. Bent over, scooping up air like it was going out of fashion. Grim had mentioned different times, different worlds before. Did he mean different dimensions, like the Twilight Zone? Or different periods of time. Same world, different eras? Alex did not even know Harry Potter. Sure, it was close to sixty years old now, maybe older. The original films were at least celebrating a fiftieth sometime soon. Maybe longer. And that phone. What sort of phone used a screen? Let alone an aerial?

'Alex.' Grayson leaned over by the top of the stairs, not asking a question, more demanding answers. 'What year is it?'

The man in the pinstripe suit looked from Safiya to Jack, then finally up at Grayson, 'Year? Seriously? Again? It's 1995.' Then, seeing a collection of worried glances from the group, added, '…Right?'

The top of the lighthouse was an open expanse, with tall, wide archways, looking out over a sea covered in the white foamy waves of an approaching storm. In its centre was a large brazier, in which it had been assumed, a fire would be lit, to light the way for approaching vessels. In these early morning hours, with the sun rising, there was no need to light to warn of danger. The cliffs were visible for miles and miles to sea. But it had not been lit last night though. Judging by the old flakes of cinder and ash, it had been lit for some weeks now.

'I don't think you're right,' Jack said. 'I don't think you're wrong, either. I think we are outside of our concepts of time now. In my world. Our world…' He paused for a moment, '…In my time it's 2026. Soon to be 2027. If I'm not mistaken, Grayson, you're from somewhere further along, right? Like the future?'

Grayson smiled a new, tenuous smile. Had Jack impressed him? 'Yea. Spot on, kid. Although, I'd prefer it if we referred to your time as the past. Seeing as I'm the only one who's seen the dark future, seems fairly likely that I'm most in the know on current affairs. You're all history. I'm the curator who's wound up with his museum coming to life.'

Jack shook his head, 'I've seen the film, Grayson. He's a security guard, not a curator. Don't start searching for things in your past and making out as if they're yours. I can almost bet the biggest thing you invented was a lie to cover your tracks.'

'All right,' Safiya sliced through the tension she could see slowly boiling around them. 'Put your cocks away. No past. No future. No arguing about who's time is right. Enough of that. It's going to give me a headache. I'm from 2020. Just. January 2nd.' She turned to look at Jack dead in the eye, as if there were something immediate about that year, or the next, that stood out for him. She would have caught it in his eye if there was. And while he did want to, he held his breath as best he could. Still, Safiya saw something there. Sympathy?

She, Alex and Jack waited, until Grayson realised that…'Oh, my turn? Erm, 2071. Yeah. I'm ain't gunna regale you with modern wonders and technology. Let's just say it ain't 1995 anymore. Far from it. You thought the virus was a bad time. Man, you are in for some bumpy years, if we ever get back.'

And, I suppose, that's why none of you have recognised me yet. Good. Let's keep things informal, then. Grayson looked back over the edge of the lighthouse and tried to picture his childhood. Just for brief second. *What had Jack's time been like? Do I remember it all correctly? It all seems so grey and washed over, like a painter mixing his pallet.*

'I think after everything we have seen in the past day, maybe discerning whose timeline is better shouldn't be on the agenda,' Grayson said. 'There are matters at hand need attending to. So, kid, where to? I figured somewhere quiet away from the breaks might put your mind at ease. I don't wanna spend longer in this place then is absolutely necessary. You get me?'

Jack nodded. He leaned back, placing his shoulders into the stone between the windowed archways of the lighthouse and closed his eyes to the world.

****

Safiya had been sleeping. When she awoke, she saw Grayson standing beside her, still gazing out into the ocean, looking like some figure from a Victorian painting. A lover awaiting his wife's return from sea.

'What was that?' Safiya asked, rubbing one eye with a balled hand.

'There's a man,' Grayson replied, looking down, 'seen him approaching from over that way. Taking his time. Looks old. Just him. I was gunna wake you when he got closer.'

The door to the lighthouse closed again, below, and the soft patter of footsteps echoed their way up the winding staircase. After many more minutes than it had taken them to do so, the footsteps reached the last two-dozen and the man from below began to whistle. It was not a tune any of them recognised and it made the whole situation more outlandish, more far-cry and more sinister.

'Oh, my.' He was a rotund, stout, and portly fellow. In every sense of every word. Almost as wide as he was short. With a thick grey moustache and long, wispy sideburns beneath a woollen, grey cap, the man stared at each of them in both awe and fear.

'Please, av got na' a penny on me,' the man said. 'You can 'ave the tower for the night, I'll make a haste elsewhere.'

'Where are you from?' asked Jack, moving closer to the man, who was still fanning himself gratuitously with his handkerchief and moping the profuse sweat pouring from under his woollen cap.

Blustered, the man replied, 'Name's Muldoon. Haggart Muldoon. Muldoon Clan. I'm no from Skane. From a wee hamlet, just south o'the rocks. Me and mine. Just the hounds. Wife did'ne make it through the pestilence. Buried her in the back here. She loved this tower. Shame she ne'er saw it glow again.'

'Skane,' Jack repeated the word, 'that's the City. Big walls. A huge cathedral? Run by, ah…' he rubbed at his temples again, '… Alderman…'

'Blackdaw. Aye,' Muldoon said, 'that's the one. Take it you boys, and lady, are from the north? Ave'ne seen nothing but corpses come down from the hills in two summers. Bless The Architect there's still people living there. Got me a son up in Kinrith. At least he was. Left with the Legions, last winter, a'put an end to all this death. In truth, I di'ne believe he'll come back.'

'What's *The Architect?*' Asked Jack, who seemed utterly enamoured with this man who had wandered in out of the cold.

Muldoon stared at Jack through squinted eyes, 'You, er, you're no from the north, are ye?'

'I'm from the north, of England,' Jack answered, which received nothing but yet another vacant expression from Muldoon.

'Nay a place I've heard of,' Muldoon eyed each of them suspiciously, 'but, I'm no one for judging a stranger's greeting. Nay prone to xenophobia. Anyways, around here, we're firm believers in The Order. Tha's what my sons died for. Wha' my pa died for. The Architect is the highest Order in the universe. The Lord of Heaven. And we take it to heart tha' we each must play our part in the fight against The Adversary, and his many wily minions. I was Architect's Voice in the Temple for twenty-five years, until the great pestilence came. I keep his lighthouse gong and guide all vessels to a worthy shore.'

'Right,' Alex half-laughed, half-acknowledged Muldoon's words, 'so it's like a cult. A religion?'

'Watch yer tongue, son,' Muldoon fired a quick glance at Alex. 'Lesser words have seen men strung up by their entrails and fed to the kraken.'

'Kraken?' Alex turned white, but Muldoon carried on, ignoring his complaints.

'It's the only religion around here, although we have our differences in theological matters. I for one, have accepted the old ways, of my pa and his pa before him. That The Architect sent the Hanged-Man in his glory to show how we might escape the coming darkness of Ragnarök. While there are those who believe the Hanged-Man to be The Architect's only begotten Son, sacrificed to us so that we might be free from the torments of an everlasting fire. And then there are those barbarians far to the south. Islanders. Who believe that the Hanged-Man is chained to a rock for eternity with crowds eating his liver, for his crime o' stealing holy flame from heaven.'

A moment of awkward silence gripped the room. Jack felt the air grow tighter and thicker. Alex had waved away Muldoon's words as the ramblings of a madman and taken it upon himself to attend to the brazier in the centre of the room. Jack took in every word, adding into the collection of lore, history and geography that was knitting together through the synapses in his mind, one by one, with much ache and pain. Safiya did not want to hear anymore of religion. She had heard enough for an age and had stopped paying Muldoon any notice some time ago; she just wanted food and a good night's rest to figure all this out, in her own way.

'Tell me, old timer,' Grayson interrupted the *lesson*, 'we're looking for an old man, wears a big hat. Got on eye. Smells a little like tree-bark. You seen him? Led us through here and then disappeared.'

Muldoon looked up at Grayson as though the man had simultaneously saved his life and taken a huge dump on his front porch.

'Are ye tossin' with an old man, son?' Muldoon barked. 'I'll no 'ave blasphemy under this roof. Tell me wha' the Hanged-Man would want with *you*?'

'The Hanged-Man?' Jack asked. 'He calls himself Grim. He led us through a doorway. Brought us to this place so that we rescue some *Skulla* of his. Some girl. She was taken by a...*creature*...called Loki.'

Muldoon made a wavering gesture with his left hand above his head, holding the smallest and index digits out, shaking them vigorously. 'Blessed be. You followed him? Truly? By The Architect's Holy House, I shall take you wherever you need to go. Aye, aye. Aye. Let me return to my house and, I-I-I'll fetch the cart. We shall go east. I shall take ye to the Black Monks and the Servants of Fire. And th...*stoop*...'

Muldoon trailed off mid-sentence, throwing himself over to where Alex was standing and batting his hand away from the brazier with all his might. A small box of matches skittered over the stone floor and cast its contents across the tower.

'Fool,' Muldoon cried, slapping Alex with a he, sweaty open palm. The sound ricocheted adown the staircase of the lighthouse. 'No fire. Ne'er fire again.'

'W-W-W...' Alex started.

'No, son,' Muldoon exhaled a long, rancid breath into his face and returned, wagging his finger at each of them, 'no fires. No flames larger than a man can crawl through. Lest the wraiths come. Through the fire.'

And with those last words, he stormed towards the stairs and could be heard cursing and muttering under his breath down and down. The door slammed behind him and Grayson watched the old man bracing against the wind, heading back into the trees.

'Uh, what the actual fuck was that?' Alex rubbed his cheek. His brow so furrowed, Grayson thought it would leave a permanent mark. 'Fucking idiot, mate. Its freeing in here. Wanted a fire.'

The others let Alex get on with his business, which was now picking up each individual matchstick, whilst uttering a different curse word, such as 'wanker', 'tosser', 'prick', 'nonce', and 'pillock'. He was busying himself doing so, without realising that sometime into his venture, that the others had given up on waiting for Muldoon to return in a hurry and had started one by one, to fall fast asleep. Except for one. Grayson had his eyes closed and by all appearances was dead to the world. A trick he had perfected time and time again. A lure. A trap. Something about Alex's nature was curious. It intrigued his anthropological mind to see such a reckless and utterly self-centred object at work within the world. Grayson was entirely convinced that the man went against all levels of self-aegis, when Alex began to carry on with his previous task, regardless of Muldoon's warnings.

'Stupid old bastard,' Alex muttered, scratching the tip of the match against the sandpaper of the box, 'cults and weirdos. Had enough of them. I'm bloody freezing here.'

Grayson felt he could either stop the man from doing something potentially dangerous and catastrophic, or he could see where the events brought them. Maybe he was truly intrigued or, maybe he was just a little bored of waiting for Muldoon. Either way, Grayson simply sat and watched as the match sparked and a small flame dropped into the brazier, catching light of the remnants of oil and kindling, before erupting into an open conflagration.

You Were Warned

ᛉ

She that war remembers, the first on earth, when Gullveig
they with lances pierced, and in the high one's
hall her burnt, thrice burnt, thrice brought her forth, oft not seldom;
yet she still lives.

- Völuspá

When Muldoon returned, the lighthouse was quiet. Giving off a warming glow, the brazier has worked its magic, sending Grayson, Jack, Safiya, and Alex into a restful, deep slumber. Muldoon had noticed the fire from some way off, crackling away in the afternoon sun. Even at its zenith, with both suns blazing, the solar hue hardly managed to penetrate the thick, almost smog-like cloud covering the sky. It appeared to hang above powerless, dying and doomed. An orange omen of pestilence and death. Muldoon hitched the cart to the post, as quickly as he could, cursing and spluttering as he did. With awkward steps, he flung himself from the cart and hobbled towards the small hut by the rear of the tower. It was a tool house, and inside he needed only one thing.

The door of the lighthouse burst open, banging against the inside wall. Muldoon's portly figure raced, as fast as his body would allow, leaping two steps at a time. He only had to stop once, half way up the stairs, to stop the pain in his chest. A feat made all the more difficult by the cumbersome wooden bucket in his hand, which was filled with sand from the beach. Up and up he wobbled, until finally he clambered out onto the landing of the tower, nearly spilling the sand over the floor.

He was shouting now, 'Bloody fools. I warned ye. I warned ye, I did. I warned ye.'

Jack arose from his sleep, jerking one foot out in front of him. The movement caught Muldoon by complete surprise and at the final hurdle, he tripped and fell, sending the wooden bucket cascading sand over the tower floor. It sounded like rain, beating down on a glass roof. Muldoon, ignoring the pain in his thigh where he landed, sat up, failing to scold Jack. There was no time. The fire needed to be put out. But how? That's when the group awoke. Not to the cacophony of the spilt bucket, but to the banshee's wail emanating from inside the brazier.

****

'Oh, Heavenly Master, preserve us.' Muldoon turned pale.

Jack flipped onto his side and saw the portly shape kneeling before the brazier, rocking back and forth on his knees, in supplication to The Architect; that he might find mercy in his heart to spare what was coming.

'W-W-What's happening?' Jack used the round wall of the tower to lift himself up, kicking Grayson beside him.

The prisoner's eyelids flipped up. Another wailing scream eked its way from the flames. It sounded as if it were closer now. Louder. Safiya and Alex took a few moments to come to, before all four of them were awake, watching Muldoon, still rocking like a madman beneath the brazier.

'Please, no,' he cried, then rocked back onto his hands and crawled from the fire as the final scream exploded from the brazier and a black, skeletal hand shot from the flames.

****

The hand took hold of the edge of the stone brazier, curling its ancient fingers around. Jack felt a huge hole open where his stomach had been. He looked at Muldoon for guidance. Anything. What should they do? And it was clear from the pallid, gormless expression on Muldoon's face, that the time to stop this madness had passed.

'No. No. No fire. No fire.' Rambling, like a Neanderthal, Muldoon rolled over onto his stomach and tried to belly crawl his way towards the stairs.

The black, skeletal hand emerged further from the fire, bringing with it a forearm, and a shoulder, draped in a tattered grey, patchwork cloak. Farther and farther, the hand extended, bringing more of the once disembodied wraith into view. It was a ghastly thing of obsidian skin, mouldy, ancient clothing and a face which seemed more feline than human. Long sharp canines protruded from the upper jaw, hanging over the lips. Jet coloured cheeks and forehead bulged under the pressure of thin strips of bone and sinew. When the wraith had almost fully emerged from the fire, it opened its mouth. No words escaped. The sound that came was so high-pitched that the others heard only the tail end of the screech. It was as if someone had blown a dog-whistle close by. Muldoon let out a terrible, gut-wrenching bellow, as the skeletal hand swiftly took hold of his upper thigh and dug sharp nails into his flesh. With the strength of ten men, the wraith snatched back, dragging Muldoon up and into the brazier. The man screamed and screamed, but the flames did not sear his flesh or even catch his clothes. Instead, he escaped the touch of the fire and was screaming because he was being pulled, limb by limb down into the depths of the inferno.

Safiya yelped something incomprehensible, as Alex pushed past her, flinging himself down the first set of stairs. Then, he was gone. Safiya moved towards the brazier and reached out a hand, but Muldoon had already been pulled so far down, that only his right forearm remained visible. The fire was red-hot and Safiya recoiled. Seeing no other option, she followed Alex. Jack looked at Grayson. The prisoner shook his head and they bid Muldoon a silent farewell, before sprinting down the stairs after Safiya, three steps at a time.

Bursting out through the lighthouse door, everyone was panicked. Alex turned right and ran until the cliff edge fell away and he was forced to retreat back on his hands, scraping his plans across the jagged rocks. Safiya headed towards Muldoon's cart. It had been pulled by two chestnut mares, who had become irritated and spooked by the noises, but had not bolted just yet. Grayson and Jack left last. A violent, blood-curdling wail followed them out. They were not sure whether the wraith had followed or even left the confines of its fiery domain, and neither looked back to check.

Grayson waved his hands forward, shouting, 'Get in the cart.'

Jack was running so fast that a sharp stitch ripped through his side, forcing him to bend over. Alex reappeared, with bloodstained palms, raving about something he had seen in the waters of the sea in his brief glimpse over, into the blue-green abyss. They ignored him and one by one climbed atop the cart. Jack took it upon himself to snatch the reins, giving the horses one quick snap. Whinnying, the beasts rolled without question for their master, grinding the wooden wheels over the rocky earth. Bumping away, the cart drove away from the lighthouse with all the speed that Jack could muster from the mares. The world was different now, in the light of day. And though it might not last long, the sunlight which fought against the now-brown clouds, pushed hard. Jack felt the ultraviolet rays reach his forehead. A brief, but sweet relief from the nightmare.

****

They had rolled on for almost a half-hour, before Jack decided to try his best to rein in the horses. He snagged in the leather straps and felt his arm tug to the right. Ahead, houses had begun to appear. At first, they had seen only one or two farms, littered across open pastures. Then, the houses became closer together and even stacked in rows, far over the fields. The cart pulled further to the left, nicking its wheels against roots and rock.

In the air, a swift and deafening quake shook the world. It seemed to come from nowhere, swooping down from the sky, bringing a plume or cloud in its trail. Not one of them saw the creator of such a calamitous sound and yet they all heard the thundering roar of its shadow.

Jack pulled back and the mares pulled again. Jack shouted something unintelligible and felt the leather pull back so hard that...snap. Jack was thrown backwards into Safiya. There was a terrible breaking of wood and suddenly the cart was moving independent of its drivers. The two chestnut horses had broken free and the cart was sailing over the field at tremendous speed.

'Jump.' Jack cried, pushing back at Safiya. 'Jump. For God's sake, jump.'

Alex was the first. He landed on his bruised palms and collapsed. Safiya leapt, landing on her feet, but felt a long stabbing pain deep into her knees. Grayson, almost shoving Jack off the cart, rolled as he touched the floor, with Jack somehow behind him, landing on top. Jack's elbow drove into Grayson's chest, but compared to the pain in his back, Grayson barely felt the blow. The horses were gone, headed back towards the sea and once more the group was alone and trapped in their unknown isolation.

****

'Enough,' Alex stood up, then forced his foot into a rock the size of a small football. There was a heavy this, followed by a tirade of curses, as Alex threw himself around in a madman's bluster.

Safiya tried to put her hand on Alex's arm to calm him down, but this only seemed to unfortunate him more.

'No. Fuck this, mate,' he barked. 'Fuck all of this. Fuck fucking doors. Fuck the fucking undead. Fucking zombies. Fucking old one-eyed men. Fuck old Scottish peados. Fuck that fucking, whatever was in that fucking fire. Fuck all of this. I've had e-fucking-nough.'

'Alex, calm down,' Safiya's tone changed, the way a mother might speak to an ill-tempered child, 'we're all going through the same hell.'

'No,' Alex cut her off, 'no we aren't. Look at you all. What? A student. A mother? A con? Do you even know who I am? I'm Alex-fucking-Wormwood.'

Each of them stared at him with blank faces.

'Seriously?' he spat, 'Oh, of course, cos you're from the future, right? And I'm just some old idiot. Well, I know what this is. I've watched TV. This is some CIA black ops high strangeness. We've all been dosed and now this is some test. It's a test. A crazy medieval video game. I'm just in a dream. Yeah. A dream.'

When no one said anything, he took that as his sign to continue, 'Alex-fucking-Wormwood. You know where I was the other day, before that fucking plane crash, mate? Huh? Vegas. Headline act. Alex Wormwood. I have sixteen books out. I have my own internet website, mate. Just for me, on the internet. I have three cars, two houses, and a bank account with more numbers than any of you have seen. Head-line-fucking-act. Vegas.'

Safiya saw his face was turning from a deep maroon into a sapphire blue, but when she tried to hold her hand out again, Alex swatted it away with such force that it left a mark.

'Get off me, mate,' he spat again, 'I'm out of here. Fuck this. Fuck you. And fuck you, Jack. Huh. You the ringleader? You're the first one I met, mate. You seemed like a druggie to me. Who do you work for?'

'You know,' Grayson pointed his finger towards Alex, who was pacing back and forth, eyeing each of them one by one, 'I knew a guy who cursed as much as you. Didn't end too great for him, you hear?'

Alex span, staring into Grayson with such force that it seemed that his eyes might begin to fire lasers, 'and, I don't know you either, mate, but fuck you...'

Alex held his palm out, as if to tell Grayson to stay back, when there was the same curious rumble as before and Grayson was hurled back with enough force to knock him off his feet. The sound of the blast reverberated across the field, sending carrion birds squawking into the air.

Jack ran to Grayson and helped him up, but before they could confront Alex, he had taken off over the field.

'I'll go after him.' Safiya said, taking up a jog.

There was no time to change her mind, she was gone. They both were. As soon as the dust settled, another murder of crows landed nearby, beginning to feast on something in the grass.

'Aww, hell,' Grayson nursed his stomach with both hands. 'Now ain't the time to be scooby-doo-ing this situation. We should stick together.'

'They'll be back,' Jack said, 'I hope; we should stay close by. Take a look around. Maybe we'll stumble across Grim.'

'Sure. Where is this place, anyhow?' Grayson puffed his chest and exhaled a long groan.

Jack searched his mind and felt the map unfurl a little more, 'Solsten. A farming community. There's a Temple here. Maybe Grim is in there. Come on.'

Solsten

ᚼ

Mim's sons dance, but the central tree takes fire at the resounding
Giallar-horn.
Loud blows Heimdall, his horn is raised;
Odin speaks with Mim's head.

- Völuspá

Not a soul remained inside the town. Perhaps it was
a little too generous to offer it the title of 'town';
more of a large village. It held nothing but peasant
houses, now smouldering ruins. A simple, wooden temple,
now littered with corpses and decaying flesh. Several larger
houses surrounded by swathes of land, that had begun to
crumble under the fires of whatever large destructive element
had bombarded their roofs, whilst laying waste to the crops,
leaving only handfuls of barley, surrounded with blackened
earth. What had happened in Solsten was nothing short of a
cataclysm. It appeared to Jack as though a nuclear weapon had
been dropped less than a mile away. The resulting chemical
blast having obliterated man and building within seconds. Of
course, it had not been a nuclear event, far from it. No
irradiated ash lay around in heaps. The bodies had not been
reduced to cinders and remained, rotting in the streets. A fair
few had indeed been charred beyond any human

comprehension, so that they resembled barbecued meat rather than one living, breathing person.

Grayson appeared to find the situation less horrifying than Jack. His mind had attuned to a taste far more inquisitive of death than fearing. As he mulled around Solsten's streets, he would stop and observe the carnage, as a scientist might observe a new found specimen; awe and intrepid thoughts calculating just what immense power had rolled across these streets, just hours before. They had heard what they had wanted to hear and negated to collect in their minds what they failed to comprehend. If Jack were to say the words to himself, it meant it was real. That these troubling woods and fields held more than man and beast. That horrors unimaginable lurked just outside his line of sight. In the depths of the night and even in the brightest of days. Had it not been enough that he must bear witness to the primordial terrors that clambered their way through the flames and that he had to watch, immovable in his dread, as the wraiths tore their way through Muldoon, then to drag him back into their hellish inferno. Into a realm of, God only knew, what lay.

Jack leapt from his skin, as a timber roof fell apart to his left, dropping its rafters onto old, kindling furniture, with such force that the front door to the house burst from its hinges, into the street. Somewhere close by, he heard something similar happen again, and again, and again. Soon, Solsten would be levelled. The great equaliser had come in the daylight to rob men and women of precious life. As for what form had it come? Jack had listened from the lighthouse and heard its screeching wings descend and still he would not believe. He had heard the rumblings of dread-creatures rising from the ground in waves and he had closed his mind to the possibilities of Hell.

'Look here,' Grayson called from across the street. He was holding a charred skull in one hand and with his free hand had begun to feel the soft tissue around the eye sockets. 'This was a flash fire. See? Skin done burnt in less than a second. Only the upper mantle of the epidermis has been scorched. I could take a guess at how, but I'd no doubt be wrong.'

Jack stared into the lidless, eyeless sockets and could not help but try to picture what those orifices had witnessed in their remaining few moments in this world. A fire so dark and so intense in its heat that not one of them had seen a flame on the sky. Not until the early evening, as the houses began to ignite had they seen a speck of conflagration.

Black-fire? he thought, *Does such a thing exist? Even here?*

Even after all the destruction. Something had to have come. Something or somethings with legs and hands and opposable thumbs, able to do intricately and delicately place these fleshy totems on their poles, and strong the still-breathing from their own entrails, across doorways and arches. It had been the last thing he had noticed, and this made the thought even more terrifying. As though the images of human remains paraded over the houses like party-decorations had been only an afterthought. The icing on the cake. Maybe even just for fun. All the destruction had been just a taste. It was only Grayson who understood. It was desecration. It was not enough to enter a graveyard and remove a corpse; you had to place the head between the legs as well when you were done. Leave your mark. These creatures, these demons, thought with a human mind. An evil, malformed, human mind. It just made it all so much more insidious. A bear will attack a camp and possibly eat the campers, but he will not place their entrails around the picnic table, like some Hell-bound buffet, for the unlucky hiker to stumble across come sunrise.

Grayson found himself drawn towards a dilapidated house, still glowing with white-hot embers. Every so often, a puff of air would blow flecks of burning ash into the air, or the crackling logs would split and cough up a phlegm of smoke. A familiar sense of darkness blew a cloud over his mind, pulling him towards the bottom floor of the house. A scent of madness on the air. It intrigued him. Called to him. He had not felt this kind of surge in a long time. It was the darkness whispering to him again, after all these years. Closer. Closer. Until, he literally stumbled upon it. A corpse. Shattered and charred. Half melted into the wooden boards. Grayson stopped, stooped, and stared at the scorched remains. His heart fluttered. Not for the sight of the crumbling bones and flesh, but because once more elation soared inside him. The possibilities of death. The opportunity which had laid itself before him, almost on a plate.

It was some time before Grayson could pull himself away from the corpse. Holding out his palm, he peered down at the silver necklace, still wrapped with strips of blackened skin. When he began to walk away, he, just for a second, believed he might finally have gone mad.

'Ahhh,' a voice, not from inside his own head, spoke, 'the death-whisperer. I'm so glad to have finally found you, wandering like a lost lamb through this dying place.'

It could have been madness. If he were in his own world, Grayson might feel the need for concern. In this place, stranger things had happened than disembodied voices. But of course, that would be all too acceptable. Nothing so simple existed here. Turning, Grayson found himself face to face with the staggering remains he had just, so ghoulishly, robbed. A corpse spoke to him with a voice like two stones being rubbed together. Scratching and grating.

'Interesting,' Grayson eyed the corpse from head to toe, not fully figuring out just how it was standing on those twisted legs.

'Mr. Grayson, I presume?' the corpse's mouth twitched with every syllable, but the black tongue did not move. Instead, the teeth merely chattered as the lipless jaw swung up and down, imitating speech. The real voice came from someplace far within and far below. Inside the hollowed optical nerves, flickers of that old blue flame sparked.

'I don't believe we have had the privilege of an introduction,' Grayson drawled in his southern-state accent.

The corpse made a gurgling sound, which might have been laughter, 'We have met many times. I have always had the pleasure of looking through your eyes when you sniffed the last inch of life from those men, women and children. Not that I am judging your past-times. I find the simplest of acts the most enjoyable. Unfortunately, this unwilling host is not viable as a temporary residence and I will have to depart soon; I would much appreciate if you would hear my offer?'

Grayson looked back over his shoulder. Jack was busy inspecting some fallen masonry some paces across the street.

'Go on.'

'Good man,' the corpse gurgled again. 'Forgive me if I make any presumptions, but let me say I know you perhaps better than you know even yourself. My offer is simple. Give up this foolish facade of the hero. Throw down your crusading sword, and in turn I shall give you not only leniency for your march against me, but I shall grant unto you, eternal life. You may remain in Altheim, or if you wish, return to your world, keeping the gifts I would bestow onto you. It is, as they say in your world, 'a no-brainer'.'

If the speaker, through with this corpse talked meant to or not, a poetic slather of brain matter oozed from the corpses head, making its way down the neck, until it slid out of view. Grayson watched, weighing in his mind both consequence and the outcome of satisfaction. What would he lose, really? Grim had told them very little and had not inferred whether they were even to make it home after his little quest had been fulfilled and his Skulla procured.

'Can I ask,' Grayson placed his hands on his hips, 'who you are?'

Gurgling became splattering of Stygian phlegm, spewing from the lipless mouth between gum-less teeth. 'You already know. I have been with you some many years; though. I will forgive your misgivings if you choose to still remain atheistic to my existence. It is my greatest gift, after all.'

Grayson huffed, 'the devil?'

Silence lingered, just for a moment, as the corpse seemed to think. 'I suppose so. Just one of many names, you see. I have been around some many years now. Humans and the like do love to name what they do not understand.'

'You're the one we met in the other place. The hel-place?' Grayson asked, giving a quick glance at Jack; still busy elsewhere. 'Loki. Right?'

'Pah,' the corpse spewed another globule of tar down its burnt chin, 'Loki is just a believer. He has his reasons for doing what he does, but in the end, he is mine. It is my will and only my will that bends and shapes these worlds. Loki serves me, just as Grim serves The Architect. How many worlds have you seen now? And how many do you believe are guided by a loving hand? No. I thought as much. You and I are kith and kin. We do not lie to ourselves like the others under a false godhead. No. We are unique. So, let me ask, Michael Grayson, will you follow?'

Jack gave the architecture one last kick before turning around. The fires were dying, slowly. Receding. No doubt the embers would smoulder for some time. They had to leave. There was nothing left here in Solsten. No trace of Grim. No sign of life to point them forward. They would have to meet back up with Safiya and Alex in the fields and try to make as much use of the coming dawn as they could. They should have slept tonight. Awoken with the sunrise not the sunset. Everything was easier in the light. But where was...

'Grayson?' Jack called, then hearing no reply, cupped his hands around his mouth and did so several more times, as he worked his way down the street, towards the ruined Nordic temple.

No reply. No sign of life to be seen. Nothing. Grayson had gone. Vanished. Jack was alone.

Vegvísir

↑

He with shields encompassed me, red and white, in Skatalund;
their surfaces enclosed me; him he ordained my sleep to break, who in
no place could be made to fear.

- Helreið Brynhildar

It was not hard to find Safiya and Alex; they had not wandered far. Jack picked up their trail and found the pair of them hiding out in the remains of an old farmhouse. Not a farmhouse, as Jack would have imagined. The roof was not thatched, but made of straw, with the occasional pebbling of slate. It was a simple, round hut, for all descriptions. Only the handful of medieval scythes, rakes, and a single broken plough placed this house above the rest. That, and it was one-eighth the size larger. Jack had to crush his way over scorched barley, feeling every crack of the plants beneath his boots. Every last motion of life leaving a dying world. Still, there was no sign of a human presence. Whatever had decimated the town had done so quickly and with utmost prejudice against every soul there. Jack heard a pair of horses, maybe a field off, and thought it might be the mares they had rode in on. It did not matter. Long, demonic screeches had forced Jack to shelter behind the broken plough as he watched more of the wraiths glided over the edges of the dry-stone wall separating the fields, before the horses were silenced. *Wraiths*, never in his life had he imagined he would see anything as utterly horrifying enough to make him pray for a swift and painless death. Jack considered them as kites, dancing, caught up in a gale. Their tattered robes and obsidian skin were stains against the dawning light. To say it was morning meant something else entirely here. No baking sun to warm the bones. A dying sun for a dying land.

It was, surprisingly, Alex who greeted Jack first. The man, perhaps ten years his older, threw his arms over Jack's shoulders and embraced him tightly.

'I'm sorry, mate. I didn't mean to go off on one. You know? It's...it's, just it's this place. I can't handle it. I just want to go home, mate. You know?' Alex had been crying. A slightly lighter shade of skin was visible on his cheekbones.

Jack nodded and implied that all was forgiven. It was hard on them all. How could it be anything other than difficult? But then, that was life, at the end of all things.

'Hey,' pulling on her shoulder, Jack woke Safiya from a feverish dream, 'Grayson's gone. We have to go. We can't stay here.'

****

Sometime, as the orange celestial glow began to creep farther towards the horizon, the group found themselves walking downhill. Jack had heard the fruitless whinging of the horses and had tried to put the image of them out of his mind; how they had been left as sacrificial lambs to the slaughter of those banshees from the fire. What world would allow such creatures to exist? What disease had so crippled this realm to allow nightmares to roam free, unchecked, raping the land? What curse touched even the sacred and hallowed flames?

'Guys?' It was Alex who spoke.

They had meandered downhill and onto the small slither of land between cliff and sea. It would not be right to call it a beach. A beach conjured images of ice cream, sun, and sandy shores. There was sun there, but it slowly died. There was sand there, but it was a dark, Stygian colour, more suited to the grave than the break between surf and turf.

****

'What in the world?' Safiya had spotted the same image, though it was not hard to see. Once it was pointed out to Jack, the sight was obvious. How had they only just noticed it?

A ship. Not some medieval knarr, or Nordic longship, as Jack would expect in a world so ancient. No, this was a modern warship. Modern in a relative term, as it happened. It had to be close to six-hundred feet long, maybe more. The only comparison Jack had to attune the ship to was an old image of the Titanic. Hulls of steel and wrought iron. This was no more a ship than a behemoth of the tides. She was rusted. Damaged beyond repair. Had more holes in her belly than a stuck pig, but she was nonetheless impressive than she had been the day she vanished from sight.

'U-S-S Cy-clops,' Alex said, in a way that made him sound far simpler than he had ever done before. This was in part due to the fact that most of the lettering on the side of the iron leviathan had been covered in oceanic entropy. Barnacles, moss, and an odd translucent goo had become almost at one with the ship.

'Wait, this is, what? The USS Cyclops?' Jack decided he was moving in for a closer inspection.

They could reach the ship, if they wanted. Half of the port side hull had become beached far up onto the black sands. There was a hole through the edge of the hull so wide and so deep that they could have stood on each other's shoulders and merely walked inside of the pleased. No, there were three holes like this. Long, serrated holes. Tears. The steel from the hull bent inwards along each of the shards.

No gun did this, Jack thought, *something big, with claws dragged this ship inland.*

'So, what is it?' Safiya nudged Jack, but kept his voice a little quieter, not to alarm the Alex if Jack were to divulge anything too...haunting.

'I don't know,' he replied, bluntly, 'it's not from here, like *us*. It's from, *our* time. Or our *world.* I can't see anything around it. It isn't speaking to me.'

Those words sounded even stranger coming out than they had entering his head when he had thought of them. But this world was speaking to him. He knew almost everything about the realm of Altheim, and yet he could voice only little of it into reason that the others would comprehend. Safiya gave him a curious look because it was so understanding. She patted Jack on the shoulder and carried on towards the ship.

'Though,' Jack called after her, 'I don't think we should go in there.'

****

They had decided that Jack was right. Somehow, delving headfirst into what they could only assume to be a wartime vessel, possibly over a hundred years old, though that was relative, seemed to be a mere invite for trouble. They wanted, no, needed, to find Grim, and if possible, Grayson. He had simply vanished. Jack had searched through over a dozen houses and farmsteads before giving up hope. Whether by choice, or by force, Grayson had gone. Something in the way the prisoner behaved told Jack it was most likely the former. There was only one way home, the *key*. Loki, that serpentine demon, had the key, and Grim was the best shot at finding him. *It*.

It was decided they would travel as a three, never splitting, unless to empty their bladder. Alex took this safety precaution one step further and simply voided himself wherever he pleased. Said tried her best to keep as close to Jack as possible, and much to Jack's disheartened comprehension; this was because spending more than ten minutes near Alex made her skin crawl. However, Alex Krieger had managed to claw his way to the top of show business amazed Jack. This revelation came not because he believed Alex to be completely inept. The man was a Magician, at least here, in this world. In their world, what Jack decided to call the 'real world', Jack had never heard of Alex Wormwood. In the real world, Alex had no supernatural ability. He was just Alex. Which meant to rise as a renowned magician, he must carry some showmanship, some pizzazz.

Jack watched the man pissing against a tree, trying to drive away the spiders, and saw not even a glimmer of decorum. Amazing, really. Then, there was another reason Jack might not have heard of Alex Wormwood. I'm that scenario, Alex Krieger was dead. Or...missing. If so, what did that mean? Philosophically? Existentially? Did they never make it home? Did they make it home, in a different time? There was also the scenario that Jack tried his best to ignore. That Alex Krieger was from 1995, and he was a famous stage performer, and that Jack Schneider was from 2026; it was just that both worlds existed apart. The mere brief glimpse into that notion, made Jack quiver with an altogether higher level of fear.

Fields after fields, after fields after fields. All of nothing. Blades of grass trampled underfoot. Cold flesh, rotting, cast over spears, shields and war machines the likes of which Jack recognised not from his avid reading. Small, ballista-type mechanisms, smaller than a man's height. Each battlefield held several and each of these weapons was littered with a dozen or more corpses. What had happened to this world? Jack tacked his mind and found only fragments. When Safiya had asked him, Jack had explained it in the best and only way he could, because he himself was struggling to understand the voices in his head.

'This. All of this. It's all recent. The death. The destruction. Grim should never have brought us here. A long time ago, this world was something that he created, or at least populated. He would bring people here. People we would call *medieval*. From *our* history. From the looks of it, they stayed just as they were, trapped in a world of magic and monsters. I don't know exactly what Grim was trying to create. But everything I can see, in my head, is from then. Before the plague and the war. I can only see how this world used to be, not so long ago. In my mind, this world is beautiful. Full of life and love and magic. That demon we met in the other, darker world; this is all *his* doing. I think he wants to bring that world, here. Or at least bring all those monsters out of hiding. What kind of creature could possibly want something like that? What soul could willingly cause so much wonton destruction? So, if Grim brought us here to stop him, that means we are going to have to face him; and that terrifies me.'

So that was that. A weight had been lifted off Jack's soul. He had finally been able to express his thoughts. His migraines formed into a narrative that exposed the truth hidden deep within his mind; from a place he was unsure had truly existed.

****

As bewildering as it was, the USS Cyclops was not the only earthly visitor to Altheim. Alex had seemed to pick up a knack for finding lost things in and amongst the rubble of the world. Making their way off the beach, he had found three photographs, stapled together. They looked old. Very old. Ancient. And yet, the date on the Polaroids read, *1982*. The picture showed a Chinese couple on holiday. The urban sprawl of Los Angeles behind them, lit up with its famous one-word sign. As they continued north, Alex had pointed out a large cylindrical shape, high up on a hill. Jack had asked them not to go, but Safiya had agreed to follow Alex. She wanted to find food, and drink. All she had found in the farmhouse before was stale bread, a barrel of foul-smelling water, and a bushel of worm-riddled apples. Still, food was food.

As it happened, the cylindrical shape was only a fraction of the object's true size, but on impact, the plane had broken into a hundred separate pieces. The largest, being the cockpit, the smallest being the half-buried suitcase not far from where they stood.

'Do you think this is my plane? The one I crashed on, I mean?' asked Alex, and Jack had to stop him from climbing aboard. The cockpit looked as if nature had taken hold before even the Cyclops. As distorted as time was, Jack doubted this was Alex's ride.

'A lot of planes go down. I don't think it's safe to go crawling through wreckage, just to find your seat number.' Jack pointed his hand to one of the smaller pieces of fuselage, a few hundred yards away. Even in the poor sunlight, they were able to make out large rodent-kindred bipeds scuttling about the wreck.

'Oh, mate. What are those things?' Alex moved back, barging into Safiya, who gave a similar, disheartened glimpse at the creatures.

Jack waved his hand towards them, as if the pair might be encouraged to look away, 'I don't want to find out, but I think they're the original natives.'

They would continue walking, until the sun disappeared over distant, snow-covered hills far ahead. In the morning, they would walk some more. Sights of plague, famine, and war spread out like a Biblical bomb over the landscape. There were things that walked the day, with two legs, but they were not human. Things that stalked the night, speaking in hushed voices, but they were not people. Every village they passed, every town on the horizon had been scorched. Some had been so badly damaged that they did not even consider approaching them to find food or water. It would have been a futile effort. Nothing except stone and bones could have survived. Even the less-travelled paths they stuck to had seen horrors. Shackled corpses strung to trees. Caged animals left to rot in the sun. Carrion birds in their flocks of hundreds blacked the sky as they circled the forests, where men had died. Children and mothers lay where they had fallen of hunger and pestilence. The dying sun would rise and fall three times, before even the faintest glimpse of hope appeared. At the first sign of frost on the morning, Jack realised that he was seeing something he had not imagined he would. Greenery and life. Tiny, glistening buds dared to open on a misty, autumnal dawn.

Knock-Knock

ᛒ

All door-ways, before going forward, should be looked to;
for difficult it is to know where foes may sit within a dwelling.

- Hávamál

A crooked city, filled with crooked spires. It had exploded on the horizon, as though the entire fortified town had suddenly been dropped from the sky, landing in the snow-bitten valley.

Safiya, Alex, and Jack had followed what they had guessed to be a disused road, up into the hills, a long way's north from where they had arrived. Safiya had guessed that the journey had been close to fifty miles. It had taken three days. They were almost at the point where hunger begun to transform itself into a more dangerous foe. They had managed to heat the icicles which had clung to the old house in the hills where they spent the previous night and quench their thirst. When the stretch of road meandered its way to the apex of the hills, they had been met with the image of a gothic painting. Nestled between the high mountain of snow and a deep river running from the East, the crooked city was a vision from above. For the last maybe sixteen miles, it seemed as though the horrors of this world had ceased. Flora and fauna were abundant. Deer, hares, and songbirds moved through Altheim without molestation. The ground was unscorched by war and the pestilential bodies no longer littered the byways and hills.

'I have to say, this doesn't feel right,' Jack said, as they closed the door of the abandoned house and headed north, towards the crooked-looking city.

'Oh, for heaven's sake. Food, Jack. If we are ever going to find a way home, then this is it. The only place for a hundred miles and you want to avoid it? What about finding the old man? Where else would he be? It's like the Emerald City, see. The Wizard's down there. Come on, what's the big problem?' Safiya pushed him playfully in the shoulder and she and Alex continued on.

Jack waited a little longer before joining them. His eyes focussed on the city. Its crooked towers and misshapen spires did not look like a haven to him. Even in the morning light, something gothic and dark seemed to linger over the bent rooftops of the townhouses and towers which looked like blackened teeth against the snowy hills.

'Because it's all too…safe', Jack called after her. 'You don't burn down your own home in war. The safest place to be, is where the enemy sleeps. He never shits on his own doorstep. Or, maybe it's just because this place looks like Dracula's Castle?'

'Cool,' Safiya called back. 'Let's see if we can find Frankenstein.' And she ran off down the road.

****

Above the door, hung a sign, only half attached by a single iron link, so that it swung to and fro, creaking as it did. An ill omen. The poorly carved letters on the sign read:

Alex and Safiya just looked at Jack, waiting.

'Oh,' he said, finally understanding that beleaguered stare, 'it says, *The Withered Horse.*'

'Nice,' Safiya grimaced, 'what a creepy name. I suppose we just head inside? It sounds full. Maybe we can get some food. Or drink.'

****

There had been a ruckus coming from the tavern that the group could hear over a half-mile away. It sounded like a party. Every few minutes, between the odd sea-shanties and rapacious roads of delight, a triumphant cheer would emanate from the drinking hall. Jack decided that the building looked German. Something you might see at a Christmas Market or at an Oktoberfest pavilion. He had seen the real deal many times visiting his Oma in Munich, though he had never stayed for Oktoberfest. Perhaps if had, he would have recognised the songs and the cheers.

Jack pushed them door open and was hit in the face with a gust of warm air, filled with stale beer, rotting food and urine. Suddenly, everything stopped. All the songs and the jokes ceased, and the tavern dropped to a silent hush, as a dozen or more faces turned to see the newcomers.

'By the Hanged-One's beard,' one voice from the party cried.

Tables had been laid out in the typical dark-age fashion. Places at either end to create long rows, on which the guests could see one another face to face. Around the hall, shields and swords hung, so many and so tightly knit, that it appeared that the roof and rafters were made of steel. On the benches, twenty-six men and women stood to attention, holding drinking horns so close to their lips they could almost taste the ale.

'Guests!' came another cry, and the tavern exploded in cheers and merriment. Drinks were tossed and scraps of meat flung from tables. In the far corner, two hounds bayed a long howl.

Before any objections could be made, hands reached out from tables; men and women rushed to their sides and dragged the threesome down the benches. They sat them in the centre of the middle row. Jack felt a long cloak thrown over his shoulders, whilst Safiya was pushed towards the table, as two fearsome looking women started to pull and tug at her scalp, wrapping the length of brown hair into braids. Alex was thrust between two of the largest men he had ever seen. Their bulging arms and long beards almost obscuring him from view, as they handed him a long horn of ale and tossed a plate of food in front of him.

'Guests. Guests,' the voice cried again. It was coming from nearby. A heavy scuttling of wood on stone and the chairs were slung back and ever person in the room took their place.

****

It's a damn Mad Hatter's Tea Party. They're insane, Jack thought, but felt an aching in his cheeks spreading wildly. He was smiling. Safiya was smiling. Even Alex was beginning to forget about the horrors of Altheim. In here, the nightmare was, not *over*, but perhaps stalled. In time.

Another sea-shanty began, and the rows of warriors began to sway to the beat, some slapping their hands on the table as the chorus picked up. When the minutes ticked over and the song reached its final chord, they all gave a below of triumph and sat as one, echoing a mighty war-cry around the hall.

'Welcome friends, welcome,' a man, roughly the size of a small bear, raised his hands. He was sat in front of Jack, on either side, sat Safiya and Alex. 'It has been so long since we have entertained. Please, eat, drink, and be merry.'

Jack felt...odd. His mind began to work overtime. Something was *off* about this hall. He picked and poked at the nooks and crannies, but somehow could not understand why he felt so charged under his skin. What was it?

Then, Alex screamed. The man fell back off his bench, flipping the plate of food away from him, so that it turned in the air, landing facedown. Jack stared at the plate, because it was moving. One by one, the contents of the plate inched their way out from under the wooden bowl.

Maggots, jees, Jack moved back in his seat.

'What the fuck, mate?' Alex scrambled upwards and begun flapping his hands, patting down his pinstripe suit, just in case any of the little critters had managed to crawl onto his flesh.

Jack expected an uproar. He prepared himself for the entirety of the hall to either begin fighting or throwing food. Instead, there was silence. The bear-like man who spoke, simply stared at his own plate, lost in some trance like realm.

'What is this?' Jack furrowed his eyes, pushing his bowl of wriggling soup as far from his nose as he could manage, without tipping it over Safiya.

Finally, the bear-man spoke, with a glistening pool in the corner of his deep, blue eyes. 'I am so sorry. It has been a long time, since we have had guests. I...often forget.'

Some ways down the bench, a woman wailed. Another man near her started to sob uncontrollably. Just like that, the world had returned to its haunted state. It brought Jack back into reality. He looked at the hall again. Closer. Every plate, every bowl, and every place had been set with festering meat, rotting vegetables, and fish, that crawled with insects. Even the horns and jugs of ale seemed to be teeming with vulgar, spindly life. Above, in the rafters, huge spiders the size of two hand's breadth weaved thick, intricate webs. Between the swords, shields and axes, tiny, watery, black-eyed arthropods looked down, watching the intruders. Even the smell seemed to change. Jack no longer tasted the sweet ale on the air. All there was now, was the scent of latrines and decaying fruit.

Closing his eyes, Jack inhaled a rancid breath, counted backwards from three, and exhaled. He looked around. The hall was a very different place now. Its people were far from the illusion he had been offered when they first arrived. He looked at the bear-man in front of him. He was hunched over the table, head in his hands, but when he looked up, Jack saw an amalgamation of scar tissue, open, festering wounds and scabs. He was a corpse.

'What are you?' Jack asked, and the man sensed he was purveying through the trickery.

'My name is Brynjolf. This is my clan.' Brynjolf followed Jack's eyes. Decaying corpses, every one of them. Even...Safiya. Jack could see her in a new light. Just like the others. Safiya's once heart-achingly beautiful face was dry, flaking and sunken. Her pallor was a green tinge, eking with sickness. To her side, rows upon rows of desiccated, decomposing cadavers wailed and moaned in their eternal death.

'We are cursed,' Brynjolf stood, and the rest of the clan stood with him, 'all of us. Doomed to spend eternity with an undying hunger and thirst. We each fought and died, trying to free this land from the *demon*, and we failed. No longer do the Valkyries ride in Altheim. We shall never see the Halls of Valhalla.'

Several of the clan started to hum in a painful lament. Just the slightest sound was enough to make Jack's own heart break.

'To the Hanged-One,' Brynjolf lofted his drinking horn and swilled down the last of the wriggling ale. As he did so, his stomach churned with a gurgling thunder, as the ale began to pour out of an open battle-wound, mixing with Brinjal's innards, as it sloshed down his tunic and hit the floor. 'Cursed we are. And cursed he may be for leaving us to rot.'

In a wild explosion, the door to the tavern rocked on its hinged and flung from the lintel with such force that it was as though a giant's fist had pummelled through the front of the building. One by one, as the shards of wood spilt over the stone, the warriors of the hall leapt to their feet and drew swords and axes.

'Do not,' a shadowy figure emerged from the daylight, into the hall, carrying a long spear in one hand and holding a wide-brimmed hat in the other, 'curse me, Brynjolf. If anything, curse yourselves for not being victorious.'

'The Hanged-One,' a woman whimpered, frightened, from the back of the hall.

'Aye,' Grim steeped inside and smiled when he saw Alex, Safiya and Jack still seated, 'and if you want your Valkyrie, I have brought one to you.' his withered, tight-skinned hand rose up, holding the spear to point at Safiya.

****

'I must apologise for being so late,' Grim made a space between Safiya and Alex, facing Jack. With a waving of his hands, he shooed away the dozen or more onlookers who had decided to crowd around them. 'For goodness sake, leave us alone. Or at least bring some ale. Tyr's hand, some people.'

'How did you get on? As I say, I was held up during our departure from Helheim. The Door can be a tricky path to manoeuvre. Luckily, you all made it in one piece.'

He seems different than before, Jack noticed, seeing the man lingered between old age and a youthful vibrancy that did not seem to fit together.

As though reading his thoughts, Grim nodded, 'Yes. This world has a great air. Suits me just right. I feel much better than I did before. Less…' he tapped his head, '…cloudy. Tell me, then, how bad are things in the south?'

Safiya was the one to explain. She had developed a certain knack for describing in great detail the utter terror that they had endured each and every day, through sight and sounds. She had done so each night before the three had slept. Safiya recounted the horrors of the battlefields, the carrion flocks over the villages, and the corpses littering the streets. How they had been driven to eating rotten fruit and stagnant river water whilst hiking through a land in which none of them should have ever set foot.

'It was not exactly as though I could have invited you, now,' Grim offered, but it did not sit well with Safiya. 'Come, now. Follow me. There are monsters and demons and strife afoot. I needed you. We all need you. If there is to an end to this insanity, then I simply had to bring you here by any means.'

'But why?' Safiya's voice rose and heads around the room turned to listen in and watch.

Grim shrugged, 'Who can say? The Norns chose you four, just as they chose the Skulla before you. I am merely a messenger and a collector. I bring what is needed, and fate unravels itself before me.'

'Speaking of the four of us.' Jack inclined his head.

'Ah, yes.' Grim sighed, using one free hand to buffer the brim of his hat, 'Grayson. I was warned he might be a problem. Still, the Norns chose him as they did you. I fear he has parted ways with our company and joined another.'

'Loki?' Jack asked.

Grim nodded. For a brief moment, he looked like a child who had done something terribly wrong, and was hoping he would avoid being found out.

'So, he's still alive?' Safiya asked.

Grim nodded again, 'Yes, I am afraid so. Not far from here, I imagine. In the Bastion.' He pointed over his shoulder and the had to assume he was referring to the crooked city looming over the tavern. 'A shame. He showed a great deal of promise, you see. I was hoping when this was all over, he might have taught young Betty how to rule.'

Rule? Betty? 'Who?' Jack asked.

'Before he could add a 'what', Grim interrupted him, 'Beatrix. She is the Skulla I was referring to. I had intended to bring her here some years ago. You see, she is a descendant of mine and holds a certain power over this world. Runs in the blood. As it does in yours, although she is directly of my lineage, and with her ruling over Altheim, I believed I could save creation from the Twilight of the Gods.'

'Ragnarök.' Jack felt his spine surge with adrenaline and fear.

'Aye.' Grim acknowledged the tone, 'a terrible fate that awaits us all. You see, Loki had several children. Hella, whose world you have already visited; it is where we met. Jörmungandr, who exists in your world and could himself wrap about the core of the earth. And lastly, there is Fenris-wolf. Aeons ago, I and the one called Tyr bound the Great Wolf here, in Altheim, lest he grow and grow until he consumed the Nine Realms. I fear that, now, without my Beatrix, Hella, and Loki will free Fenris-wolf and using my key, bring him the Midgard. Your home. There, the three will destroy the Tree of Life and free the armies of the dead and the great dragon Nidhogg, thus plunging the cosmos into a dreadful darkness, from which it may never return.'

Alex had not been paying very much attention to Grim, or to either Alex or Safiya. The whole time they had been speaking, he had been practising a little trick he had learned some nights ago, lying awake as his stomach churned with hunger. He focussed his mind, trying to recapture the feeling when he had levitated Safiya from the cliff's edge; a power he had only caught glimpses of so far. Now, he could open his palm and bring an object from the table directly into it, without moving a muscle, with little effort. The jug of ale zipped across the table with such force, that it toppled and spilt over his now dreadfully soiled suit.

'Getting there,' Grim smiled at him, 'it has been a long time since I met a *Seidr*.' Then added under his breath so only Safiya could hear, 'They were not as empty upstairs, though.'

She giggled and turned red when Jack did the same. 'What exactly did you do to me? I am dead? am I dying? Am I a ghost?' she asked Grim.

The old, one-eyed man made a barking sound which turned out to be laughter, 'Gave you? You are each my kin. Descendants. You have had these gifts all along. Altheim simply engorges them. Gives them strength. Consider yourselves lucky, most souls have to actually face death before they can move between worlds.'

'Lucky?' Jack felt a rising fire in his veins, 'lucky? You call all this luck? We've been through hell.'

'Aye,' Grim smiled, 'quiet literally. But you are all in one piece. Yes? And perhaps even the better for it.'

Jack's mouth flew open, but no sound escaped. He looked at Safiya, his eyes wide with a burning rage. Expecting her to back him up, she seemed to sink a little, offering no support. Closing his lips, Jack sucked back the anger and hid it deep inside.

'And as for you,' Grim placed his hat on his head and coiled an arm around Safiya, 'you are not dead. Your metabolism had slowed to a halt. Have you not felt the power of the Aesir flowing inside you? A calming storm? A paradox of life and death? You are a Valkyrie, my dear. You have been given a mighty spear, and wings with which to wield it. Give it time. It will come to you. You will need it in the coming days.'

'So, there's a plan?' Alex spoke for the first time, 'to get us back home?'

Grim scoffed, 'yes, I suppose home is the goal. Still, there is work to be done beforehand, yes? It seems as though I need not bring you to your army, anyhow Safiya; you appear to have found them on your own.' Grim looked around at the men and women in the tavern, their curious faces seeming not to appear as if they were eavesdropping. 'The universe is a curious place, indeed.'

With those last words, he waved his hand across the table before the three, and before they could watch his fingers move, the plates of rotting meat and wriggling soup had regenerated to the sight of their former glory. There was food and drink enough to feed twice as many.

Bastion

"**S**o, what's the plan?' Safiya asked as she strapped the leather belt around her waist. The sword she had been given, a long, serrated blade almost as thick as her arm, hung inelegantly by her waist. Brynjolf had asked her to raise her arms and dropped a heavy, rusted shirt of mail over her head. The chains rattled as they sunk over her breasts and landed by her stomach. Its weight lessened over the time she wore it, as if she were breaking in a new pair of boots. As Brynjolf had said, 'You might not need it, but tis better to have it on.'

'The plan, my magnificent Valkyrie,' Grim eyed her from head to toe, quite impressed at the remarkable change, 'is simple in its intricacy. Take your warriors, Brynjolf will show you the way, and steal your way beneath the city walls. Once inside, you must fight your way to the inner keep and head for the Crooked Spire in the centre. I believe that is where Loki will be hiding.'

Safiya shook her head, 'Right. Castle. Demon in the tower. I suppose I need to slay the dragon on my way in?'

Grim gave her a curious, one-eyes stare, 'heavens no. My dear, I slayed that creature years ago. No dragons left. Though, you will have to enter through the sewer and up into the crypts. Bound to be the odd native down there, along with the odd Draugr.'

She shrugged, and his reply was 'You shall see in good time. Now, let me look at you once more. My dear, you are radiant as ever. A true warrior.'

'I've never even been in a fight,' Safiya crazed her cheeks.

'You'll learn. It's in your blood.' Brynjolf slapped her hard against the back, sending her staggering forward. The rest of her warriors let out a ruckus of laughter, beating their weapons on their shields, as one by one they stormed out of the tavern.

ᛗ

Be not so rash alone to go, daughter of heroes!
to the house of draugs: more powerful are, in the night-season,
all dead warriors, than in the light of day.

- *Helgakviða Hjörvarðssonar*

Brynjolf had led his warriors on no less than twenty-three skirmishes across Altheim. He had lost only ten men in his life as Hersir. That had all seemed an age ago now. No longer did Valhalla call to him as it had in his youth. No longer did victory taste so sweet. For, now, he felt no taste. No sweet sugar of mead. No crackling pork. No sting of death. When the blood-plague arrived, many of his kith and kin fled north, into the mountain passes; through treacherous paths, fleeing an invisible enemy. He had stayed. With his Úlfhéðnar, there was only one way to live and the way to Valhalla lay not in the mountain pass. Brynjolf's Úlfhéðnar were uniquely apart from the world. Altheim generally consisted of two types of people;

the gifted and the cursed. The gifted; Men, Elves, Dwarves, Druid, Fae, Hanged-Worshippers, Hildefolk, all praised by The Architect and by the gods, for they possessed the gift of death. One day, their hour would come and into the next life Odin would call them by horn and by name. The cursed; Draugr, Infernus, Unhallowed, Vampyr, Valravn, Dark Elf, Ghouls, Troll, Jötunn, Frost Giants, Fossegrimmen, Kraken; yes, some could find release in their deathbed, but it was no gift. Only Helheim awaited their souls. Only Naglfar would call to them. Only Hella. Others eked out their immortal days and nights as the undying. Never to see the great halls of the Aesir.

As for Brynjolf, and for Jargun, Astora, Eric, Bjorn, Bolf, Bruni, and the rest of his company, they were trapped. Caught between the land of the living and the realm of the dead. The cursed einherjar; afflicted by a berserker's rage and a passion for battle that Grim's resolve only protected them from Loki for so long. At the rising of their blood, Brynjolf and his own would become that which is often unspoken, even amongst veterans of the shield-wall. The berserker. The blood-raged beast. The Úlfhéðnar. The wolf-warrior. As painful as the t5ranformation came, its misery fell short of the curse of a tasteless, loveless existence.

Ahead, Lucien's Bastion rose. Kissing the cloud of mist and fog. Caressing the shape of the Hollow Mountain. The Crooked Spire, however, pierced the veil of grey, like some heaven-bound spear. Oh, Gungnir of the North.

Bjorn led the passage over hill and down into the valley, as the Úlfhéðnar wound like a fiery serpent in the darkness, their torches ablaze beneath the starry sky. Safiya, their Valkyrie, kept close to Brynjolf, as the wind called back a mountainous howl and strange visions of the cursed ones stalked the treeline, watching the band of wolf-warriors close in. Having decided to negate the bridge, leaving that path to others, the Úlfhéðnar journeyed below. Crossing marshland and river, the bear-like Brynjolf lifted Safiya over a deep pass of water, which ran up to his ribs. He held her like a lover, as towards the Bastion's under-crofts and sewers, they moved. Small hamlets dotted the valley under the Bastion, spread across the unnervingly beautiful fields of green. Brynjolf had not noticed Safiya's curiosity, as a small cart, loaded with furs began to trundle its way from the villages out into open pasture. Safiya had wanted to call to them; Brynjolf knew that. Which is why his rough grasp against her mouth hurt all the more. Only weeks ago, he had felt the pangs of humanity.

'No,' she looked up at him, as the bear-like semblance of a man shook his head.

'There is nothing we can do for them now. Pray to the Hanged-One; their presence goes unnoticed.'

How curious it was that he could lie so easily. He expected the sound. Knew it to come, and yet, the ferocity and sheer dread stabbed his heart like a seax. Brynjolf placed his huge palm on Safiya's shoulder, when he caught her eye turn to witness the remains of the cart spilling onto its side. A creature, more wing than limb, carried a still-shrieking soul off into the ether of the Hollow Mountain. More blackened wings, spurred on by bloodshed, escaped their roosts of the Bastion, filling the air with a chorus of flight. They descended on the villages, to catch the fearful unawares, dragging more thralls back into their master's keep. Over the next hour, the constant march was halted only by the occasional scream from afar.

Astora was the first to enter the sewage pipe, which led up into the mountain; into the Bastion. She crawled into waist-high filth and runoff from the houses of the keep. Bjorn held the iron grid above his head allowing the rest of the companions to crawl into the stinking darkness of the tunnels. Maybe ten feet wide, a river of waste flowed down and out into open rivers. Pipes, flows, and waterways formed a mediocre and ancient sewage system. Brynjolf knew from the days of his father that they could follow the tunnels half a mile, then into a brief climb, to reveal the Forgotten Tombs where their ancestors lay. Deep in the bowels of the Mad King's castle. The Mad King himself, Lucien Bonehand, had insisted upon construction of the keep and the Crooked Spire, that the honoured dead of his kin be forever interred, never to see their realm grow cold and dead in the bleak Fimbulwinter to come. So terrified of Ragnarök was Lucien, that he grew insatiable in his love for all things twisted, misaligns and malformed. Issuing decree after decree that, 'Not a tunnel may run without curve, nor a tower stand upright. No window to hang in prefecture, lest the children of the night come crawling in and Volva enter one's home and one's dreams. We are the children of The Architect and we build to serve the light.'

These decrees, upheld by tradition, years after Lucien's death by his own hand, of course, made traversing the bowels of the Bastion somewhat troubling. Tunnels led for miles only to lead into dead ends. Caverns of pitch-black darkness. Ceilings sloped and fell in the hope of trapping frightful intruders beneath stone till Ragnarök come. In parts, this series of labrynthian puzzle had worked. Creatures entered, never again to see the light of day. Then again, some learned to adapt, to live down here amongst the imprisoned existing through cannibalism and interbreeding rituals. Far below the Crooked Spire there were rumours of beings, come into existence that should not be.

Luckily, Brynjolf and Astora knew by memory a way through the labyrinth.

'Hush, hold still,' he pushed Safiya against a cavernous wall, seeping with water from some high spring until it soaked through rock and bone into the festering waters of the sewer.

Some faint figure ahead cast a silhouette across the wall, carrying torch by its side.

'An ill sign,' Brynjolf whispered, as the torchlight faded, 'that men still do the bidding of these overlords. What dread vestige of courage falls when they cannot die for their kin?'

Whatever magic Alex Krieger had come to possess in this world had not the faintest touch on the romantic verse this bear-like warrior could utter. Safiya found herself blushing again. Yet the man looked at all times as though simple English verse would confound him.

'Who are they?' she asked him.

'Thralls,' Astora spat at the floor cursing the thought. 'Lackeys of the demon Loki.

'I will break them,' Bjorn gripped a heaving palm around his hammer.

Safiya let a shrill giggle escape, which at first embarrassing was joined by others.

'What?' asked Bjorn, dumbfounded, as they moved again, 'I WILL break them.'

'I know brother, hush now.' Brynjolf saw a tunnel ahead, leading to the right, lit by a mystical green aura: the inevitable burning, of *balefire*.

Conjured only by necrotic magic, balefire burned like swamp gas. Almost untouchable by wind, flames of green lasted long after their combustible source had faded. For tonight, it was the smouldering heads of traitors to Loki that gave fuel for these witchy blazes. Safiya tried to ignore what she had seen. That what burned nearby, held to the wall by iron nails, was not the charred remains of a young boy's skull but just a fantastical falsity; a Halloween decoration for the mentally corrupt. No creature of feeling could boast upon such a desecration of a soul.

There came a guffaw from nearby. Brynjolf held his hands low, signalling his companions to keep their heads down and breath quiet.

'I just don't see why it's always us that gets the maggoty ones,' a voice gurgled from the dark ahead.

'Oh, shut up, would you,' a second, high pitched voice snapped.

'I's hungry as all, nothing but scraps of flesh for a week now.'

'When the Great Wolf is released and the new Queen is crowned, the coronation feast will be every bleeding soul in the Nine Realms, you stinking troll,' pierced the second.

'And how long's that, eh?' barked the first, 'just because we's undying now, don't mean we can't starve.'

'To death,' the second corrected, 'we can't starve *to death*. Now come on.'

'And I'm not a troll,' the first voice called, close by now, 'my mother was a hag and, urgh.'

Brynjolf spotted the creatures appear in the balefire before Safiya had. Luckily, as the hideous, pustule-covered figures emerged, Astora and Bjorn had placed themselves lying in wait. Before a voice could yell, 'guards', two long seax's drove into the creature's necks, sending thick pulses of coagulated blood shooting onto the wall. The corpse they carried fell into the sewage by their feet, carried away on the festering current. Brynjold nodded and the companions moved forward again. Safiya took one look below and felt sick. Enough to force her stomach to physically churn. Once she had received a phone call from the coroner's office reporting a death nearby. Safiya had grabbed the pad and pen, but when asking the crucial question, 'And the date of death?', had received only the reply of, 'Ooh, err…the police say the last electricity bill was paid in December.' It was then March when the call came. Still images of a bloated corpse. Lying naked. More bed than man now. Skin moving with insect life. You'll find a cat also,' Safiya had told the police escort, 'half his face has been eaten.'

Tunnel after tunnel led the companions up a winding staircase, through a small empty cavern, until a stench unplaceable to Safiya greeted them. She had smelt death a great many times. But not old death. Ancient death. The archaeological remains of what death had once been. To her the description could only be associated and attributed to the word, mould.

'The Mad King's crypt,' Brynjolf said. He drew a small torch from his belt and used one of the balefire totems to ignite it. The fire did not catch green, but orange, the colour of untainted fire. 'Be careful here.'

'Why?' Safiya whispered back. 'Did you see something?'

His large hand moved to a nearby tomb, 'This one is missing. And he will not be alone.'

Of course, he was right. A heaving thud of broken stone ahead was caught in balefire, the lid of a tomb breaking in two, crashing from its place.

'Draugr,' Bjorn cried and heaved his hammer above his head, awaiting battle.

Astora sparked another torch, just in time to see the shuffling bodies come around the next corner.

Zombies, is what Safiya had thought. For a second her mind flitted to a source of pain her mind had forced her to forget, until now. *Madge*.

The feeling was fleeting, eluding her again, as the two-handed sword flew headlong out of the near-darkness towards them. Caught by surprise, a voice called from the rear, chocked out by a last gurgle of pain, before falling silent.

'Magnusson.' Brynjolf recognised the face caught in the torchlight.

A rage set amongst the warriors like a disease.

'Valkyrie,' Brynjolf growled, as his hand broke with bestial shards of bone, 'be best that you stay back.'

She took the torch from his hand. Now she could see clearly what was causing him such pain. His eyes, once pools of blue, now yellowed and bright. His knuckles sprouting with tufts of hair. His back breaking, elongating and twisting. A snapping of muscle and sinew, forced Brynjolf to stoop. Half-man, half-beast. Safiya told herself that she understood, but her fear told her she did not. Around her the Úlfhéðnar had transformed into wild, ferocious beats. Stripped of the clothes and even their own skin, they bayed as a pack and rove their claws into the stones of the crypt, rallying forward into the fight.

Úlfhéðnar. Wolf-warriors. With renewed strength and resolve, the bones of the dead began to fall once more beneath their claws. Several times, as she tried to keep the torch in place and see what was happening, she heard the whimpers of a dying dog. She rushed ahead to keep up. A corpse lay by her feet, one she recognised; Jargrun. An axe splayed out from his impacted chest cavity, allowing his blood to run rivers through the corridor. *These were no zombies*, she though, *they fight like living soldiers.*

Claws snapped on bone. Swords cleaved at fur. It was a mess. A bloody mess. Bodies old and new began to pile up in heaps as Safiya struggled to follow the carnage. Some shrieked.

Some howled their last. She felt a whistling arrow fly past her cheek, grazing it slightly. Ignoring the pain, she ducked, seeing a Warhammer come crashing overhead, shattering not one, but two coffins. The ash and bone-meal remains spilt over her hair, turning it a deep grey. Another bow twanged and a curious sensation started in her toes, working its way upward. Pain. Delayed pain. Glancing from side to side, she finally felt it. An arrow, jutting from her forehead. And yet it felt nothing more than splinter. Tearing the iron and wood free, Safiya stared down at the bloodied tip and laughed. A Valkyrie? Could she truly believe it? Not undying. Not undead. Something other. Something new. And she allowed it, finally, to consume her.

The spear glinted at her, as if winking through the darkness like a lover. She grasped the shaft of the ancient weapon, still sharp as the day it was forged. Safiya hurled the weapon with everything she could and even saw it strike at the Draugr ahead, shattering his corpse. Ducking and diving. Weaving and bobbing. The fluid strikes came as naturally now as breathing. She just had to let it all go.by the time the last of the Draugr fell, a half-worm-eaten bearded soldier, Safiya had used axe, sword, bow and spear as though she had trained for this night since childhood.

'They won't stop coming,' Safiya yelled, cutting down her thirteenth victim. Its ashy-blood coughed over her in a cloud of age and an aroma of cold, damp soil. Graveyards dirt. They had fought on and on, through the chambers of the crypt. Draugr had appeared, like rodents, crawling from the floor. Burrowing down from the ceiling. Worming their way through their graves. Hand expelled randomly at corners and heads appeared from every nook and cranny. The world above and even time had forgotten these men and women, now raised from their tombs by the necrotic magic over the Bastion, Brynjolf and his companions had to slice their way tooth and claw until they broke through into a chamber, below a well, filled with moonlight. Sacred, purest air swam down from the world just feet above. Safiya knocked her arrow, pulled her string, and let the bow send forth the arrow, seeing it split the next Draugr's skull into three splintered pieces. She screamed for her warriors to fight, 'fight on.'

Handfuls of the unhallowed dead still climbed from the crypts entrance, as the companions burst out into the open air. Their exit, a large mausoleum, located in the centre of an empty, unused fountain. They now stood, under silver clouds, in the circular formation of houses and towers which made up the very centre of the Bastion. Lingering over them, like a dark totem, was the Crooked Spire.

Safiya held the long blade in both hands, clinking its edge against the stone wall of the fountain, as if inviting for more, more battle. Around her, the Úlfhéðnar rolled back their grey heads, gave paradise to the celestial god Selene; howling a chorus that entered every house hearth and heart in the castle, so that even the demon in the tower would know that the wolves of Altheim had come for his blood.

Yellow eyes opened under the veil of shadowed streets and alleys. Red eyes awoke from daylight slumber, greeted by the scent of meat and bone on the wind. A shrieking reply came seconds after the howls had stopped. Their greeting had been heard.

Cloak and Dagger

"**O**kay, mate. While she's off galivanting about, what do you expect me to do?' Alex was tying a black cloak, the least moth eaten he could find, around his shoulders. 'And you promise, like swear down, cross your heart, if we do this, we'll make it home?'

Old Grim chuckled, 'Yes. If you do as I say, and do it correctly, I swear an oath on my armring, Draupnir, you will see your own world again.'

ᛗ

Fierce ravens shall, on the high gallows, tear out thy eyes,
if thou art lying, that hither from afar is come the youth unto my halls.
- Hávamál

Hearing the screams of war echoing through the alleyways, Alex decided it would be more beneficial to his survival, if he were to avoid the moonlit streets and instead make his way between narrower byways. Being that Safiya had entered the city through the sewers and this had created a ruckus so loud, the mountain folk would hear, beneath the streets was another option he ruled out.

Dark shadows played on his mind, as Alex stepped between two tall, storied houses. It took him back to his busking days, standing beneath the Tudor houses of Chester, plying his street magic to children and the occasional awestruck adult. That life seemed a bygone age, now. Even the starlight's of Vegas and NYC felt as memories belonging to an altogether different man. And it had been, what, a week? Seven working days since Flight 715 from Nevada had screamed out of the sky, falling from the heavens like a castaway angel. Alex had put little thought into the passengers of Flight 715. In the end, what had happened...had happened. If he was the sole survivor, whatever outcome prevailed, did it matter? As Old Grim had said many times: 'fate is an inescapable huntress.' Perhaps, since the moment he was brought into this world, Alex Krieger has been destined to walk these narrow, uneven streets and carry out Grim's will, whether he had booked his flight, or not. In another life, he had fallen overboard and washed ashore in that nightmare forest. In another, his train had bypassed King's Cross and arrived fifteen minutes late at Terrorville; population, five.

It's Jack's mind to think about that rubbish, Alex thought, squeezing himself into a stony tunnel, leading away from a deserted road. *Let the Philosopher worry away his life. There's a job to be done.*

He focussed his mind on both the job at hand, and the fact that should it be done just right, Alex would spend the next fortnight in a luxury hotel room. He would fill the hot tub, order in the escorts and not leave the room until management had knocked at least three times. Imagine if my case had made it out of the flight, too, Alex kicked himself, a couple gram of 'Charlie' would make this experience at least a little more bearable, if not just slightly more intense. *Intense* might even have been an understatement. Alex had never felt so in edge. Even standing before a crowd of two hundred clapping punters, his heart had not felt a beat so strong. It was exhausting, every second, feeling the unending grip of adrenaline and anxiety pulling through his veins with every step and every breath. One gust of breeze became the breath of a nightmare beast. Every scurrying rodent became a hellhound. Every shadow stretched until it seemed hellbent on consuming him. *Just pull it together, for God's sake, man, get a grip. It's just the wind.* Pushing out of the tunnel between the houses, Alex saw two large blackbirds, perched atop a slanted fence. A rat scuttled out of its cuniculus, pattering along the alleyway. Stopping then starting. Stopping then starting. The raven's eyed the pest with curiosity, but did not swoop to snatch their prey. Strangely, they seemed far more focussed on Alex.

'Bloody place,' he scowled, exiting the crooked archway.

'Bloody place,' cawed one of the birds, mimicking Alex with a whistling croak.

'Oh, shut up,' Alex barked, wafting a hand to bat the avian away.

'No.' It clicked, and to its side, the second raven whistled a similar reply.

Alex considered the birds for a long moment, before finally dawning with the realisation of what Grim had meant by the words, 'Oh, do not worry, you shall not be alone.'

'Don't tell me,' he asked the Stygian crows, 'you're the help?'

'Help, help,' the slightly larger of the ravens cawed. 'Feed the plague. Stop the hunger.'

The sound of the bird stretching its feathers, made Alex start back. He had not expected the wings to be so loud, nor so big. The raven cocked its beak towards him, piercing Alex with a jet-black stare.

'Follow,' the second squawked.

Blustering, the pair lifted from the fence and took off into the night, passing by the vision of the full moon, adding a fateful omen to the night. They did not travel far, coming to land on the crooked rooftop of a taller house, some fifty yards ahead. They both cawed, calling Alex forward.

Sure, why not, he stepped further into the moonlight and made his way towards the ravens.

'Beware,' a raven landed beside him, on the window ledge, 'Valravn. Valravn. Valravn.'

Again, Alex shooed the bird away, to stop the incessant cawing, 'piss off, mate.'

It disappeared overhead, with a repetition of the same word, 'Valravn.'

Alex had followed the fence all the way to a row of houses and now the wooden struts formed a high, locked gate, for which there seemed no apparent way through. Guess I could always climb; his, though, was cut out by the second screeching bird, 'Door, door. Enter.'

Looking to his left, there was indeed a door. Surely it was, no, not locked. With a shrill creak, the wood fell back on its hinges, opening into the type of house that Alex had only seen in museums. A small hearth, the main feature of an otherwise empty loving quarter, held only embers and ash. A small stairway led into the upper rooms, of which Alex had no intention of entering. The streets had been empty, yes, but the houses might not be so fortunate. An image of himself being confronted by some half-dead native, crawling from its slumber towards him drove any notion of the stairs from his mind. These houses must be connected somehow. *I mean, how thick could these medieval walls be?* Seeing a figure as he turned into the next room, made his heart leap into his ribs. Alex stared in horror at the man, until he recognised the sombre look and matted hair. A bloody mirror, Alex chuckled aloud, but when a sound from the room above mimicked his laughter, his blood froze in his veins. He turned through the next room and thought his eyes to be deceiving him. A long, narrow hallway running down through the centre of every house. They were connected, one to another, build so tightly on top of each other that it was possible to just walk into the next building. *I'm losing it,* he thought, *this doesn't make sense.* Bumping into tables and chairs, Alex moved swiftly down the hallway, and stopped abruptly when he saw that the next room he entered was exactly alike to the one he had just left.

Did I...get all turned around? By his side, perched upon a dining table, sat a curious object. A book. *This can't be real?*

Alex flipped quickly through the pages of the book on the table. Images struck him like bullets. Skyscrapers. Satellites. All the indexes of the modern age, here, now, in this medieval place. Again, the cackling sounded down the stairs, closer now. A freak of floorboards, and Alex was running into the hallway. He felt a presence enter the room behind him, and dare not turn to see just what had emerged.

'Just run! Just run!' he screamed aloud, seeing his terroriser burst out at him from the hallway. With a piercing crack, Alex felt his body crash though yet another mirror, that had not been there just a moment before. *What's happening? Oh, God, what's happening?* Behind the mirror, stood two, claw-like feet. He wanted to look away, and still, some morbid curiosity drove him to inch his way upwards, seeing the mass of fur covering the legs, the awkward protruding bones arching out from the waist and atop the wolf's lower body, sat the chest, wings, and beaked head of a raven. Would Alex have been so ashamed to admit to the others than in that moment he had lost control of his bladder? That the warm remembrance of childhood flooded underneath him? Would he tell them that as he lay crouched, before the hideous totem-like monster, that he felt such terror that Alex Krieger had begged the creature to leave?

'Please. No.' It's reply to Alex was nothing but a grotesque mocking laughter. He turned and fled. Back down the hallway. Back out into the street. Or so he thought. Moving through the door, he opened his eyes and recognised the same room. The same hallway. With that same reflection of Alex Krieger standing at its centre. Alex screamed. Heavy footsteps ran across the room above, bounding down the stairs, as the Valravn mocked him. This time, when Alex saw the book, the pages held images quite different. This time, Alex saw the horrific visions of war. Deserts of glass, as soldiers marched under banners he could not recognise. Forests, burning with a conflagration, as aircraft he had never seen hovered overhead and the sparkling lights of gunfire rang past hill and creek. This time, Alex picked up the book with both hands and hurled it over his head. His reflection before him opened its mouth to laugh, as the pages shattered the image. As the mirror burst, Alex saw pages explode like a library, sending an avalanche of photographs spilling outward, each one of himself. They landed by his feet. One after another, after another. Every imaginable and creative way that Alex Krieger might meet his end. Sword. Gun. Car. Cancer. Knife. Suicide. He saw himself reflected in a hundred different timelines, and in each and every one he died suffering. Behind him, a board creaked under the weight of something large. Alex had no need to look. He knew what was there. The awful, totem-like monster. The Valravn. Legs of a wolf. Body and head of a raven. Soul of a demon.

'Enough,' he spun, and with every ounce of fear coursing through him, Alex let loose the sensation he had felt when first he arrived in this treacherous world. With a pop, gales of wind emanated from his palms, pages, photographs, tables, chairs, all exploded away from him. No longer did the Valravn laugh. Instead, the creature shrieked with pain, as it was thrown back into the hallway, collapsing against a far wall, as feathers and blood puffed out from its chest.

Woah, Alex turned his fingers over, and saw power. Real power.

This time, when Alex left the hallway, the room was different. The houses, no longer connected, allowed him to leave. Outside, the street was empty still, and the moon had not budged from where it hung before. As though he had stumbled onto the set of one of his more obscure sets, Alex Krieger found himself easing open the rusted gates of a graveyard. Complete with rolling mist, which cling to the edges of the headstones like morning dew.

A heavy sensation that he was being watch, pushed down on him, enveloping him like the fog. *It's fine. Yeah, this is fine,* he told himself. *It's like one of those, things, right? The creepiest place in existence has to be the safest, right? Monsters don't actually hang out in cemeteries. It's a misnomer. It's lunacy. Of course, it's lunacy. Everything in this goddamned hellhole is lunacy. I could have been home. Got some beers. Had a nap. Gone to the New Year's party at Elle's. No. Here I am. In a goddamn cemetery and...what the hell is that whistling?*

It was coming from nearby, eking over the headstones, drawing him in. Alex knew the tune. His memory was a little cracked lately. A little hazy. *Name that tune,* he thought. 'Blue Danube'? No? Is it? A solitary sentinel eased atop the headstone. If it had not eventually moved, Alex might have guessed it was part of the monument. Like those Victorian shrines, where the grave would be guarded by the stony figure of a weeping angel, or even the grim spectre of the reaper. As though the graveyard did not seem ominous enough, the figure rose on its feet and started to, clink, clink, scraping at the earth with a long, iron spade. Whatever had possessed his mind in that moment, Alex realised that this world had changed him. There would have been little to zero chance that Alex Krieger would have either the social prowess, nor the manners to ask, 'Excuse me?'

Expecting the figure to reply, Alex watched as it simply carried on in its task, wrenching another spadesful of earth from the grave, before shuffling it away into the growing pile of dirt by his side.

'Excuse me,' Alex said, louder this time. Still nothing. It was not until Alex actually patted the man's shoulder, that the figure jumped and turned with a start.

'By the Hanged-One, you startled me, boy.' An elderly, drawn, thin figure lived within the cumbersome, heavy clothes. It was a word Alex would not have used to describe what he was wearing. Rags, really. Tattered, moth-eaten, filthy rags. 'Whatever are you doing out at this hour? Don't you know this time is reserved for the dead?'

Scraping another line of earth, the man eyed Alex curiously, but passed the notion by that he was anything other than human.

'You're the first person I've seen in this city. Where is everyone?' Alex asked, leaning forward on the headstone and stretching his back until it popped with the sound of burning wood.

'Oh, boy, they don't mind me. The creatures,' the man said, 'I care for the dead, and so they leave me be. Was a time I was shunned from this community. I suppose it takes a new sort of caretaker to understand that the dead need more care than the living. Especially when the dead feel the need to return from their graves so often. I've just finished opening this one again. Its master comes and goes from time to time. Best to make it easier for them, you see. Otherwise,' he chuckled, moving his brow with a dirty handkerchief, 'it would be such a mess when they crawl back out again. Soil everywhere. This makes my job much easier; you see.'

What a creep, Alex felt that this conversation was due to be less educational than he would have liked. He needed information and the ramblings of a madman in a graveyard just were not going to cut it. 'I need a path. Need to get there,' Alex moved his finger upwards, until it faced the Crooked Spire.

'Oh,' the man chuckled again, 'Hoho, you wouldn't want to go there. No, no, no. That's where the master lives, now. He wouldn't take kindly to a visitor with your...pallor. Much alike me and him. Prefer the company of those who... talk less, you see.'

Something whipped past one of the headstones a little way ahead. A shadow in the fog. Alex felt each hair raise on his neck, telling him in that old, primal sense, that he was once again being watched.

'There's a creature following me,' Alex admitted, unsure why, 'like a big black bird, but it's got these hairy feet.'

'Hoho,' chortling, the man scraped more earth away from the grave, 'the Valravn. I see. I'd best make you a bed for the night. Won't escape him, you see. Death-bringer that one. An ill omen. An ill omen, indeed. Needs blood, you see. Like them.'

Alex had not noticed the coffins before. Aligned in a row. When the man pointed across the headstones to where the stacks of wooden caskets lay, it was hard to look elsewhere.

'Vampyr.' Shrugging, the man spoke the word of horror, as though it meant little, of anything, to either of them. 'Fresh ones, you see. Only just reborn. Were plenty of fresh meat-sacks in this city for them to feed on. Shame. Sometimes, I didn't mind the little ones. It was the older ones that shunned me. Often, the children would talk to me, while I worked. I'd say there's only a handful of live ones left here; you see. Was a great reckoning when the master came. A black and terrible summer. Suppose there's no need to fear the pestilence anymore. What's a plague to the dead and the damned?'

'Right,' feeling a sudden urgency to get as far away from this old coot as he possibly could, Alex just added, 'be seeing you,' and began to walk away with purpose.

'No,' the man called back, 'you won't. Not with that Valravn on your back.' Then, he tutted and started once more to whistle the 'Blue Danube,' as Alex picked up a hasty pace.

Wulfric wafted the torch before his face, seeing a slight glint reflect back in the iron gate. It glowed, up ahead; a familiar vestige of his time spent down here, in the dark. Wulfric had never believed, not in the age of the sun, that his life would be spent behind the cold, dreaded dark of the Bastion's dungeons. The solitary rusted key almost fell to the floor, as he swapped the flaming torch to his left hand, drawing the small 'unlocker' from his surcoat pocket.

You'll amount to little, Son. His father's voice crawled to the forefront of his mind, complete with a, possibly unrealistic, memory of his ghoulish face. Had he really looked that gaunt and shrivelled and so utterly haunting?

Slamming the door behind him and twisting the key, Wulfric heard a low, 'Keep it down out there, you bastard,' echo from one of the nearby cells. They were aligned, in rows, so that each cell had no view of another and only gazed out at bare, stone wall. Neighbourly affections not supplied under the new ruling class above. And how long ago had it been, since Wulfric had heard that name, Loki. One named 'usurper' by loyalists and 'master' by thralls, or those looking for an easy life, free from pain and torture. What a wicked weave has been spun here. Only months ago, before the war came so close, blue skies had shone over Lucien's Bastion. The Crooked Spire had been a beacon of hope, justice and solidarity. Not just in the North, but across all of Altheim. The Bastion had kept the darkness at bay. Held a wall against the tide of Helheim that managed to somehow slink their way up through the bowels of the Hollow Mountain. Then, he had come. Loki. And with him, the barrier had broken. All creatures of the night had wrenched themselves free from the Hollow Mountain, towards the Crooked Spire and consumed Lucien's Bastion with mouths salivating with hunger and a lust for blood, unquenchable to the damned and indescribable to mortal minds. Why had Wulfric been left standing? When so many around him had perished? Some small saving grace, was that he had only to bury his parents. Others had aid farewell to sons, daughters and lovers. The word itself, bury, had become a tainted word. How oft had Wulfric seen the hallowed dead return from their graves? Still, whatever fear could be held was negated by the fact that he, Wulfric Gunarsson, had been chosen. Chosen to be one of only a 'skeleton crew' remaining to man the ancient fortress of the Bastion. Perhaps the only man within hundreds of feet whose heart still beat and whose blood still ran warm.

At the end of the corridor, past the cells, Wulfric saw the movement of a shadow in the thin slithers of moonlight that made their way so far below ground. He recognised the mismatched shape before his torch, as the creature came closer on uneven feet. The odd protruding bones. The patchwork of skin. The glowing, seeping, pus-filled scars. The deformed cage of ribs, holding in its soulless heart. It was one of HIS creations. The Necromancer. He had appeared only days ago, and somehow had already littered the Bastion with his abominable blasphemies. Dead, reanimated husks, devoid of feeling, doomed to repeat their endless devilments of this Necromancer and his master.

'Say name,' the grotesque uttered with a broken, guttural voice.

Before being taken b7y the blood-plague, Arnhold, Wulfric's superior had called them 'Infernus', which in a distant, foreign tongue meant, 'faceless one'. For the vestige before him it was more than apt. Without ears, tongue, lips, nose nor eyes, this creature spoke only through a necrotic magic.

'It makes for a far more subservient worker,' Arnhold had explained. 'Thus is the nature of our new lords in their castle.'

Perhaps Wulfric himself was as such? A pitiful wretch, subservient in his work as he had become. Did it matter anymore? What existence in Altheim remained, was due to die a slow, relentless death, and even then; it was not always the end.

'Wulfric. I am the warden here,' he replied, trying not to gaze into those lidless holes. 'Let me pass, I have to make my rounds.'

A pang of anxiety crossed him as he spoke to the Infernus, as it just stood and watched, motionless. The moment passed, as the monster ebbed to one side, allowing the jailer to slip by, unmolested. It gurgled something unintelligible as Wulfric started to descend the winding staircase to the lower level.

Lit by sconces in the walls, the 'Pit' as it was most commonly referred to, harboured prisoners no more; instead it was home to the abominations the Necromancer created and some of those the master, Loki, had dragged with him from Helheim. It sat below the innermost courtyard of the Castle, that should they be required, these abominations could be called upon to drag themselves up from the Pit, to feast on the living therein. Lucien's Bastion was no longer a fortress, it was one behemoth lure and trap for anything still living. It was Wulfric's job to pass his torch by each cell, making sure everybody accounted for; and to do this thrice per night. This night, as those before, Wulfric had no stomach for such devilry. He had performed this hideous task only once, fully and the images he had seen scarred his dreams. A defilement to everything holy. Against The Architect himself and the Hanged-One also. Never would he willingly look upon those blasphemous creations again. His pace even quickened with each cell he passed, feeling dread eyes in the dark, eyeing the taste of his flesh and the feel of his skin over their own bones.

Wulfric felt the ache of sleepless nights weighing on his mind. Each step another slip down, into fatigue. Sleep now a fleeting menace. Always there, just out of reach. It was not like him to see demons in the dark, at least where they were not. Ghostly vestiges where only stones lay. Tonight, as the third hour approached, Wulfric felt his primal hairs erect at almost every waking minute. Something in the air felt wrong. It had dredged up something like the scent of death on the wind and with it came images of those abominations. Feeling the last few cells disappearing by his side, Wulfric slid the key into the lock, slid over the iron bolt and let loose a terrifying shriek.

The face before him was a pallid and horror-stricken expression, forcing Wulfric to recoil and brandish the torch at the figure, as if trying to abate a woodland creature.

Alex leapt back from the flame, waving his hands like a madman. He shouted at first. Then dropped his voice to a gruff whisper, remembering where the tunnel had brought him. Seeing the man recoil and pull the key free of the lock, Alex placed his palm on the door and closed his eyes. Wulfric watched, as the mechanism clicked, slid out of place and unlocked. The door opened.

'H-h-h?' Wulfric questioned.

'Magic,' whispered Alex, as he disappeared down the corridor.

A choice crossed over Wulfric path. A chance encounter in the dark. Immediately, he knew which of the paths open before him he would choose. Rather than see himself a bitch to these hideous blasphemies, Wulfric clutched at the torch and chased after the figure.

Wulfric heard the blast before he saw the blue flash of light. Upon turning the corner, at the top of the stairwell, saw the Infernus, scattered into a dozen or more pieces around the alcove. Spattering of intestinal matter and pus covered the stones where the creature had been fired backward.

Alex was standing, with an expression of utter bewilderment on his face, as his eyes gazed unbelievingly down at his own hands.

'Whoa, mate,' he puffed, turning his hands over, inspecting every vein, every line, every crevasse, as if there, writing would appear and read, *Yes, this is magic.*

'Who are you?' Wulfric asked, still gripping torch and dagger, though strangely feeling more at ease now, in front of this witch, than he had standing before the moulding face of that blasphemous Infernus. Another monster fallen, at the very least.

'Alex,' he held out his hand and gave a shrill snort, when he saw Wulfric recoil away, sensing some ill omen within his skin.

'I'm guessing,' Alex continued, 'since you haven't stuck me with that thing, that you aren't in the business of this…Ragnarök? Amma right, mate? Yeah. I thought so. I know conviction to a stage when I see it, and mate, you just haven't got it. So, do us both a favour and either follow me,' Alex pointed down the hallway, 'or fuck off,' his digit pointing down the stairs now.

Lips parting, tongue moving, no sound could be heard from Wulfric's mouth. This curious newcomer in his attire of stripy under trousers and striped tunic had allowed Wulfric to follow a new leader, before he had even realised, he was doing so. How odd.

'May I ask, see you, where we are heading?' Wulfric questioned, holding the torch closer to Alex than he seemed comfortable with.

'All right, Shakespeare, mate, I don't need you to come with me, really. It was just a kind offer, seeing as it's so, *you know*, down here. You look like a big guy and I'm not so good in a fight. Hate to see wasted talent when I see it. Just stay close and keep the fucking flames away from my face and the pointy end of that thing behind you.' Alex waved, forcing the seax to turn in Wulfric's hand.

'What magic,' the warden exclaimed, beaming.

'Yeah, I'm full of surprises, should see me walk through fire.'

Wulfric sucked in a deep lungful, 'Surely not. By the Hanged One,' clasping his fingers around his father's parting gift; a small silvery cross, attached to his neck with the snarling mouth of a wolf. 'Are you here to rid us of the master? So long now his yoke has trodden us underfoot. Not even the Southern Armies made it north or gained foothold on the Bastion and here you are. With such magics, would you dare stop him? Could you?'

'Just think of us as the bloody SAS, mate. Small in number, but we get the job done.' Alex span about his now-stubbled face eerily close to the torch. 'But I'm no fucking hero, and I don't want you falling at my feet. I'm just following orders. I don't know where I am or what the hell I'm doing here. Really. We just do as the octogenarian says and everything will be hunky-dory. Okay?'

Wulfric smiled and nodded. A lot. He repeated the words he did not underrated, as though it were some confirmation that he did, '*octegariun*,' '*essayas*,' 'hunkeedoorey.'

'Atta, mate. Let's go.' Alex lightly slapped Wulfric on the cheek. Then took his hand back seeing Wulfric's gormless expression and wiped the greasy palm on Wulfric's cloak with a grimace before headed down the hallway.

'Watt Tyler was right,' Alex muttered ahead, 'these peasants are bloody revolting.' Then, as they passed the first row of cells, he asked, 'Who's locked up down here, anyway?'

A slither of moonlight wound its way through a crack, far up in the foundations of the Bastion, making the stone shine with a watery, pale reflection.

'Dead men. Monsters. Abominations. Blasphemies. Grotesqueries. Reared for the fighting Pit and the master's bidding.'

'All right, mate, calm down. 'Alex waved at him frantically, seeing the redness of Wulfric's irritation gush across his cheeks. 'I didn't need a bloody walking thesaurus. Come on. And keep quiet.'

Cold and ethereal, the Crooked Spire twisted from their feet, up into the ragged crags of the Hollow Mountain. Alex felt a little less queasy now having left the dungeons. His new carry-on, Wulfric was, although dreadfully annoying, rather helpful. Using those huge arms and thick head, Wulfric had opened gates with ease. Alex, on the other hand, would have had to sit and contemplate a while to figure out how best to not use his hands to literally bring the walls down on top of him. No, the warden was a much simpler method of extraction. Having mystical powers was all well and good, but one wrong move and, poof, who knew. Might turn himself into a newt. Wulfric was surely, as well, much better company as the living, than that gravedigger had been. The thought made Alex shudder and tussle his fingers.

As if conjuring what he saw in his mind's eye next; manifesting it into reality, like some horrifying, deified *tulpa*, a crash of wings broke the silent air. Alex saw the Valravn leap from the night, into their path, standing on its beastly legs, between the travellers and their quarry, the Crooked Spire.

Both of them froze in terror, as the Frankenstein-monster-mashing of wolf, raven and man screed high into the stars, craning its long, black beak skyward and digging its yellowed claws into the earth.

'For Valhalla.'

Wulfric had cried and begin to charge before Alex could scream at him to stop. He tried to move in the warden's path, but was too late. Alex grasped out with his mind…with his hands and…almost…pulled. It could not stop Wulfric's charge. The pull only managed to trip the warden, so that he now ran, headfirst, seax to the side.

'Aww, you twat.' Alex sighed, cursing himself.

As easily as swatting a fly, the Valravn fluttered its wing, colliding with Wulfric. It sent the warden skyward. Alex was turning his head in time, just to see the mind-bending altercation. No sooner had he looked, then it happened. In the blink of an eye. A momentary crack in space. In time. A purple twang in the night split reality. An illusion of daylight and it was over. Wulfric hit the anomaly mid-air, with the sound of a flailed whip cracking, vanished, emerged again in a fraction of a second. When his remains hit the earth, being all that remained of Wulfric, mere bones; they scattered over the mud and soil of the courtyard. Alex was only just seeing now that Wulfric's remains lay not alone, but that the courtyard was almost teeming with shattered remnants of warriors and citizens alike.

'Aha, that's different all right,' he swallowed a lump of fear in his throat. Retched. Then tried again.

They moved as quickly as each other. Not knowing where it came from, a surge of strength flowed through Alex. Fear? Terror? More like. When the winged-chimera advanced on him, shrieking like a fire-alarm, so did he. It seemed as though he were tearing at an invisible plastic sheet. Tough, resisting his pull, the Valravn stood still feet away, broken in its stride. The Valravn screed, as its muscles and fibres began to tear apart from their roots. Its molecules at the centre, breaking down. It screeched in pain. Tearing, with every shred of power he had, Alex felt rapid waters rushing through his blood. He heaved. Finally, with a ripping, squelching last tug, Alex pulled apart his arms, letting them shake in their sockets.

Ten feet away, the hideous, beastly amalgamation wrenched in two. Hell, Alex was ready to say, 'cleaved in 'twain'. The critter split down its centre, almost perfectly symmetrical and fell to the earth in half. All its loose internal organs dropped by the middle, forming a small heap of blood and guts.

'Aww, fuck, mate.' Alex cocked his head to the side and heaved. A projectile spew emerged across the ground. 'that...was bloody brutal,' then he retched and heaved again as the smell finally reached him.

Grim's Road

ᛙ

Broken was the outer wall of the Æsir's burgh.
The Vanir, foreseeing conflict, tramp o'er the plains.
Odin cast [his spear], and mid the people hurled it: that was the first
warfare in the world.

- Völuspá

It was beautiful, Jack thought. *A beautiful, haunting painting.*

It hung against the backdrop of a picturesque mountain scene. Above, the clouds gathered, obscuring the highest peak of the highest mountain. Beneath this crooked hill, whose peak touched above heavens, sat their destination. Nestled in the valley, surrounded by bodies of running water and fields of green grass. The castle, clung partially to the mountain itself, jutting out on a triangular plateau. A long man-made bridge stretched out like a giant's stone finger, reaching the cliffs on the valley's far side, where Grim's cart rolled along a treacherous cliffside path. Jack peered, uneasy, down the edge of the cliff. One stumble. One loose rock. And the cart would fall hundreds of feet, to the broken earth below. Yet, the cart had not stumbled once, even on the roughest of stretches, when the path had been even less width than the cart itself. Grim was in all utterly at ease with his strange eight-legged mare taking control. So much so that barely gripped the reins. The name of the horse, Sleipnir.

'The slippery-one,' Grim had called the animal, pulling a draw of smoke into his mouth, as the cart petered onto a smoother terrain, with woodland either side, clinging to the side of the cliffs with long-dead roots.

'He is, unfortunately, also named Lokisson, and carries with him the curse of Loki. Though, I would allow Sleipnir to carry me unto the ends of the world. Without fail.' Grim reached forward and gave the steed's rump a slap, to which it replied with a friendly flick of the tail.

'Behold,' Grim said, tapping Jack towards the crossing over the valley, 'the bridge of the Mad King.'

Sleipnir rolled the cart to the left, away from the cliff's edge, where it was greeted with the visages of two mighty Valkyries, paving the way onto the *very*-lengthy cobbled bridge. The bridge would carry them over field and field until they reached...

'... Lucien's Bastion,' Grim did not smile, 'once the seat of the Mad King himself. Long ago, in the Golden Age of Altheim. Behind her fabled walls, lies our foe, Jack. Be prepared to witness a sight not oft seen by mortal eyes. For a shadow has long since grown on the accursed place. Blood-drinkers, skin-changers, and fiends of old from the Hollow Mountain's depths have rescinded their dark abodes. Now, the Bastion is nothing more than a castle of death and despair. Of the living in souls within its walls, I sense a fear rising. Loki's plan to set in motion the Gotterdammerung stirs both beast and demon from slumber. A greater foe than he has awoken, below even the pit of the Hollow Mountain. Do you hear it screaming? Calling to its kith and kin?'

Jack caught the old man's eye and nodded, 'Yes, The Adversary?'

Grim turned back to Sleipnir and whistled for the horse to ease on his pace. Jack took the opportunity to fulfil the strange desire in his heart and peek over the edge of the bridge's crumbling walls. Far beneath, rivers twisted around the pillared foundations, buttresses of unfathomable height, kissed by the silvery waters of moonlight-touched streams. Roosts of bats swarmed from their twilight homes, into the forming mists of the night, gathering like vortices upon this haunting, gothic painting of ancient stone.

Some ways over the bridge, the usually calm and peaceful Sleipnir began to buck and bray. Ahead, through more attuned eyes, something wicked had spooked the animal. It was only as the cart rolled closer that the animal actually became calmer, once it had seen that it was no beast stretched wide across the narrow bridge. Jack thought similar, at first glimpse; that the desiccation and desecration and dissection had been the outline of a large, winged creature. It was, in fact, a man, whose arms had been stretched by wire and whose skin had been cut and shaped and pulled away from its person. The ribcage had been cut and the lungs pulled from the back of the spine, letting the man 'spring-open', hacked at the rear, to give the visage of an eagle, in flight.

'By the Tree.' Grim's voice faltered, as he barked furiously all manner of curses. 'Too far this demon has gone. Too far.'

The old man released the body from its poetic torture and held it in his arms, folding everything back into its rightful place.

'A blood-eagle,' Grim spat, 'reserved only for the greatest of treacheries. For what this man has done I feel no taint so strong on his soul.'

With those words, Grim folded the limbs to the body and placed the corpse in the back of the cart, without need for Jack's help. It was only when the cart jerked and rolled on again that Jack could look back and see the eyelids fall open and the cavities of blood beneath, lay empty. Visited again by horror, Jack heard the curses uttered by Grim as Sleipnir rode on over cobbled stones, past men and women and children, all dead. Their heads arranged on spikes, like some grotesque royal welcome for these weary travellers. Other suffered a greater pain. Heaved over the edge of the walls, their stomachs bulging, as long staves punched from bowel to chest, there to be impaled, until their fleshless, skin-eaten bones fell into the rivers below. Cages chained the side of the bridge with human remains. Barrels of bloody matter and a viscous sanguine liquid. Overhead, more bodies hung in gibbet's, leaving flesh exposed for the carrion birds encircling. Still, they were able to provide sustenance for their avian assailants, who swooped from on high to carry away fleshy morsels for their young. With such a freely offered feast, the birds came in their murders, adding to the endless sight of blackened wings over the moonlit keep of Lucien's Bastion.

At the end of the cobbled bridge stood the infamous Traitor's Gate. Built not to withstand an approaching army, for no army ever thought daring enough to assail the Mad King's fortress; this gate stood for only one purpose, to let those crossing the Valkyrie's Bridge to know that to defy the will of the king was to be punishable by death. To have your skin removed from your body in one long pull, whilst your lungs still took air and your heart still beat. Your skull finally becoming another level in the stone foundations of the keep. Jack saw tonight a glimpse into the long-dead mind of the Mad King Lucien, yet also saw with what utterly astonishing power he ruled to create such architectural wonder from such barren rock. Not a single roof in the castle or surrounding villages was equal to its neighbour. No tower wet unbent or slanted. The houses and hovels dropped down and down, clinging to the mountain, till they spread out around the bottom of the plateau and cliffs. A small, slip carved into the mountainside, the only way for his subjects to reach the Mad King. Though, as Jack and the others knew, there was more than just a few runways, secret passages and crypts through which to enter the castle.

****

Jack easily kept up with Grim, though the old man held a powerful stride, as they approached the unnerving, towering walls of the Bastion.

'See the gate?' Grim asked, and it had been somewhat of a rhetorical question. There was way to miss them. Two behemoth iron doors, the size of twenty men in height, held the city walls closed. Bodies, wretched, decaying, and festering isn't their own filth, had been hung for the gatehouse above, left to rot in the moonlight. A murder of crows made their presence known as they swooped in for another morsel of flesh.

'With what army do you intend we break that down?' Jack asked, eyeing the sheer weight and size of the doors.

'We do not. Break it down.' Grim spoke as if Jack had purposed the most belligerent question. 'We are going to knock on the door and ask to be let inside.'

Sure, Jack was in a mind long since able to worry about the trivialities of simple reason. 'Why not, eh?'

Bastion's houses rose and fell in awkward, mismatched patterns. Each roof seemed to follow on the from the next at an entirely different level, as though a dozen different architects had designed and build the city to appear altogether misshapen and bent. Some windows hung at peculiar, diagonal angles. Others had been placed onto overbearing walls, so that the only view from inside would have been the ground. Stone and masonry bulged in places where it should not and sank in places where it should. Still, once every seven or so houses, there would be an almost perfect design placed between them. Jack understood that these houses were designed not to break from the misshapen architecture, but to draw attention to them. This is what a house should be, and these are what you have been given. Oddly unnerving.

'Mad Lucien,' Jack said aloud.

'Yes. The insane designer of this forgotten little berg, nestled in the hills. I believe, as the story goes, he designed one large abode in particular and trapped himself inside, ever building so that none would find him.' Grim pointed, through the spaces between the mediaeval shanties towards a building woven into the face of a rock.

Jack almost asked why, before racking his mind. What he found in those memories he never chose, haunted him. 'A vampire?'

Shrugging, Grim replied, 'Naturally. I do not suppose one would wish to lock themselves away for all time because they simply cease to care for sunlight.'

Although no human presence was to be seen, the streets of Bastion were not entirely empty. Shadowy figures loomed out of their dwellings, into the moonlit night. Eyes of sanguineous crimson flickered from alleyways and dark, moving shadows slipped in and out of windows, ever watching as the pair strode on towards the Crooked Spire.

'Are these vampires?' Jack examined the nightly figures.

'Some. Yes.' Grim acknowledged several of the shadows gathered in an upper window by tipping his hat towards them. 'Others are simply ghosts and spectres. Memories who have long since lost their humanity and cling to their souls like barnacles on a ship. It would take a great deal of prying to release them from their snares. I suggest we do our best to ignore them.

'I believe, we are here.'

Curving around one of the inner streets, the road opened up. Houses dropped away and led out onto a great courtyard. Once, many years ago, as Jack remembered, the Kingly expanse had been host to festivities and great regal pomp. In its place, there had been erected a vile and hideous construction. Walls of wrought iron and steel encircled a pit, filled with mud, bones, and decaying remnants of warriors. Jack was immediately reminded of an ancient coliseum. An arena, in which slaves would fight to the death for the enjoyment of their superiors and owners. Behind the fighting pit stood the base of the Crooked Spire, and looming far above, its curving, twisting frame extended high into the night.

****

As easily as brushing aside a net curtain, Grim waved his hand over the gates, watching them swing open on rusting hinges. The sound screeched for miles around and Jack wondered if Safiya and Alex had heard it, wherever they were. *God, tell me they are all right.*

Jack followed Grim into the arena. It was in no uncertain terms, a trap. There was no other notion that could be possible and yet they willingly strode inside and awaited their snare-master's appearance. Still remembering the face of that slithering demonic presence in Helheim, Jack was all too happy to wait just a moment longer, before Loki materialised into their presence. His wish was denied. Several feet above, on a tall parapet of the encircling arena, a single obsidian shape emerged to greet them.

'Grimnir,' Loki was as naked as before, with only his blackened skin shielding the various stings, cuts and scars from view. He was tall. Maybe taller here. His bright, luminously white face contraposed grotesquely with his epidermis. 'It has taken you much longer than I thought. Then again, what is waiting, when you have given me all the time in the world?'

It was obvious that Loki was referring to the runic key, as he rolled something gently between his long claws.

'Jack, is it?' Loki snapped his neck towards the man beside Grim, syllabising every word with a demonic hiss. 'He has told me much about you. And your friends. Am I to assume that they are the reason my Draugr have been awoken?'

'Enough of this, Loki,' Grim smacked the shaft of his spear into the mud, sending a reverberating wave of static around the arena, to show he still had some power left, especially in this realm. 'Release the Skulla, Beatrix, and return her to me. Ragnarök can wait. Fall on your knees and I will show you mercy. You shall not return to your cave, I swear.

Even the Aesir might see fit to allow your soul entrance back into the halls of the gods.'

What shrieked around the arena was no less than the cry of a menacing eagle, but the sound itself came from Loki, who hunched over, dizzying with laughter, 'The gods? How many are left, One-Eye? Soon, the Twilight will be upon them and Götterdämmerung will see the dawning of a new age. Everything shall fall, and be replaced with a new order. One of death. Why await Valhalla when I can bring Valhalla to the Nine Realms? No more men. No more elves. No more dwarves. Nothing but the armada of the damned to sail the Naglfar on a voyage across the stars, reaping world after world until only the strongest of shadows remain.'

'But this is a pointless rebuke, Grimnir. None of you shall see the Black Dawn rise. None of you shall witness as The Adversary is awoken from the Great Cage below. I will allow nothing of you to remain, lest you look on in horror, as The Architect himself is destroyed. I shall at least, once-brother, spare you that terror. And not by my hand shall your reckoning come. There is much to be done. Shall I offer a small reacquaintance as my parting gift?'

As the wicked form slithered away from the parapet, it was replaced by another, smaller figure, but one that Jack found no less horrifying, no less intimidating and no less heartbreaking.

'Grayson.' Jack called up and saw the figure wave him away, instead turning to Grim.

'Well, well, we meet again, old man,' Grayson smiled. He had changed, drastically, not just in voice, tone and manner, but in appearance. Instead of the long dancing ponytail by his neck, nothing but a smooth and tattooed scalp remained; etched with images of grotesqueries and abominations. He had discarded the white, prisoner's jumpsuit and emerged wearing what seemed to be a priestly or monkish vestment. Long black drapes hung from his shoulders, touching the floor. His gnarled fingers wrapped themselves around the shaft of a dark staff, itself carved with sapphire runes.

'Good God,' Jack had wanted to scream the words in his head but found them barking from his mouth like a rabid dog, 'what have you done?'

'Don't address me, kid. It's the old man I've come for.' Grayson spat down into the pit. 'Look at what fate has drove us to. You drag me through hell and high water and stand there looking as though you ain't done a damn thing wrong. I'll tell you now, old man, there's a reckoning to be had.'

Grim stepped forward, pushing Jack back with his spear as he did, 'Michael, that is enough. Turn your sword elsewhere and we can end this.'

Chuckling with a mouth of browning teeth, Grayson spat again, 'Yeah, yeah. Sure. Let's all play happy families and forget trespasses and whatnot? I knew, deep down, with every life I ever took, that something greater was calling to me, from the abyss. A terrible darkness that glowed with warmth. All it took, was a little shove through a door, and bingo, life awakens within me once more. I should thank you, old man, before I dissect you and find out how you work. You saved me, in a way. The way a bullet saves a starving mutt.'

Quick as lightning, Grayson slammed the staff into the parapet and the fighting pit shook to life. Shots of blue light swam from the staff, swimming about the edges of the pit, before descending into the litter of corpses strewn on the bloody, muddy ground. One by one, the blue aura began to illuminate and grow within the bodies, bringing each of them into a reanimated existence. Bones and flesh rendered and snapped into place, as two dozen or more warriors clambered from their graves, twitching and gasping for an air they could no longer consume.

'Jack, take this.' Grim flicked back his cloak and a dazzling glimmer caught his eye. Whether or not it had always been there mattered not, Grim drew the blade and tossed it to Jack, who caught it feebly, almost dropping it under the unusual weight. 'Its name is Tyrfing. Let the blade do the work, boy.'

As if guided by a hand not his own, Jack felt the sword snag in his palm, directing its way forward. On the first slash, as a rotting corpse closed in on him, Tyrfing gleamed with an inner light of fire, before sweeping sideways and back, severing the revenants head from its shoulders. With a gurgling gasp, the blue light fell from the corpses eyes and it lay still on the ground once more.

All right. All right. Let's do this, Jack heaved a deep breath and again let Tyrfing drive him on.

Another corpse fell, splitting in two. Then another and another. Jack swung and slashed, chopped and hacked through an army of decaying muscle and bone. The feeling of each strike made him queasy, noticing every foul cut nick across sinews and marrow. Several times the sword became lodged in a skull, or a spine and Jack had to use his feet and both hands to pull Tyrfing free, ready, just in time, to turn the blade on yet another revenant. By his side, almost step for step, back-to-back, Grim lunged and drove Gungnir through open bellies and twisted torsos, flinging the human remains around the pit as if they were ragdolls.

Above, Grayson yelped a cry of rage, as the last of the revenants was slung over Grim's shoulder, the aura vanishing from sight.

'Thieves,' Grayson smacked the staff into the edge of the parapet and cursed them, seething with anger. 'These gifts I've been given. You have no idea, kid.'

'You have those gifts from me, son.' Grim flicked back his cloak, standing as tall as he could manage, though Jack heard the old man's chest heaving with strain.

'Silence.' Grayson lifted the staff and with both hands drove it so hard into the wooden floor that it splintered. 'I have something truly special for you two. Behold.'

Something grating moved under the pit. Jack had to leap to one side, as the floor shook in its place and started to open. Corpses of the fallen fell one after another, down into a pitch-black hole in the centre of the arena. Mud and earth sloshed over the edge, dripping into the dark abyss. A terrible groan emanated from the hole, as behemoth limbs stretched out from the murky shadows below. What crawled forth from the depths was nothing less than an utter abomination. A Frankenstein creature, made of the bones of dead men. An amalgamation of horrors from the grave, bound together with rope, steel and whatever dark magicka Grayson had infused the creature with life. Every hair, every fibre of Jack's being stretched outward, wating to break free from his soul and flee from the dread anathema. Chunks of fat and meat still clung to the human remains, as the nightmare finally released itself from its cage under the pit and hunched over. Standing tall, it would have dwarfed the tallest of giants. Grayson roared with madman's laughter, as the creature, the creature rattled its way forward, towards Grim.

'A *Gravelord*. Never again.' Grim showed for what Jack saw to be the first time, sheer fear under the face of the abomination.

Grim used his hand to toss Gungnir through the air, a spear woven with such runes that it would always deliver a killing blow. The spear soared through the arena and caught the ribcages of the Gravelord, spinning away into the mud. Without flinching or pausing, the abomination continued to lumber forward.

'Run,' Grim cried, turning away.

Jack did not need telling twice. He turned on his heels and fled. It was hard, trying to break his feet free of the mud each time he pushed on. Behind, he did not need to see or hear the creature, he could feel its presence shaking the earth and the shadow of its form blocking out the moonlight. When he fell, Jack felt his life flicker for a moment, teetering on the possibility that with one crushing blow, it would be all over. Jack closed his eyes, throwing his hands over his head like caught prey, ready for death.

****

As though a gust of wind passed over him, Jack felt the air move. Behind, the abomination staggered and began to howl. Again, and again. Jack heard movement dashing all around him. Side to side, the pawing of pads across the earth drowned out the creature's protests, when Jack realised it was not the Gravelord who was making those sounds. Turning over, still flat to the floor, he saw six, large wolf-like animals leaping and howling at Grayson's necrotic creation. Jack had seen this before; hounds baying at a hunted and cornered bear. He did not know where the huge wolves had come from. He was not even sure if they were, so to say, 'on his side'. At first, he did not care. Jack took the brief opportunity to scramble to his feet and make his way towards the gate of the fighting pit.

There, Grim waited. Looking back, the pair watched on, flinching are the abomination struggled against the animals, when Safiya came bounding through the gate beside them. Paying them only a hesitant glance, she rushed in to join the fight. Jack looked at Grim. The old man smiled and followed. One of the Úlfhéðnar rose up on its hind legs, using them to grapple up onto the abomination. There came w violent screech, as the Gravelord clutched its sinewy palm around the wolf-warrior and squeezed, spilling innards and entrails onto the floor, steaming as they sank into the cold earth. Seeing their brother fall, the berserkers raged, howling a chorus of anger, before attacking as one. Swatting and swiping, the abomination roared with ten heads, that writhed and screamed atop its skeletal form, trying to tear the Úlfhéðnar free. Teeth sank into its legs and arms. Below, three of the wolf-warriors tore at chunks of flesh and remnants of human corpses, dragging pieces of the Gravelord out and tossing them aside, just as it had done to them. The largest of the berserkers managed to pounce up onto the abomination's upper torso, snarling with fury, and bury its head, neck deep, into the steel and bones, like a fox digging for a trapped rabbit.

After a moment's struggle, the wolf was inside of the carcass of the Gravelord, ripping and shredding its way out again through its amalgamation of ribcages; bursting through its chest and releasing a mighty, blood-soaked howl. Cocking its many heads towards the heavens, the abomination roared its chorus, before staggering backwards and dropping to one knee. Each splint of steel holding its limbs together came loose, from the ferocious and insatiable claws and teeth. Again, and again. Relentlessly, the Úlfhéðnar removed corpse after corpse. Skull and chest and skin, till all that remained were the bare bones of the Gravelord. With a terrible pop, it dropped to both knees, though still towered above the arena. Between its shattered cages of bone, the amalgamated corpses wailed, as one by one they were torn from their hellish behemoth and cast to the floor.

The Gravelord roared, using the last of its might to wrench free two of the wolf-warriors. Using every last morsel of strength, it brought the heaving hands together, and the berserkers clashed into a chaotic pile of guts and hair below. Another of the wolves tried to limp away, critically injured from below the waist, when the heaving fist of the Gravelord fell from above, breaking through the spine and pushing the hound into the mud, where it did not move again. Safiya had been watching her warriors fall, one by one, enraged beyond any realisation that she could feel this fire within her veins.

Drawing her sword, Safiya timed her position and moved swiftly between the fighting. Dodging limb and bone, she manoeuvred with an ease she had not felt since her youth. Finally, as the seventh Úlfhéðnar was crushed and she had seen enough death, Safiya rolled under the shadow of the abomination and used the blade the cut two heaving blows into the upper thighs, cutting the steel and cord binding the legs in place. Roaring, the Gravelord's torso fell down, splitting between its legs, as the upper half cracked, falling backwards.

Wooden beams of the parapet shook, and the foundations crumbled, bringing the arena wall thundering upon the abomination. Through snaring, bloody canines, the Úlfhéðnar scampered around the decimated ruin of the Gravelord, craning their teeth moonward for a triumphant, choral howl. Not a soul saw Grayson's body fall, yet it must have been somewhere within the rubble and smoke of the collapse. It was not until Safiya saw the wretched, tattooed hand crawl forth from steel and splinter, that any sign of life remained. Without hesitation, her teeth gripping together, Safiya rushed, dancing over the ruins of the abomination, finding her sword drawn and pointing down at the scarred face of the Necromancer.

'Do...it,' Grayson choked out a lungful of dust. One eye had been horrifically removed by a large steel bolt, tearing a chunk of flesh from cheek to forehead as it carved through Grayson's face. 'Please,' he added, as a pool of blood emerged from his lips. He coughed again and doused Safiya in a shower of sanguine rain.

'No. Stop.' Grim sprinted spryly, teaching their side before Safiya could deliver the killing blow. 'There is another way. I realise the pain he has caused in you all, but allow me to try and heal his soul.'

With his gnarled fingers, Old Grim gently touched the tips to Grayson's temples. There was a great awakening, somewhere deep inside the Necromancer. Deep in a realm long thought forgotten. Where wild beasts roam the dark forests and vultures pecked at what shreds remained of the prisoner's soul. One by one the images fled, deeper down into the recesses of Grayson's mind, to be locked away, in that shroud of immemorial shadow, where they had grown so many years before.

'When he awakes, I can promise you the demon's taint will have gone.' Grim told Safiya, but had to reiterate that, 'he is still the wretched killer he once was. That I cannot change. His sins are innumerable. I leave his gate in your hands. Be the judge I cannot be.'

Only one eye opened. Safiya met Grayson's gaze with a curious wonder. She waited, hoping to see that powerful soul she had met all that time ago, in the forest of nightmares. In Helheim.

'You,' Grayson blinked his remaining eye, 'I'm glad it's you, girl.'

The sound of steel grating on steel was the last sound of the battle. Grim, facing away, held his breath. With both hands, Safiya clutched a hold of Grayson and pulled him out from his dusty grave. Her sword had been sheathed and Grim exhaled a sigh of utter relief. They would need the Necromancer, in what was to come; though the thought of leaving him alive still filled him with a sickening dread.

The Crooked Spire

❖

The sun darkens, earth in ocean sinks,
fall from heaven the bright stars,
fire's breath assails the all-nourishing tree,
towering fire plays against heaven itself.

- *Völuspá*

J ack looked at Grayson. The man could not help but stare
back, with that care-not attitude, the blasé façade that Jack
knew to be nothing more. It is when Jack himself held the
gaze, that Grayson flitted his eyes towards the floor, just for a
moment.

'Look, kid,' Grayson said, as though he were trying to
justify stealing a wallet or lifting a bag of sweets from the
corner shop, 'I'm ain't in the business of apologies. I am what
I was made to be. Ain't no-one can change that. All of ya'll
best not start getting sentimental and preachy, cos I'll just walk
away. I can do that. I can walk away right now, from all of this.
I'm choosing to stay, right here, and finish this. And this ain't
about redemption or some need to change-my-ways. All I'm
after is revenge. Can you dig that? Something real dark, darker
than I ever felt, got inside my mind. Made me…see things I
ain't never seen before, kid. Drove me into a maddened, rabid

state. Look what it created.' He kicked the corpse beside him, still trying to crawl away from its abominable amalgamation beside them, shaking his head, 'Look what I did.'

'It was a great taste of power,' he continued, 'truly mesmerising. But I've seen a piece o' Hell I ain't never going looking for again. Even in my most...curious days...I never thought such a wickedness could truly exist. I'll help you take down this monster, kid. Not for you, but for me. I'm gunna place the dagger in his heart myself. And then, I'm gunna leave y'all be. Nothing left for me now, in any world, 'cept Hell itself.'

Jack nodded once and held out his hand. It was a feeble gesture, but it had to mean something, right? Grayson bit his lip, shook his head and grasped Jack's wrist with his hand. Jack did likewise. There was embrace. No happy ending. No friendly reuniting under the moonlight. Just this. Only this.

Up they climbed. Through the Crooked Spire as the stairs wound and wound and wound endlessly into the sky. The Spire itself had sparse rooms below the zenith. An occasional broom closet or armoury would emerge to their left, but no room for accommodation; nobody lived in the lower levels of the tower. Everything that needed to be, was at the very top. Mad King Lucien had insisted it that way, which is why he had named his upper throne room, a wide-open hall at the very top, the Aerie. Directly below the Aerie and around its edges were small, narrow bedrooms and one kitchen. The structure itself began at one-hundred-and-ten feet by the same amount, squared. At the centre, before sloping a little to the left for several dozen feet, the tower was less than half as wide. Architecturally, it made no sense. Should not have been. Rumour was, that a travelling master mason, speaking a dialect unheard of, had been captured by the Mad King and imprisoned until the work was complete. The finishing touch on his masterpiece he would call the Bastion. Directly below the precipice of the Hollow Mountain, the Crooked Spire was structurally chaotic and for that reason, unsettling.

At its peak, resting atop the Spire's apex, sat the golden statuette of a bear. This finial capping must have had some connection, though now lost, to the Mad King. Like the castles across Europe that Jack had often seen in his travels he felt a strange familiarity gazing around at the Bastion. The gothic annulets of the pillars aside the fluting inlays, from a nearby temple. The gargoyles hanging from the tall flying buttresses. The stone grotesques hanging within. At the highest point of the temple, just below the oriel, sat a beautifully carved rose window, within each and every stained sheet of glass was depicted a separate, fantastical scene of sea-voyage and naval battle. Quaint, shanty houses, with white-painted upper floors and hammer beams extending out into the streets, which twisted without focus downhill and over bridge.

Jack waited, at the top of the winding staircase. Around him, he saw tall, monumental statues of indescribable beings. Some with more legs than arms, some with more heads than eyes. Others of an arachnid species, with the torsos of women and the udders of a milking cow. There was a single inscription over each of these gargoyles, running sequentially, beginning with Titan I and finishing with Titan IX. Jack turned his back on them, as their marble eyes seemed to follow his own around the foyer. When the others reached the top, Jack waited expectantly, for this final showdown and had eagerly readied himself for Grim to speak. Give some voice to what might come. Prepare them. He did not. Instead, the old man slammed his spear, Gungnir, into the marble floor and with a swift kick, let the two arching doors fly open, revealing a twilight throne room, with only one source of light.

Hanging there, without string, rope or chain, was a single, pulsing organ. At the centre of the throne room, it defied all logic of physics and philosophy. Why it hung there was knowledge only few possessed; the darkest and most twisted. A remnant of an antediluvian and obscure form of magic, no longer spoken by mortal tongues.

'The Black Heart, Grimnir,' Loki's serpentine tongue slithered out of the darkness.

'Blasphemy,' Grim rebuked, peering ahead and seeing only the single source of light in an otherwise, only partially, moonlit hall.

He slammed Gungnir into the floor again, allowing the echo of the sting to drive away a growing, haunting chant which had started to emit around the hall from mouths unseen. Dark alcoves and obsidian chambers littered the edges of the room, with hungry, piercing eyes staring back from the shadows. Jack did not want to imagine what he might see, should those beings emerge into the pale light.

'To some, it is blasphemy,' Loki snarled back.

'Am I to guess that it is with such magic that you altered my Key, twisted my greatest creation and made that blasphemous Black Door? A foul trick Faubartisson, oh, Loki of old,' Grim spat at the darkness, still unable to see where the voice of Loki came from. Wherever it sounded to originate, was surely far from its real location.

'It was not with my witchcraft that I performed such a deed, I merely acted as the instrument for *his* newest creation.' Loki hissed.

'The Adversary.'

'The Adversary, yes.' Loki seemed to almost flash an appearance. Almost. Just another shadow in the dark. 'It took years to find. For an age I festered in that cave, as poison dripped into eyes, burning my flesh. Sigyn held the bowl as best she could but, still she would falter, and Midgard would tremble with my rage. Surely you felt it, Grimnir, and knew I would one day spill that rage into your precious worlds. How pleasing do you think it was that when breaking free, that I found you had abandoned Midgard, for a new world. This world. Trying so hard to keep your precious people alive. More slain to build your walls, ride with the *Wilde Jagd* and follow you into Valhalla. Because they have new gods now, don't they, in Midgard. A different Hanged-One rules now. All of you children under The Architect, the *false one*. We all know the dark gods rule and the *old ones* will return, when The Adversary is freed. One-thousand years of fire, to begin with. All I required was one last piece of the puzzle you had so cleverly schemed. I took from you your princess. The lady Beatrix will now be crowned instead, Queen of Helheim. And my daughter, Hella shall ride with me upon the Naglfar as we retake Midgard and the Nine Realms. With her armada of the damned, and the might of Fenris-wolf, I and my kin will bring the glory of Ragnarök.'

'Silence.' Grim barked, slamming his spear, the way a judge would bang his gavel.

'Not this time, Grimnir,' Loki emerged, momentarily from the dark, if only to give each of them a clear glimpse at his twisted, necrotic face.

'What need of you for Beatrix? Why not simply ride out with Hella?' Grim asked, coyly.

Loki sniggered, 'you know why, Grimnir. You know why. One must always have a ruler in Helheim, else the sting of death would not taste as sweet. What use would Ragnarök be if there were no souls to collect?'

'You would place a child on the throne of Hel?'

'Why not?' Loki flashed in front of Grim, before fading into stygian mist. 'You did.'

It was…true. He *had* done such a thing. Taking Loki's child from its mother, damning her to reside in *sick-bed* for all time. What he had done, he had done to *stop* Ragnarök. Had he not? Was that not all that mattered?

'Every piece you have played. Every step you have taken. Every game you have created, I have been there to witness, and I have been there to turn the tide against you.' Loki laughed, a hearty, throaty laugh, filled with victorious glee. 'You made the Silver Door; I made the *Black Door*. You founded Altheim, I *twisted* it with monsters and demons. You inspired men to follow you, I *infected* their minds and broke them. You sought to hide my children from me, I took *your descendant* from you. You came to stop me, and I *allowed* it. There is only one last move for me to make, and once Fenriswolf is free, I shall use *your* Key to open the Silver Door to Midgard. The Tree of Life shall burn and all who rest on its limbs. For this, I thank you, Grimnir. For all the years you hid from fate; you have made it so.'

'You know so much, and yet you force truths from me. Tell me Grimnir,' Loki's voice turned curious. 'Did you know all and now are simply stalling for time?'

'Yeah,' the Necromancer stepped from the shadows, cracking his knuckles, as if about to enter the ring with an old rival, 'looky here, he brought back up.'

'Aye,' the Philosopher came to stand beside the two.

'Leave the girl alone and leave, demon,' another voice, the Valkyrie walked towards the Necrotic Orb at the room's centre.

And finally, the Magician followed, 'yeah, face it, mate…the job's fucked.'

'Such is the fate of the deceiver,' Gungnir slipped with ease from Grim's hand and before eyes could see it move, the silver-tipped spear had pierced through the Necrotic Orb, and shattered the Black Heart of The Adversary. A quiver of light rippled out from the Crooked Spire. Every dark being across Altheim, even across the Nine Realms, felt a stiff sting of pain in their souls.

Loki screeched with anger and leapt forward from the shadow. His body fell to the floor, arms out in front, as he tried in vain to catch the Black Heart. It touched the marble floor with a thud, as Gungnir stood erect from the organ, mighty and triumphant. Loki was fast in his vengeance, but the Magician was faster. With all the power he had learned to focus, he pushed out his palms, sending the demonic Loki cascading through the air. Moonlight filled the room, from every window, nook cranny of the stone walls. The Black Heart's strange power subsided, and the Crooked Spire was itself once more. With a sly, owl-like scree, Loki dragged himself up from the floor, crawled hand and foot towards the throne, lifted himself from the dais and slumped down onto its golden-filigree seat.

On the ground of the throne room, was engraved a symbol. So large, that it encompasses the entirety of the hall, from wall to wall. Depicted thus, was the image of an Ouroboros, a snake which eternally devours its own tail. Devoted to time and the persistence of change, the snake coiled itself about a perfectly equal triangle, whose upper tip touched the dais. Hanging from the walls, was an altogether different symbol. A burning tree, of white and red set against a black flag. It summarised much the same; being the passage of time. But instead of eternal glory, there was persistent chaos.

'The Architect and The Adversary,' Loki was slunk over the throne of golden filigree inlaid oak. It was the only chair in the room. No seat for guests, nor concubines.

He uttered a single, guttural word and a figure, larger than any in the room, came forwards, clutching a familiar face between its grey, gnarled hands. The Princess.

'Let her go,' the Valkyrie seemed to burst with rage, so that the others could feel an electrified sensation brimming about them, across every primal hair.

Loki puffed out a retort, mockingly, 'Come get her, oh, *valiant* warrior.'

Before the Valkyrie could make it more than a foot, yet another figure emerged from behind the dais. It was a young woman. Not much older than the Princess herself and yet, with each turn the girl took, she changed. One half, young, beautiful skin and radiant blonde hair. The other half, a rotting, disfigured corpse, with a pallor of flesh that had marinated in saltwater for a week. Green, sickly, and broken. Her tongue lolled from the side of her mouth, through lipless gums.

'Hel,' Grim warned them, waving even the Valkyrie to move away, as the sick-girl shamble towards them. One foot stood upright. One bent and crooked as the Spire itself.

Hel screamed. A mixture of girlish cries and a dead tongue. From the shadows an army of moulding cadavers shuffled, calling out groans as she wailed with her armada of the damned. Grim and the others were surrounded.

'Fight. Fight for your lives.'

They did.

Sending back wave after wave, the Magician parted the dead like a breaking wave. Windows shattered under his casts, sending body after body against wall and stone. Limbs, so forced by the power, wrenched from their sockets, adding to the growing, festering stink. The Valkyrie fought the dead as she had fought them in the crypt. Her spear was like a tree-limb in the wind. Her spear-tip a falling star in the night. Each celestial spin forced her foes to kneel before her and taste their second death. The Philosopher and the Necromancer fought side by side. Body after body came, fell, was made whole again to fight their own kin. Slowly, but surely, the Necromancer forced his will and his might back into the fallen remains, returning them with a vengeance to stalk the armada of the damned. The fight was over before it had even begun. Loki gazed on in sheer fury. Not that he had underestimated his own power, but that not even his trickery could have seen such a deception from the old man. How could he have known who they were? How could he have known what power this world could instil? Perhaps it was not Loki, Faubartisson, who held all the unseen cards?

'No.'

All eyes turned to the edge of the tower. There she stood, out on one of the Mad King's balconies. She had moved slowly, unseen, and in her hand, dangling so close to the edge – was Beatrix, as Hel wrapped her bony, paper-thin fingers around her neck.

'I believe,' Loki started to clap with great emphasise, 'that she will drop the child, if you do not surrender this farce.'

****

It was far too late for Jack to shout. Too late to beg. Too late to stop Grayson from moving forward. The Necromancer yelled, hurtling at full speed towards Betty. Around Jack, time slowed to a heartbeat's pace. Hella launches herself through the air, pouncing, fingers extended like curling adders. Had that second passed again, what a different world might have been. Grayson felt his arms cling around the girl, holding her tight. The throne room boomed with Jack's voice. Grayson felt the floor loft from under him. Felt the air turn cold and sour. Then, just as he expected, the ground opened up around him. Betty fell on her back, as the pair collided above her, into a formless shape of blurs. She managed only to see Grayson's gleaming smile, as he tumbled over the edge of the tower, holding the queen of Helheim in his arms. They each rushed over to the edge. Jack, Alex, Safiya, Grim, and Betty. The five companions looked on in horror, at the shadow of blood on the stone so far below their feet.

The Wolf at the End of the Story

ᛗ

Trembles Yggdrasil's ash yet standing; groans
that aged tree, and the jötun is loosed. Loud bays Garm
before the Gnupa-cave, his bonds he
rends asunder; and the wolf runs.

- Völuspá

The Crooked Spire was empty. Rejoicing in their victory, the few people left living under the shadow of Lucien's Bastion had risen up, called down from the mountains and the valleys, to take back their beloved city. Tribes of warriors claimed their streets, driving the creatures of darkness back out into the cold wastes of the North. The Jötunn and their stunted, malformed kin retreated far underground, as the flags of The Architect were raised once more over the walls. As the madness had come to a closure, not a soul had seen Loki retreat. Somehow, the trickster had managed to leave the city unmolested. Grim had an idea that Loki, who had once possessed the ability to morph his shape into any form, simply became a doppelgänger, stealing human form, before slipping away into the night.

'We cannot allow him to escape. Not again.' Grim had warned them, as the five companions gathered around the crackling pyre, upon which their friend, Michael Grayson, had his body lain.

Smoke rising, almost as high as the Crooked Spire, send a message far into the heavens that Grayson had paid at least part of his due and each gave a prayer to The Architect, that this last act of selflessness and care might go in some way to negating the Necromancer's crimes against God and man. But they would never truly forget who or what he was. A man whose duality never ceases to struggle within his soul. Plagued by a shadow. Given hope by companionship. There was no time for feasting. No time to rejoice in the revelries of Fallangr. Altheim itself was far from safe.

Every world that clung to the Tree of Life remained, as it had before, in utmost danger. Loki had lost only one child that night. Grim knew that there was only one destination, one direction he could go. Further north, where the mountains fell into rolling hills of ice and snow. A barren, lifeless desert of wraiths, where only the Jötunn themselves dare tread. It was there, all those many aeons ago, that he, his son and Tyr had bound the monstrous beast, Fenris-wolf. That ancient leviathan from the bitter cold, who if set free amongst the cosmos, would set into motion the Twilight of the Gods.

Ragnarök has yet to be stopped. Rolling through the treacherous, mountainous paths, Grim had called on his people to return to him his horse, Sleipnir. Bound to a heavy cart, the eight-legged mare hiked its way over hill, carrying the five remaining companions in a cart laid over with a white tarp, so that along with the white mane of the horse, allowed them to remain an unseen hunter. Betty slept most of the journey, as did Alex. Safiya and Jack knew that safety was a luxury they could ill afford; not yet, not until all of this had been finished. So, they stayed vigilant, together, whilst Grim himself had not felt the touch of sleep in some hundred years.

Rising and falling twice, the dying sun of Altheim began to set on the third day, when the mountains finally broke and the cart, pulled by Sleipnir rolled away over a frozen lake, beneath which creatures never seen by man, slinked to and fro in their briny abyss. Wolves, called to the frozen north by their great master, Fenrir, gathered *en mass* in the hills, but merely watched the travellers pass, ever present watchers in a barren wasteland. Only eyes on the storm now. Piercing yellow glints. Hints at what was waiting, just out there, beating the veil of snow and shadow. Wolves, patiently waiting as the companions made a brief camp, under the only shelter available. A poor construct. The cart was placed at the top of a small ridge and gave only a modicum of added protection from the hail of ice.

Grim had to shout, over the wind sweeping across the endless desert of snow, 'We have to find the chains. They cannot be far. Jack, my son, stay here and await our return. Come, Safiya, bring something warm.'

They and Alex threw a couple of woollen coats over their backs and set off away from the camp. Jack watched as their feet sunk to almost knee height, trudging very carefully through the snow. By his side, Betty wrapped the last of the blankets around her legs and climbed down under the ravine. Jack followed. Immediately, the wind dropped by twenty decibels, no longing ringing through their ears. He was now able to make out what Betty had tried to say several times before; 'I'm scared, Jack.'

They were in a sleep like state when the others returned. Not dreaming. Not quite awake. Such cold did that. Clamped right into the bones, like a vice and gripped until the eyes closed and the heart slowed. At least they stayed cold. Survival Rule No. 14: Warm in cold, never old. One of the last signs of death by severe hypothermia.

Hunched beneath the snow-covered heath, Betty and Jack sat impatiently and waited for news to return. It had been some time since the others had left to find help. Whether the small fishing village, in its isolated wilderness, had been abandoned seemed too depressing to contemplate. Jack tucked and trimmed the large animal hide, so that Betty was comfortable and warm. Overhead the icy shards of a winter's gale passed by like bullets. For a moment, Jack felt as if he were in the trenches of Normandy. Jerry's hail of metal firing into the distance of no-man's-land. They were not safe here, he knew that, but they had enough shelter and enough warmth to keep them alive for a good while. He prayed that time was, as they said, 'on his side'.

'Jack?' Betty moved sideways in the hovel, so that her head leaned onto his shoulder.

The feeling was uncomfortable, but he allowed it. 'What?'

'Grim said there's a monster waiting for us? Is that true? I don't wanna see any monsters. Why can't we just go back home. Momma is gunna be furious with me.' Betty sounded far away. Perhaps she was thinking of home. Jack was not sure if he had remembered exactly where, or when, Betty had said 'home' was. Without thinking too hard, he guessed Kansas, sometime in the thirties. Maybe that was just Hollywood encroaching into his mind again. Perhaps the Cowardly Lion and the Scarecrow would be waiting just over that next hill? A tall green monolith, welcoming them to the Emerald City. He doubted it. This did not seem as if it were a Hollywood story.

Not an American one. This was a tale much older than the ideals of 1776. There were things out here in the vast unending darkness that had seen the dawns of new stars and the births of galaxies.

Here, he thought, *there be dragons;* picturing on old pirate's map on the desk of a captain's quarters.

'You know,' Jack had to speak a little louder, as the gale blistered over another round of machine-gun fire hail, 'my Oma used to say—'

'What's an Oma?' Betty interrupted without looking up.

Jack chuckled, 'it means grandma, in German. She used to read to me. Stories. Stories you'll know well. Cinderella. Sleeping Beauty. But, the originals. Not the reboots. By the Brothers Grimm.'

'Like *Mr.* Grim?' Betty asked.

Jack's mind had not made that connection before, 'Possibly, yeah. Anyway, the original stories are much darker and much scarier than the Disney stuff. Oma used to say that at the end of every good story, there was a wolf.'

'Is that the monster that's waiting?' Betty moved in a little closer.

Jack shook his head, but felt she was not looking, 'I'm not sure. But that's the point she made. There's *always* a wolf at the end of the story. It's sort of the obvious conclusion to a story in a country where all there is, are trees and mountains and wolves.'

'And what, then? Let me guess, the hero saves the day?' Betty sighed, louder than the gale, and Jack knew she was thinking of Grayson. He was not sure if there would ever come a point in which he could explain to her just what Grayson was. The others had hinted at his past, but even at fourteen, and a bright fourteen at that, Betty had missed the tone of the conversations.

Jack shook his head, 'No. No, not usually. I kind of think now, that maybe the moral she was trying to get across was that *we* have to be the hero. Nobody is going to come riding out of the hills on a white horse and save the day. Remember, these weren't the Disney stories. They were old German folktales. If you want to survive the night, you just have to understand that there are wolves out there. Make yourself ready. Make yourself strong.'

Just like that, at the closing of his lips, the world ahead of them erupted into a howl so loud that it seemed to frighten the wind. As it came, bellowing from the shadows of a midnight realm, the ground that followed it quivered and trembled towards them.

Betty moved in so tight, squeezing so loud that Jack thought they might suddenly pop and become one entity. He managed to hear her ask, 'what was that?' in a petrified wail.

What came next, he was unsure was spoken aloud or in his mind, *It's the wolf at the end of the story.*

****

Grim and Alex launched the coats and blankets back into the cart. He had explained that they had found a lead, a chain, not far. The links led northward, into a land where the hills began to slope again. The cart rolled on, through the snow. Another deep, deafening howl silenced the wind and brought with it a reply of choral wolves, baying from their watchful posts. Jack had seen something tall, carrying a stone almost as large as itself, wandering high upon a hill, covered in snow. The naked, humanoid figure must have been over fifteen feet in height. Everything out here in the wasteland felt overbearing. As though every living creature so longed for the remnants of that lingering, dying sun, that they had grown skyward; like a tree seeking the light. Jack supposed the wolves, judging by the height of their eyes, might have even dwarfed Sleipnir, who had managed to haul them through hell and high water without breaking a sweat or offering a single complaint. Grim often talked to the horse and sometimes the two large ravens ever soaring high above the clouds.

Jack wondered if they replied. Not in words, but in their own speech. Or maybe in words Jack just did not comprehend? Eventually, the cart was following the chain. A huge link of steel lifting out from the snow. Big enough to hold down the largest iron ship, maybe even a fleet, it stretched along the wasteland, like a steel vein across a white-giant's back. Once, the chain shifted, and the sound it made echoed through the very core of the world. They followed the path of the chain for three hours, until it had finally started to rise out from the snow and into the air, where it would meet its captive. In the eye of the storm, Jack saw only a huge black mountain approaching. It was shaped, oddly, like a sleeping wolf.

'Grimnir.' The mountain...spoke. As the rumbling awakened, two great moons flashed before them, as an immense, coal cave opened from the floor, releasing a gale of rot and decay.

Jack saw first, what the others had failed to understand. These were no moons, hanging in the sky; but eyes. It was no cave that wrenched free of the ice, but a colossal beastly maw, complete with jagged ridges of razor sharp, yellowed teeth. This was no mountain shaped like a wolf; but a wolf. Larger and more tremendous than anything Jack could have imagined or described. So intense was the thought of this creature, that he had to focus only individually on aspects of the wolf. An eye. A tooth. A nail. To put such things together would create a tapestry from which Jack could never again look back. It would consume his mind, just as one small inhale and the wolf itself would consume them all. And still, Grim released the reins and stepped out on the snow, never hesitating, never faltering, to confront the beast.

'Fenris-wolf,' Grim called over the winds and the snow and the ice, and the mountain shifted, 'I hear another, calling, from Gnipahellir. Shall I inform him, there is to be no Ragnarök? Not on this day.' Great quakes shifted the cart sideways by several feet. Sleipnir finally whinnied in uncertainty. Behind them, vast open fissures broke over the frozen lake and creatures long though lost saw their first glimpse on light in ten-thousand years.

'Ah, Garmr. He will be expecting the Corspe-Hall opened. And yet,' the mountain boomed, 'I send my sister's presence not in Helheim. Tell me, Grimnir. Where is Hella? Did you slay her, oh, Hidden-One. It would be much like you, to take life, from fate, into your own hands. Ragnarök can always be delayed, but it can never be stopped.'

'Fortunately,' Old Grim barked back, as loudly as he could manage, 'I believe it can. Lo, oh, Great Wolf, forgive me. So long ago should I have let you free. What an ally you would have been to the gods. No?' In just a simple act of nodding his head, Fenrir caused the cart to lift momentarily from the ground. Gungnir's shaft trained under the strength of Grim's tightly curled fingers, as the black mountain released a cacophony of laughter.

'I could have slain more enemies of the gods than even the Thunder-wielder,' Fenrir howled, 'but for your fear, you left me bound in fetters and shackles. Like my father was bound, also.'

Grim stepped several paces closer, placing on foot behind the other, 'your father was bound, as you were bound; because within the like of Laufey, the blood of the Jötunn resides. It is this fire that cannot be at peace. It will, unfortunately, consume all. And, for all it is worth...I am truly sorry.'

His foot slipped past the other. Dashing forward, Grim lifted and released Gungnir. With a splitting crack, the spear span through the snowfall, faster than a bullet. The mountain howled and shook, rocking the world. On distant shores, trees fell, the foundations of houses cracked, and a great avalanche rolled across the frozen lake. Deafening, Fenrir's howl of agony forced the companions to shield their ears and curl together. Jack thought the sound might echo into eternity, as the great wolf roared and roared. When it began to die, the world was left with another sound; one that caused Jack to look up and feel a strange guilt stain his soul.

Whimpering, Fenris-wolf shuddered, twitching, over and over, as the chains loosened, and the mountain started at once to recede. After a long, silent reprieve from the whimpering howls, Jack could see that Grim was striding forward towards a man-sized figure on the barren flats of ice. Jack wanted, no, he needed to see. Looking down, at first, Jack had expected what almost anyone would have expected to see. A wolf. Now the size of a man. Pierced. Defeated. Dying. Jack had expected to feel guilt. Sympathy. Finality. Reprieve. Elation. Instead, Jack saw a man. Broken and beaten, and it was all he could do not to feel a new emotion, hanging between despair and vengeance.

'Tricked once again, Grimnir,' Loki laughed, spewing a river of blood as he spoke.

The sanguine life spattered the virgin snow and left it tainted, melting. Steam rose from the earth, as the man choked out his final cackle. Loki resembles nothing of the obsidian-skinned demon, as he lay dying. His hair, a soft brown, seemed well-kept and slick, adorned with braids and beads. His face was clean shaven to the bone, showing that his eyes no longer bore crimson pools, but rather shone with a golden hue. Grim remained silent. Loki had been defeated. One ghost finally put to rest; at what cost? He wrenched Gungnir from Loki's side, spurring another torrent of blood across the purest snow they had ever seen. Then, it dawned on Jack, just what had happened, and his heart sunk so low into his stomach, it made him physically sick. Fenrir was free.

'There is no time.' Old Grim howled over a rising storm of ice that had appeared with a powerful, vengeful feel, across the frozen lake. Perhaps one final gift from the old trickster.

He whispered something, a word older than tongues, older than mankind, upon the face of the key. There it was, again. No longer tainted with the obsidian, stygian curse, stood the Silver Door. Grim felt it call with a strength so unnerving that he was unsure whether to burst into laughter, or tears. But not all was finished. Not yet.

'Go,' Grim grasped at Safiya with one hand and flung the handle of the door inward, into the nothingness between, with the other. She saw a bright, silvery light, drawn to it like a moth to a flame. Something warm and safe called her through, and with that, she was gone.

'Now,' Grim clutched Alex's arm, and before the Magician could spin to call to Jack, was thrown backwards into the ether.

'I shall leave last, please,' Grim offered a hand to Jack, seeing the look he gave the old man. A want to see him leave this place. A mistrust in what would come. 'No more tricks, Jack. Please, take her with you.'

Thundering, the edges of the frozen lake closed in around them, until only a high wall of snow was visible. In its centre, Jack took hold of Betty's hand in his. She nodded at him, though shivered uneasily.

'Trust me. Don't let go.' Jack gave one last smile and with that, the pair vanished from sight, just as the world behind them was engulfed in ice.

The Silver Door had opened again.

Epilogue
Ragnarök

ᛉ

Home ride thou, Odin! and exult. Thus, shall never more man again visit me, until Loki free from his bonds escapes, and Ragnarök all-destroying comes.

- *Vegtamskviða*

Jack was the first to come around. His face was lying still, on a pillow of ice. A cold tingling crept into his ear and over his hair. It was *snow*. More snow. They had not left. They were still out there, in the barren wastes of...*London?*

He looked up. There it was. The Tower. Its stone and brick monoliths extending around the medieval fortified keep. He was just outside its walls. Along the street leading beside the Thames. A snow fall, a deep snowfall like he had never seen, blanketed the Capital. And, *my God*, so harsh was the winter's grasp that for the first time in over century, the river itself had frozen over. For a moment, as he glanced at Tower Bridge, extending over the icy Thames, leading towards the great keep of the Tower, he thought that maybe, just maybe, it had all been a dream? A hallucination? Had he been drunk? Drugged? Everything was here though.

And the others? He was alone. Not completely. He saw an old man wandering towards him through the snow, which had been so poorly scraped from the path that the elderly, stooped figure in his beige trench coat and hat, had to walk knee-high through the white powder, sending small flurries into the air, as even more snow started to fall. The figure came slowly closer and Jack laughed, when he noticed it.

Probably from the war, he thought, staring across at the shuffling man with an eyepatch above his left cheek.

Easing himself upward, Jack found that his head had been resting on a small mound of ice, covering, only partially, a newspaper. The old black and white fluttered gently in a gust of wind, as Jack pulled it free from its icy prison. Dusting off the snow, and breaking apart the pages, he read what he could, that had not been weathered away,

BRITAIN SET TO FACE ITS SECOND YEAR OF WINTER

For the nineteenth month in a row, climate change disbelievers are encouraged to look around at the world as it is now. A never-ending winter has gripped the British Isles and most of Northern Europe. There seems to be no end in sight to the snow, the ice, the hail and the rain (which is not unusual). His Majesty the King has ordered the Armed Forces to begin the second phase of rationing and that all those seeking to find refuge over the Channel are to do so through the proper legal paths. International committees are no longer accepting new migrants, as the wave of the new Virus in Southern Asia has begun to reach critical levels. It is a grim outlook for the world in these troubling times.

****

Jack then quickly flicked back the top corner of the page to read,

August 12ᵗʰ, 2029

He could not believe his eyes. It was, just, all so surreal. He had stepped out of the proverbial frying pan and landed straight into the burning hob. But it was not real? Was it? There was only one more readable headline that Jack was able to see,

RAVEN-OUS OMEN SIGNALS END OF MONARCHY?

The infamous ill-fated omen has finally come to pass. Two winged residents of the White Tower have taken flight. Ravenmaster John Humphreys if dumbfounded as to how the birds were able to escape. Not only that, but he is the only officer to have let such a tragedy pass since the foretelling of the odious words, 'If the ravens leave the Tower, the kingdom will fall...' So, what does this mean for our King and his New Britain? Is this relentless winter only the beginning of the end for our sceptred isle?

****

Ravens? Towers? Bridges? Winter? It was all getting a little too close for comfort for Jack. Hitting home a little too hard. Which is when she finally returned to his thoughts. *Lucy.* But if it really was 2029, and he had not aged a day, then... He rubbed his temples with two fingers, massaging away the throbbing headache. He could not think straight. Could not see everything as he had done before. Those old memories of that place. Altheim. The Crooked Spire. Alex. Grayson. Safiya.

Jack decided it was best to take a walk. If he knew London, and he thought he did, there was sure to be a tube station near here. He could board a train, head north, back home and maybe even try to pick up the shattered pieces of his life. Everyone would be old now. His mother. His brother. His nephew. How long was it until they declared someone legally dead? What about money? What about...'All right stop, just calk down,' he told himself. But felt the quickening of his heart again, when he saw the sign in bold black letters, stood out opposed to the bright yellow of the snow-covered barricade,

NO ENTRY
BY ORDER OF THE KING

Jack felt sick. Sicker even after, as the image of the lone, shaggy dog wandered from behind the edge of the wall surrounding the entrance to the underground. Its long, black fur carrying a coat of snow. It looked at him with yellowy eyes. Or maybe he had imagined that.

Weird, he thought, *why some dogs look so like dogs, and others look like*; what had he meant? Wolves? No wolves in England. Not for a long time. No. it was a dog. Probably a stray. Big enough that Jack felt it could hold its own in a fight. It walked sort of cocky, too. Probably the alpha of the lost-and-founds of London.

Above, clouds were rolling in ever so smoothly from the edges of the horizon. Closing in around London, and the Tower, as though it were the eye of some great and coming storm. In the space between the clouds, Jack saw small twinkling stars beaming down through an evening sky. It would be night soon and he was not sure how he felt about that.

He wanted to ignore the signs. Ignore the voice. Chalk it all up to a bad dream. Bad food. Some horrible life-altering mental breakdown. He wanted to, so much, just close his eyes and pretend that the voice had come from inside his own head, when all his reasoning and rational mind could tell him was that, no, it was real.

'Alex?'

But the voice had not called to him. No. The voice had run past him. Kicked snow over his boots and closed in on another man, sitting on a nearby bench. The man stood, he looked familiar. Then a voice called, 'daddy', and a young girl joined the couple who seemed so familiar. Not only by face but by the way the tanned-woman moved her arms. The way the man slipped his fingers behind his daughter's ear and pulled out a £2 coin. The way the girl laughed. So familiar and yet so distant, back in a world he could no longer remember.

'Oh, wow, Daddy, look,' the girl tugged at the man's sleeve, pointing up into the rolling clouds.

'Oh, yeah. Babe, do you see that?' the woman asked.

'Huh?' replied the man, 'Yeah, I see it. How weird.'

Jack looked up. He followed the girl's arm, leading into a finger that pointed accusingly at the sky. A shape in the clouds. It was noticeable without having to try to see it, the way you sometimes have to when someone points out a thing that is, to them, obvious, and to you has to be imagined. But there it was. The shape in the clouds. Forming the eye of the animal, the moon glared through a misty evening cumulus. Two wide plumes had been formed for its jaws, whilst the odd arrangement of jutting trials of vapour formed what were quite apparently teeth between them. The haze of the wolf seemed to roll as gently as the coming storm. It moved across the sky without changing shape, as clouds do. One by one, the emerging celestial lights disappeared inside that beastly maw, as if being swallowed.

Anthropomorphism:

- The attribution of human characteristics or behaviour to a god, animal, or object.

Tonight, Jack had another word for it. One that would describe what he was seeing in the heavens. It was a sign. It was an omen. It was the wolf at the end of the story.

It was Ragnarök.

Sources

https://www.sacred-texts.com/

Henry Adams Bellows, *The Poetic Edda*, 1936.

The Poetic Edda, Snorri Sturllson, translated by Carolyne Larrington, Oxford University Press, 1999.

The Project Gutenberg EBook of The Elder Eddas of Saemund Sigfusson; and the Younger Eddas of Snorre Sturleson, by Saemund Sigfusson and Snorre Sturleson.

Neil Gaiman, *Norse Mythology*, Bloomsbury, 2018.

WYRD WOLF

Author Bio
Author Eric Schoch

Eric Schoch creates worlds of fantasy and horror which have developed from his own personal experiences and expanding imagination. His love of all things Norse and Viking has culminated in his latest novel – *Grim's Door.*

From working in settings such as prisons and mortuaries, Eric always finds he has a story to tell, from the macabre to the downright bizarre; which he shares in his short stories by Wyrd Wolf – *The Unhallowing.* Upon completion of his Theological degree, Eric has been studying further and further into the religious and the esoteric, finding his way into secret fraternities and druidic communities. A keen reader and an avid rambler, he can often be found either lost between the pages or lost somewhere on a mountainside in Wales with his Collie named Colin.

Blessings /I\

He can be contacted and found on social media via @wyrd_wolf or thewyrdwolf.com.

Lightning Source UK Ltd.
Milton Keynes UK
UKHW022011090223
416682UK00013B/1121